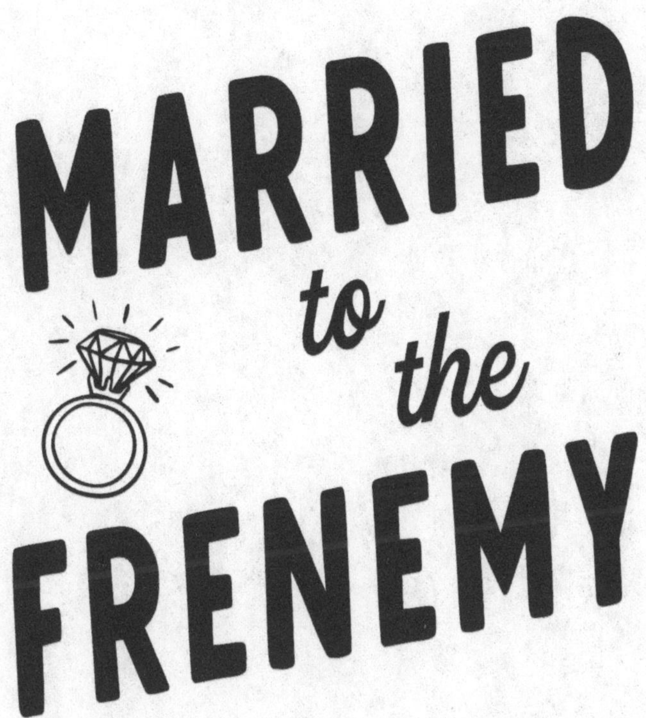

MARRIED to the FRENEMY

T.K. LEIGH WRITING AS
TRACY LEIGH

MARRIED TO THE FRENEMY

Published by Carpe Per Diem Publishing, Inc

Cover Design: Cat Head Media, Inc.

For a full list of all of Tracy's books, including recommended reading order, please visit her website:

www.tracyleighbooks.com

Books and reading order for her spicy billionaire romance alter ego, T.K. Leigh, can be found here:

www.tkleighauthor.com

For exclusive sales and excerpts,
sign up for Tracy Leigh's VIP list!

https://www.tracyleighbooks.com/subscribe

Or scan the code below

To everyone who can't get enough of those "my wife" vibes…

This one's for you.

ONE

Haley

"Not again," I hiss under my breath as I scurry through the employee entrance of the casino, my short legs not carrying me as quickly as I wish they would.

This is the third time I'm late this month.

And it's also only the third day of the month.

To say I'm batting zero lately would be an understatement. Between the upcoming holidays and learning the woman I've been renting from is selling her house, requiring me to find another place to live within my meager budget, I'm more stressed than I have been in a while.

The icing on an already shitty cake is having a boss who seems to find pleasure in yelling at me for everything he can. Which is exactly what he does the second I barrel into the employee break room.

"You're late again, McBride!" He berates from behind the desk in his office without even glancing up at me.

"Sorry, Frank. My daughter has an earache, and the pharmacy took forever to fill her prescription."

He scoffs and finally looks up, his eyes filled with disdain. "I don't give a shit about your kid. What I do give a shit about is that all the people on the floor spend as much money as possible. Do you know what makes them want to spend money?"

"Alcohol," I grumble, having heard this lecture countless times.

"Yes. Alcohol. Now get that pretty little ass out there and make sure they keep spending money."

"Of course." I head to my locker, shoving my coat and purse inside.

I'd love nothing more than to quit this job, but as a single mom, every penny counts, especially now that I need to find a new place to live. This job may involve dealing with sleazy men and their wandering hands, but it also brings in good tips most nights.

Just as I'm about to close my locker, my phone buzzes in my purse. Stealing a glance at Frank to see his attention focused on the papers in front of him, I retrieve my cell and find an unknown number flashing on the screen.

Hoping it's good news from one of the rentals I've applied for, I discreetly answer.

"Is this Haley McBride?" a voice comes over the line.

"It is."

"This is Malcom Harris. You came to look at the property listing I have a few days ago."

"Yes. How are you Mr. Harris?"

"Good." His tone falters, and in that split second, I know exactly what he's about to tell me. "Unfortunately, the owners have decided to go with another applicant at this time."

I squeeze my eyes shut, pushing down the ball of frustration building in my throat from losing yet another rental opportunity. In the small town where I live, finding affordable housing is no easy feat, and I hate the idea of having to move to a larger city.

But with limited options and a tight budget, it may be my only choice — even if it means uprooting my daughter and taking her away from all the friends she's made in preschool.

Even if it means uprooting *my* life, too.

"I appreciate you calling. Thank you for your time."

"Haley! Floor! Now!" Frank bellows. "If I have to tell you one more time, you can kiss this job goodbye."

"I'm going." I shove my phone back into my purse and slam my locker shut, practically running down the hall. I don't stop until I reach the serving area where a group of women dressed in identical tight-fitting black dresses huddle around a bar, waiting for the bartender to fill their drink orders.

"There you are," a tall blonde says upon my approach, giving me a hug.

"Sorry. Maggie has an ear infection."

Ivy's expression falls. "Is she okay?"

"She's fine. The pharmacy was just backed up and I didn't want her to go without her antibiotics."

"You're a good mom." She squeezes my arm. "How's the apartment hunt going?"

I groan in frustration. "I'm beginning to think it's hopeless. So far, every place has turned me down. Probably because they're worried I won't be able to make the rent. As it is, I'm not sure how I'll come up with the down payment I need, especially with Christmas coming."

"I'm sorry, Haley." She gives me a sympathetic look, her perfectly manicured nails tapping against the bar. "You could always…you know."

She doesn't come right out and say it. She doesn't need to. I'm painfully aware of how some of the cocktail waitresses here supplement their income through prostitution. Hell, some girls ended up quitting and doing it full time when they learned how much they could make.

There was only one time I came even remotely close to crossing that line, thanks to unexpected medical bills for Maggie. Luckily, I came to my senses before I did something I'd regret, no matter how much money I could have made.

"It'll be worthwhile. Especially for you." Ivy leans closer. "Blondes are a dime a dozen around here." She nods at the sea of blonde-haired cocktail waitresses. "But a natural redhead?" She toys with a tendril of my auburn hair. "Men go wild for that. A few of my regulars ask about you. Want to know if you're available." She places her drink order on her tray and carefully lifts it off the bar.

"I'll keep that in mind," I respond with a tight smile.

"It's not as bad as it seems," Ivy reassures me as we make our way onto the casino floor.

The air is thick with the smell of tobacco and alcohol, mixed with the scent of sweat and desperation. The cacophony of slot machines ringing and patrons cheering is almost deafening, forcing us to raise our voices to be heard.

"The first time is tough. Fucks with your head. Now, I just kind of turn it off, ya know?"

She means well. But the mere thought of doing that makes my stomach churn. This isn't the life I want for myself or my daughter.

"I'll figure something out," I tell her.

But with every passing day, my options seem to dwindle. I fear I may soon have no other choice than to do what I swore I never would.

TWO

Beckham

"**D**on't tell me you're going in to clean the tanks, too."

I look up as I'm about to slip into a pair of rubber boots, a man with a cane slowly making his way down the rows of stainless steel vats.

"It relaxes me," I tell him. "Helps me think."

"You're a better man than me," Grady replies with a deep chuckle, amusement dancing in his dark eyes. "When I was just starting out, it was my least favorite thing to do."

"There's something therapeutic about getting in there and scrubbing away every last trace of what was in there before."

"A clean slate," he remarks.

"Exactly."

He knows better than most people how much I like the idea of a clean slate.

Unfortunately, I've learned past mistakes aren't as easy to wipe away as the sediment in these steel tanks.

"I'm assuming you made some progress in the lab, then?"

"Sure did." I move toward a long metal table against the wall and grab a test tube, handing it to him.

He brings it to his nose, taking a moment to inhale the rich aroma before taking a sip, allowing the flavor to settle on his tongue. It's not mature yet, but it's important to sample the wine throughout the process. You work as a winemaker long enough, and even those early tastes give you an insight into how the final product will taste once it's had time to age in the barrels.

"Nice job, son," Grady remarks with a twinkle of pride in his eyes.

"Thanks."

I take the tube from him and return it to the table. I'm about to yank on my gloves and join the rest of my crew in the tank when he places a hand on my forearm.

"Can you spare a few minutes? I need to talk to you."

Something in his expression tells me whatever he needs to discuss is serious. Grady isn't a man of many words or long, heartfelt conversations. He's been a father figure to me nearly all my adult life, especially after my own dad passed away from ALS, but we've never had the type of relationship where we sit down and talk about our feelings.

Then again, I don't have that type of relationship with many people.

I prefer a more…solitary life.

It's one of the reasons I love my job as head winemaker so much. I oversee dozens of employees, but most of my days are spent checking on the vines or in my lab experimenting with different combinations of flavors to enhance this year's product.

"Sure thing."

I set the gloves back on the surface and signal the rest of my crew to carry on without me. Then I follow Grady into my lab, his cane echoing against the cement floor.

"What's up?"

I pull out a stool from underneath the gleaming steel table that stretches along one side of the room. Test tubes line the wall, each one identified with various percentages for my reference. Sheets of paper are littered over the surface, filled with tasting notes and my own thoughts in the hopes of improving the next round of experimentation.

Being a winemaker is so much more than just growing and picking grapes. It requires a great deal of chemistry, as well as luck.

Despite the long hours and sometimes backbreaking work, there's nothing else I could imagine doing. Nothing brings me more joy than seeing someone's face light up after tasting one of my creations for the first time.

"I've been thinking about this a lot lately," Grady begins, leaning against the desk opposite me.

At seventy-six, he still has a full head of salt-and-pepper hair, probably because he never married or had kids. Instead, his vineyard is his life, and each wine release is like a child to him.

What more could anyone want?

"I didn't come to this decision lightly." His weathered features betray a hint of hesitation.

"What decision is that?" I ask guardedly.

"I'm selling the vineyard."

My heart plummets in time with my stomach as air whooshes out of my lungs.

"What? To who?"

I knew there would soon come a day Grady wasn't my boss, but I didn't expect it so soon. I thought he would die here, on this land he's poured his heart and soul into. Without him, there is no Vivanza Estates.

"I've had quite a few offers from various Napa and Sonoma wineries that want to expand their reach into this area. As well as a few development firms, hoping to turn this place into a combination vineyard and boutique hotel. When they first started approaching me several years ago, I had no desire to sell. But these days…" He pushes out a sigh as he nods at his cane.

"I'm not getting any younger, Beckham. It's time for me to slow down and enjoy life. I'll be reaching out to everyone who's expressed an interest in buying over the years to see if they still are. I just wanted you to be the first to know."

I stare at him, unsure how to respond. All I can think is that I hate the idea of some commercialized vineyard destroying everything Grady worked so hard to build here.

That *I* worked so hard to build here, too.

"I don't want you to worry about a job. I—"

"How much?" I interject.

Grady blinks, confusion knitting his wrinkled brow. "Excuse me?"

"How much do you want?"

"Beckham, I—"

"Just tell me. What's your asking price?"

"I'm not only selling the land. I'm also selling the years I put into cultivating these vines."

"I understand that." I cross my arms in front of my chest and widen my stance. "What are you asking? You have fifty acres plus on-site processing, cellar, and tasting room. And the house I've been living in. I'm guessing five million."

"Seven and a half."

I run a hand through my hair, blowing out a subtle laugh. While I'm in a better financial position than most people my age, thanks to my lack of personal relationships and Grady giving me a share of the profits every year since I became head winemaker, I still don't have *that* much money.

"Would you take five?"

He pinches the bridge of his nose, exhaling another long breath. "I worried this might happen."

"What? That I'd want to buy this place so someone doesn't come in and ruin it?"

"I'd love to sell to someone who will treat the land with the same care and respect as we have."

"Then what's the problem? Other than the fact that I'm severely low-balling you?"

He waves me off, as if that has nothing to do with it. "When your father was sick, I swore I'd always look out for you. Especially after…everything."

"And you have. You gave me a job when no one else would. Taught me more about wine than I would have ever learned in college."

This vineyard has been more than just a job to me — it's been my home ever since Grady hired me, giving me a chance no one else would. He's taught me everything he knows about running a successful winery. Even sent me to vineyards all over the west coast and Europe to learn different wine-making techniques I could use to make our product even better.

For the past thirteen years, this vineyard has been my life. I can't stomach the idea of someone destroying it.

"I gave up a lot to keep this vineyard running," Grady continues. "Owning your own business, having people depend on you, it can be extremely stressful. For years, I lived and breathed this place. Hell, I still do."

"And it shows in the wine you've created."

"But because of that, I missed out on a lot of other things." His words are laced with regret.

"Like what?" A sinking sensation forms in my stomach.

"A wife. Kids."

"Grady, I—"

He holds up his hand. "I kept telling myself I'd get around to it when things slowed down. But things never did. Here I am, a seventy-six-year-old man with nothing to show for it."

"What are you talking about? You have plenty to show for it. Your wine is consistently ranked among the best varietals every year. And each release gets better and better."

"There was a time when I thought that was all that mattered. But you know what they say. Hindsight's twenty-twenty, and all that." He approaches me, gently squeezing my bicep. "I don't want you to make the same mistakes I did. Don't want you to miss out on having everything you deserve. If I sold you this vineyard, I fear that's precisely what would happen. You'd end up just like me. Old and alone."

"You're not alone," I argue. "You've been a part of my family for as long as I can remember. Plus, your employees love you."

"I have no one to share my life with. I don't want that to be you. Your *father* wouldn't have wanted that to be you, either."

I don't say anything for several protracted moments, speechless not only over the idea of him selling, but also the fact he won't sell to me because he's worried I'll miss out on certain things.

Things I don't even want.

Maybe I did once upon a time. Once dreamed of having a wife and kids.

Not anymore.

"I'll let you get back to the tanks," Grady says. "I just wanted to let you know."

My eyes follow him as he makes his way toward the door. But before he can disappear, I blurt out one last question.

"What if I were married? Hypothetically speaking, of course."

He faces me, his brows scrunched in contemplation. "If you were married, and I was confident you were putting your family first, then yes. I'd sell you this place, even at a lower rate. But seeing as you haven't gone out on an actual date in years, it's a moot point."

I remain silent, in no mood to get into the technicalities of my dating life with him.

Or anyone, for that matter.

"Don't worry, Beckham. You've been the head winemaker here for several years. Anyone who buys this place will no doubt want to keep you on, especially with your expertise."

"What are you going to do with all your free time?"

"Something I haven't done since I bought this land thirty years ago."

"What's that?"

"Take a much overdue vacation."

I can't deny he deserves to spend the rest of his years doing absolutely nothing.

But I still hate that someone else will soon own the land I've worked with my own hands.

Unless I get married.

THREE

Haley

"What do you think, peanut?"

I steal a glance at my daughter, my heart warming at the wonder and excitement filling her expression as we meander along the lakefront area of Holley Ridge, the annual Christmas Festival in full swing.

"This is amazing." Maggie's gray eyes sparkle as she takes in all the sights, sounds, and smells surrounding her. The air is filled with the scent of freshly baked goods, hot cocoa, and pine from the Norway spruce towering nearby.

As we weave through the crowd, it seems the entire town has come out for the annual tree lighting ceremony, as I expected would happen. After all, it's a tradition around here. I just hope it continues to be.

Parker, my best friend and the woman who now runs the property, is also going through some financial issues.

She hasn't let that dampen her spirit, though. Instead, she's confident she'll find a solution to her problem because she manifested it.

Maybe that's what I need to do.

At this point, I'll try anything so I don't end up homeless.

So my *daughter* doesn't end up homeless.

A voice in my head reminds me there's one thing I could do to earn more money, but I quickly silence it. I'm not that desperate. Not yet, anyway. Like Parker says, if there's any time a miracle is possible, it's during Christmas.

I just hope I find my miracle before I'm forced to live out of my car.

Or worse.

"Auntie Parker! Auntie Parker!" Maggie's voice pulls me out of my thoughts, and I watch as she darts toward a tall blonde woman, her arms outstretched.

Parker gracefully crouches down, sweeping her into her embrace. "Hey, Magpie."

Maggie's expression turns serious. "Grandma says no one should call me that. She says my name is Margaret, and that's what people should call me."

Parker glances my way, and I roll my eyes.

While I try to limit Maggie's exposure to my parents, on rare occasions, they remember she exists and stop by unannounced to see her. Afterwards, I always regret it, but I foolishly keep hoping they'll realize what's important and want to have a real relationship with her.

"What do *you* want to be called?" Parker asks.

Maggie's face lights up. "I like it when you call me Magpie."

"Then I proclaim you Lady Magpie of Holley Ridge."

Maggie squeals as Parker sets her on her feet.

"It looks beautiful, Parker." I give my best friend a quick hug.

"Thanks, Haley."

We stroll through the rows of festive booths, each one adorned with twinkling lights and decorations, where dozens of local businesses sell various holiday-themed items, from decorations, to cookies, and even wine.

"How's the apartment hunt going?" Parker keeps her voice low so Maggie can't overhear.

"Not great." I heave a sigh. "The downside of living in a small town. There aren't many rentals to begin with, and what *is* available is way over my budget. I'm not exactly raking it in as a dog walker and cocktail waitress. At least not enough to compete with all the snow bunnies who come in for the winter season to ski."

"From what I understand, Beckham Lawrence still

has his townhouse he rents out. You could always see if it's available."

I dart my wide eyes toward her. "Beckham Lawrence? Are you crazy? Absolutely not. There's no way he'd do me any favors, like rent to me, especially when I wouldn't be able to pay him anywhere close to what he can get for a short-term rental."

Not to mention, our history is strained, to say the least.

"You'll never know if you don't ask," Parker sings, gesturing at the booth directly in front of us. Then she disappears into the bustling crowd, presumably to give her speech before the main event — lighting the towering Norway Spruce by the lake.

"Mama! Mama! Can I have some juice?" Maggie grabs my hand and drags me toward the booth in question, my heart rate picking up the instant Beckham's dark eyes lock on mine.

A charcoal beanie covers what I know to be a full head of dark hair, his square jawline sporting a bit of scruff. He's wearing his usual attire of jeans, Henley shirt with the sleeves pushed up, and work boots.

Even as a teen, Beckham was tall and muscular. His physique has only become more built over the years, all broad shoulders and defined muscles. A pang squeezes my chest at the reminder of *why* he's as muscular as he is now. While working the fields at the vineyard certainly had something to do with it, it's not the only reason.

"Mama?"

Remembering where I am, I snap my eyes away from Beckham. "That's juice for adults, sweetie."

"Actually, I've got a little something special for you," Beckham says in his raspy voice, throwing a wink at my daughter.

Turning, he opens one of the coolers and grabs a juice box. It doesn't escape my notice it's the only one, as if he brought it just for Maggie.

Which makes no sense, considering Beckham acts as if he can't stand the sight of me.

"Thanks, Mr. Beck!" Maggie says appreciatively when he hands her the box with the straw already inserted. "I like your pretty pictures." She points to the tattoos covering his forearms.

"Thank you," he responds with a chuckle.

I'd be lying if I said the throaty sound doesn't make my girly bits flutter a little.

There's something about Beckham's laugh that makes me forget the strain that's existed between us for over a decade now. We used to be friends. Hell, we used to be more than friends.

In the blink of an eye, it all imploded.

"What's that one of?" Maggie presses, oblivious to the long line of people hoping to taste some of the wine Beckham spends hours perfecting as the head winemaker of the local vineyard.

A feat, considering he's only thirty-two.

Then again, he's worked at the vineyard since the

day he turned sixteen, with the exception of the year after he graduated high school. He started out hand-picking clusters of grapes during the annual harvest. Now he's the one responsible for the finished product.

"It's an old pocket watch, like the one my father gave me."

"He crossed over the rainbow bridge, right?"

"Umm…" Beckham glances my way, obviously unsure how to respond.

"Humans don't cross over the rainbow bridge, sweetie," I chime in. "That's for animals." I look toward Beckham. "Belinda lost her cat a few weeks ago. It's her first exposure to death."

"Then he's in haven?" Maggie asks eagerly.

"Yeah. My dad's in haven." He smiles, not bothering to correct her mispronunciation of the word.

"Do you miss him?"

Sometimes I wish my kid wasn't so inquisitive. Especially when her curiosity keeps me in Beckham's presence longer than necessary.

"Every day," he replies softly.

"Let's not bother Mr. Beck anymore," I say, noticing his forlorn expression. Regret squeezes at my chest, considering the role I played that prevented Beckham from being there when his father passed. "Auntie Parker's about to light the tree. Plus, you don't want to miss out on seeing Santa. Do you?"

Maggie's eyes instantly brighten. "I'm going to tell him all about the Barbie camper I want."

I do my best to keep my expression even, my stomach churning at the idea that I won't be able to get Maggie most of the items on her wish list. It doesn't matter how many times people have told me it doesn't make me a bad mom if I can't get her everything she wants.

Just once, I'd like to give my daughter the Christmas she deserves. The Christmas I always dreamed of spoiling my kid with.

"Santa has millions of boys and girls to get presents for, sweetie. Maybe ask him for something a little… smaller," I suggest, even though I really want to ask her to pick something more affordable.

The excitement in her eyes flickers out, her smile turning into a frown. But instead of throwing a fit like some kids would, she lowers her head and says, "Okay."

As I turn from the vineyard's booth, I can't help but feel like I just shattered my daughter's dreams. It's not the first time. And it won't be the last. But I still hate feeling like I'm a failure.

"Thanks again," I say to Beckham, then usher Maggie through the crowd.

After a few feet, I steal a glance over my shoulder and see Beckham's gaze trained on us, his expression unreadable.

He's the last person I want to ask for help. He's the last person who'd *want* to help me.

I have to remind myself it's not just about me anymore, though.

It's about Maggie.

I need to swallow my pride and try for her.

Even if I'm the reason he spent a year of his life in prison.

FOUR

Beckham

"Come on, boy," I yell after Monte, my Australian Shepard mix, as he pauses to sniff around the tangled vines.

The crisp early December air fills my lungs as I stroll through the rows of grapevines. Despite the chill, this time of year has always been my favorite. The leaves on the vines have changed colors, displaying a brilliant quilt of reds, yellows, and oranges, all set against a backdrop of rolling green hills in the distance. In a week or two, the leaves will fall to the ground, and the cycle will start again. For the time being, the vines lay dormant, giving me a short reprieve from worrying about their health. Instead, my focus is on turning the grapes we harvested into the best wine possible.

Although lately, whenever I've worked in my lab, my thoughts are consumed with the idea of Grady selling the place that's been my home for the past decade. I know he won't sell to someone who will destroy everything he's created here. I just wish that person could be me. The only way that will happen is if I get married.

I don't foresee that happening anytime soon, especially since I haven't been on a date in months. If you can even call what I do dating. I'm not the type of person a woman can bring home to meet the parents. Not with my past.

As I make my way along the dirt path, Monte barks excitedly, then takes off toward a figure approaching in the distance, the setting sun behind them making it difficult to see who it is. I squint, expecting it to be Grady. But as I get closer, it becomes abundantly clear it's not.

Not unless Grady miraculously turned into a petite redhead with brilliant green eyes.

I stop in my tracks and rake my gaze over Haley's frame, my pulse kicking up as she draws near. It happens every damn time I see her.

And every time, I hate myself a little more for still reacting to her this way.

But my body hasn't seemed to get the message. Or maybe it simply doesn't care.

"What are you doing out here?" My voice comes out gruffer than I intended, and I wince slightly. But I don't apologize. It's better if she hates me.

"I didn't mean to interrupt." She nervously fidgets

with the hem of her coat, shifting from foot to foot. "I went to the tasting room and Grady said I could find you out here. If you're busy, I can come back later."

"It's fine." I shove my hands into the pockets of my jeans. "What do you want?"

And again, my words come out harsher than I planned. It's just how I am around her. As if the ruder I am to her, the less I'll care about her.

Hell, I *shouldn't* care about her.

But no matter how much time has passed, there's a part of me that will always have a soft spot for Haley McBride.

"It's just…" She pushes out a long breath, tilting her head back to take in the blue sky before returning her gaze to mine. "I was wondering if you were still renting out your townhouse."

"I am…" I draw out, my eyes tracing over the pale skin of her face, a smattering of freckles dotting her cheeks and nose, her full lips seeming even pinker when compared to her fair complexion.

"Would you want to rent it out to me?" She looks at me hopefully. "I can't afford a lot," she adds quickly. "But I'm not asking for a favor. Or maybe I am. I don't know. Belinda's selling the house and moving to Santa Fe to be near her kids and grandkids. After spending the past few weeks trying to find a place I can afford, I'm beginning to realize how good I had it. Everywhere I look is so far out of my price range, it's laughable." There's a hint of defeat in her voice, breaking through the tough exterior she's worn nearly all her life.

"My place is booked solid through the end of March. You know how busy this place gets in the winter with all the ski bunnies."

"Right." She forces a smile, but I can tell it's to mask her disappointment.

Or maybe frustration.

"Well, thanks for your time." She spins and all but runs from me, kicking up dust in her wake. She doesn't even look up as she rushes past my brother, keeping her head lowered.

"What was that about?" Jude asks as he moves toward me, briefly glancing over his shoulder at Haley's retreating form.

Monte wastes no time in abandoning me, heading straight toward him and sitting obediently at his feet, a single paw raised.

Jude reaches into his coat pocket and holds out his hand, allowing Monte to gobble up the treats he always carries with him.

"Nothing." I shrug, praying he doesn't push the conversation.

While I have a good relationship with all my siblings, I'm probably closest with Jude. Not just because we're less than a year apart, but also because we're in similar lines of work, although we often argue over whose business requires a higher level of expertise.

Jude studied chemical engineering in college. While

he was there, he started brewing his own beer out of the garage of the fraternity house.

His first batch was a huge success and led to him dropping out after two years to open a brewery here in town. While it was initially just for distribution, he now also has a taproom, which has become the popular hangout amongst locals and tourists alike.

I still say my job is much more challenging. He's not responsible for his product all the way down to the type of soil his grains are grown in. Not like I am.

"Where Haley McBride is concerned, it's never nothing." He gives me a knowing look.

"She was asking about my rental. That's all."

"Ah." He widens his stance, crossing his arms in front of his chest. "I heard Belinda's moving."

"So it seems."

I steal a glance at the parking lot outside the tasting room, relieved to see Haley's dark SUV pulling away. I whistle for Monte to follow me and start toward the barrel building.

"What did you tell her?" Jude presses, trailing behind me.

"The truth. I'm booked through March. There's nothing I can do for her."

"Or," he prods.

"Or…what?"

His lips curve into that mischievous grin I remember from our childhood. The one that usually led to us getting into trouble.

Still, I always went along with his crazy plans.

"Or maybe you could both help each other."

"What are you talking about?"

"She could be the solution to your little problem with Grady. In exchange, you give her a place to live."

I come to an abrupt stop and face my brother. He's only an inch shorter than my six-three frame, his hair the same dark shade, although not as long.

"What are you suggesting? That I marry Haley McBride so Grady will sell me the vineyard?" I bark out a laugh at how ridiculous it sounds. "No way. Grady would never believe it."

"On the contrary," Jude retorts as I continue down the path. His footsteps crunch on the dirt beneath his feet as he catches up. "If Grady's going to believe you married anyone, it's Haley. He knows you've had a thing for her since you were kids."

"He also knows what I did to her."

"It was an accident. When the hell are you going to stop beating yourself up over one stupid mistake?"

"One stupid mistake that nearly sent her to the goddamn morgue."

Jude doesn't insist I'm being ridiculous. Instead, he glares at me.

"We barely talk," I add, pushing down the memories of that summer. Of the night that completely changed my life. "We're not even friends, let alone close enough for anyone to think we've suddenly fallen head over heels in love with each other."

"You can try to deny it all you want, but I see how you look at her."

I open my mouth to argue, but he cuts me off with a raised hand.

"You still have feelings for her. I see it. Anyone with eyes can see it. Which is why Haley's the perfect woman for you to fake marry."

I stare at my brother, convinced I must be hallucinating. Or that I'm asleep and this is a dream. Or, more appropriately, a nightmare. That can be the only possible explanation for why my normally practical and even-headed brother would suggest I ask Haley to marry me so I can buy the vineyard, especially given our past.

Years ago, I swore I'd stay as far away from her as possible. That I'd never ruin her life again. Asking her to marry me and living together? It's a disaster waiting to happen.

"You've lost your mind." I pick up my pace, practically jogging toward the barrel room.

"I prefer to say I'm thinking outside the box." He touches a hand to my arm, forcing me to come to a stop. "You want the vineyard, don't you? Don't want all your years of hard work to go to someone who's never stepped foot on this land?"

"Of course."

"Then this is perfect. Haley needs a place to live. You need a wife. It's a win-win. If you want Grady to believe it's real, she's your only option, Beck."

As much as I hate to admit it, my brother does have a point.

Grady knows all about our history. How we were inseparable when we were kids. How we were each other's first kiss. How we didn't see each other much as she got older. How we reconnected right before we were both supposed to go off to college.

How neither of us were able to go.

Instead, she spent what should have been her freshman year learning how to walk again.

And I spent mine in prison.

"You know I'm right," Jude cuts into my thoughts.

"She'll never agree to this."

"You never know. She might just be desperate enough to agree to marry you, you asshole."

"And an asshole is exactly what I'd be if I offered her somewhere to live, but only if she marries me."

"Then make sure you sweeten the pot."

"Sweeten the pot? How?"

"Give her an offer she can't refuse," he says, doing his best impression of Marlon Brando. Then adds, "and I'm not talking about your dick, since history indicates that's an offer she's more than happy to refuse."

I punch him in the bicep. It's not a hard jab, but it's not exactly light, either.

"Asshole." He rubs his arm.

"You started it," I retort, just as I did when we were kids.

"Think about it, Beck. Are you ready to walk away

from all of this?" He waves at the acres upon acres of vine-covered rolling hills, the setting sun casting a mixture of shadows and light on the stunning landscape.

"Getting married doesn't guarantee Grady will sell to me," I remind my brother.

"No. But it'll at least get you in the running. Do you always want to wonder what if?"

I could argue that I'll be fine. That I can always find another piece of property to buy or accept one of the myriad of offers I receive from other vineyards on a regular basis. But I know this land. Know this soil. Know these vines.

Am I ready to give up without a fight?

Better yet, am I willing to pull Haley back into my life even after I swore I'd stay away?

FIVE

Haley

The numbers on the legal pad in front of me blur and swirl, making it difficult to focus. One thing I've become painfully aware of is how hard it is to come up with a reliable budget when so much of my income depends on tips. Which depends on how busy the casino is. It doesn't help that Christmas is around the corner, so money is tighter than usual, which stresses me out even more.

My only saving grace has been the support system I've built over the years in Parker and Grandma Estelle, who isn't a grandmother at all. Still, she's well-known here in Sycamore Falls and loved by so many people, especially me.

Ever since I moved here after giving birth to

Maggie, she's been more than willing to watch my little girl whenever I've needed her to, allowing me to pick up extra shifts at the casino.

But even with extra shifts, I'm not sure it will be enough.

Since I live so close to Lake Tahoe, everyone has been raising rent prices to take advantage of the seasonal tourists who flock here for skiing in the winter and lake activities in the summer. A single mom who works as a cocktail waitress probably isn't their ideal tenant.

But the more time that passes and the more rejections I get from potential rentals, the more I fear I may have no option but to move to a larger city with more affordable housing. That or start sleeping with men for money.

Maybe I should take a page out of Parker's book. She's always been a strong believer in manifestation and the law of attraction. Maybe that's what I should do. Manifest a solution in the hopes the universe is listening and will give me what I need.

Closing my eyes, I push out a long breath, doing my best to eliminate any negative thoughts from my mind.

"I will have a place to live," I announce.

While the skeptic in me struggles to believe any of this will work, I'm willing to try anything at this point. Like make bold statements to the universe.

"It'll have an enormous yard, with lots of grass and trees. But also lots of good hiding places so we can play hide and seek." My heart warms as the image of the dream home where I can raise my daughter takes shape in my mind. "The inside will be spacious but not impersonal. There will be a few stains on the rug, some chips in the paint. But that's okay, because it's a kid's home. And no one will yell at Maggie for spilling her juice by mistake."

The more I speak, the more excited I get about the picture in my head. The more real it feels.

I open my eyes and scribble down notes on the pad. "She'll have her very own bedroom, painted a combination of pink and teal, since those are her current favorite colors. And it will have a loft bed with a slide and a secret clubhouse underneath, like the one I'd love to be able to buy her." My heart warms with excitement as I imagine the look on her face when she sees it.

"Our home will be filled with love and laughter and everything I wished for when I was her age. That's what she deserves. What we both—"

A sudden loud knock interrupts my train of thought, and I dart my eyes to the door, wondering who it could be after ten on a Tuesday.

The only person I can think of is Parker. It's not completely unusual for her to stop by when she needs to talk, since she knows I can't leave Maggie.

Standing, I walk the short distance toward the door and pull it open. "Is everything—"

I snap my mouth shut when I see the person

standing outside isn't a tall blonde, but a muscular grump with a permanent scowl etched on his face.

At least when he looks at me.

I don't fault him for it. He has every reason to hate me.

Even so, I can't deny how attractive he is in his winter jacket and beanie, a bit of scruff dotting his jawline.

"You're not Parker," I blurt out, breaking the uncomfortable silence.

"Looks like your eyesight is still good."

"Sorry. I just… She's the only person who stops by."

Beckham stares at me for several more seconds, the tension becoming increasingly awkward.

It always does whenever we're forced to interact with each other.

Maybe because I still don't know what to do or say around him.

"Is there a reason you're here?" I ask when I can't take the tension any longer.

He pinches his lips together, seeming to contemplate my question. His expression is so serious, so pensive.

"Can I come in for a minute?" he sighs. "There's something I'd like to talk to you about and I'd rather not do it on your stoop."

My curiosity piqued, I step back, pulling the door wide for him to enter, even though I hate the idea of Beckham Lawrence seeing where I live.

It's not a bad place. Belinda's husband built this

addition years ago when his mother was older and couldn't live on her own anymore. There's a bedroom, as well as a tiny kitchenette and living area, not to mention my own private entrance so we don't have to bother Belinda. But it's definitely cramped.

In the beginning, I didn't need a lot of room. It was just me and a baby. But now that Maggie's older, she requires more space. Most nights, I sleep on the couch and let her have the bedroom.

"Keep your voice low. Maggie's sleeping." I gesture at the slightly ajar door just off the cluttered living area.

"Of course," he whispers as he takes off his beanie and shrugs out of his jacket, draping it over the back of one of the chairs by the tiny bistro table.

I can't help but admire his rugged good looks, especially now that he's more mature than he was all those years ago. And just like all those years ago, my heart rate picks up in his presence, particularly as my eyes focus on his lips.

"Can I get you anything?" I quickly look away. "Whiskey? Beer? I have some wine, too, although I'm not sure it's any good." Smirking, I nod at the bottle boasting the familiar label of his vineyard.

"Believe me, Haley. That's a good one. Would put any of those Napa wines to shame. But no. Nothing for me. I won't stay long. I..." He trails off, his eyes focused on the notepad I left on the table.

Panic shoots through me and I move quickly toward it, but before I can snatch it away, he picks it up.

Great. This is exactly what I need. Beckham Lawrence learning how much I'm struggling financially. He'll probably tell me this is what I deserve.

He's probably right.

"Is this what you make in a month?" His eyes lock on mine, something akin to pity within.

Which irritates me even more.

"I'm only able to work part time. Plus, this may come as a surprise, but a lot of employers don't like hiring a single mom because they're worried about me having to miss work whenever Maggie gets sick. And she's a kid. She's going to get sick. So—"

"I know. I just…" He shakes his head, seemingly at a loss for words.

"Why are you here, Beckham? Other than to make me feel like a shitty mother?"

I cross my arms over my stomach, doing everything I can to hold it together. It's getting more and more difficult with every passing day. But I refuse to cry in front of him.

It's bad enough I asked to rent his townhouse and he turned me down.

"You're not a shitty mother, Haley," he soothes, a break in his normally aloof demeanor. "I see how happy Maggie is."

"Yeah. Well, we'll see how happy she is when we're living out of my car."

He steps toward me, dropping his voice. "Is it that bad?"

"Yes. No. I don't know." I throw my hands up in frustration. "I'll figure it out. I always do. What did you want to talk to me about?"

"A solution, actually."

I tilt my head. "A solution?"

"Yes." He gestures to the chair with a brow raised, wordlessly asking if he can sit.

I nod, and he sits down as I assume the chair across from him.

My eyes remain locked on him as he draws in a deep breath. Which only increases my unease about whatever this solution may be.

"You need a place to live. I have a place for you to live."

"Did your renters cancel?" Hope builds inside my chest.

"No. It's still fully booked. In fact, there's a waiting list."

"But—"

"On the vineyard. With me."

My breath catches. "With…you? Why would you do that?"

He taps his fingers nervously against the table. "Because I need something, too."

"What's that?"

He slowly lifts his eyes to mine, several protracted seconds passing as I wait for his response.

Then he finally says, "A wife."

SIX

Haley

I must be hallucinating. Or even dreaming. That must be it. I must have fallen asleep while I was manifesting and dreamed I was presented with a solution to my problem. That's the only possible explanation for why Beckham Lawrence is suggesting I marry him. After all, the man has barely muttered more than a few words to me over the past several years.

"I'm sorry. I think I misheard," I finally say once the shock wears off. "Did you say your solution is for me to…*marry* you?"

"I did."

"Beckham, I—"

"Grady's selling the vineyard. I offered to buy it.

Unfortunately, he doesn't want to sell to me because he's worried the vineyard would become my life."

"Become?" I scoff. "It already is."

"Regardless, he promised my dad he'd always look out for me. I guess he doesn't want me to make the same mistake he thinks he did by putting the vineyard first and not marrying."

"And if you were married…"

"He'd sell to me, even if someone else came in with a better offer. He'd rather it go to someone who cares about the land."

"Don't you think he'd be suspicious if you announce you're getting married so soon after he tells you he'll only sell to you if you're married?"

"We won't get married right away," he explains, making it clear he's given this some thought. "We'll wait until closer to when Belinda moves. That's the end of January, right?"

I nod, fidgeting with my glass of water.

"We'll get married then. If you agree, of course."

"Why me? Isn't there some other woman you could ask?"

He slowly shakes his head. "There's no one, Haley."

I struggle to suppress the relief filling me at the idea that he's not currently dating anyone. I shouldn't care. That ship sailed years ago. Hell, that ship never even left port.

"It needs to be you. If there's anyone Grady will believe I married, it's you. He knows all about our…

history." He lifts his dark eyes to mine, so many emotions swirling within.

Regret. Guilt. Fear.

It's the fear I can't quite understand.

"So, what?" I ask. "We'd pretend to date for now?"

He furrows his brow, his brown eyes darkening with confusion. "Why would we do that?"

"Won't people get suspicious?"

He shrugs. "We'll tell them you didn't want Maggie to get attached in case it didn't work out."

"And I don't." I lean across the table, dropping my voice. "Have you thought about how this might affect her?"

"Of course I have. It's one—"

"Because it doesn't seem like it, Beckham," I interrupt. "If you want people to think our marriage is real, if you want *Grady* to think it's real, then Maggie has to believe it's real, too."

"Why?"

"This may come as a surprise, but four-year olds aren't known for their ability to keep secrets. Hell, most forty-year-olds aren't, either. Especially in this town."

His shoulders fall as he peers into the distance, a furrow creasing his brow. "I didn't think of that."

"We wouldn't only have to pretend in public. We'd have to pretend all the time. Share a room. A bed." My cheeks flush at the thought, but I quickly push it down. "Not to mention, what will she think when our sham marriage is over? She'll worry she did something wrong."

"I'll still be there for her."

"Don't make any promises you have no intention of keeping." I pin him with a heated stare. "Your track record in that department isn't all that great."

He swallows hard, but doesn't offer an excuse or an explanation. After this long, I doubt I'll ever get one.

"Every decision I make is with her in mind," I continue, ignoring the giant elephant in the room. "What's best for her."

"I can respect that. Which is why I'm willing to take care of her preschool and daycare expenses, along with groceries, your car payment. You'd even be able to go on my health insurance. You won't have to worry about a single thing."

I straighten, opening and closing my mouth several times before asking, "Why would you do that?"

"If you're willing to go along with this, there should be some sort of incentive besides a roof over your head. Plus, it would allow you to save money and maybe finally open the bakery you always dreamed of. If that's still your dream." He averts his gaze, laughing nervously.

I have to hand it to him. He knows exactly what to say to make me give serious consideration to this crazy idea. We may not have spoken much over the past several years, but he still remembers the dreams I shared with him during that one fateful summer.

Owning a bakery has been my dream for as long as I can remember. And not just any bakery, either. Sure, I'd sell the typical cakes, muffins, and cookies, but I hoped to specialize in hyper realistic cakes. I've always loved art and baking. This combines my two passions.

Even with my hectic life, I practice making cakes that look like everyday objects every chance I get.

It's not as easy in my tiny home, but Parker lets me use the kitchen at her inn between meal service. I've been lucky enough to make cakes for a few weddings, thanks to Parker recommending me to brides looking for a more non-traditional wedding cake.

I'd love to be able to quit my crappy job at the casino and bake all day, every day. Have somewhere Maggie would be welcome. Do something that would make her proud, instead of wearing a skimpy dress as I serve drunken men with wandering hands.

"How long would this marriage have to last?"

"I'd like to stay married for at least six months after the sale goes through. That way, Grady doesn't get suspicious. At that point, there won't be anything he could do even if he were to find out the truth…"

"But you still don't want him to know."

Beckham shrugs. "He's done so much for me. Especially after…everything," he says evasively. But I know what he's talking about.

Grady Belanger was one of the few people in town willing to give Beckham a chance after he was released from prison. He refused to let one mistake define him.

Even if Beckham still allows it to define him.

"I'd rather he not learn I lied just so he'd sell to me."

I nod, processing everything he just offered. It's definitely an appealing proposal and would solve quite a few problems.

But I'm not the only one this affects.

"Can I have some time to think about it? There's a lot I need to consider." I gesture toward the bedroom door.

"Of course." He stands, shrugging on his coat and returning his beanie to his head as he walks toward the door. But before slipping outside, he pauses, glancing back at me.

"Even if you say no, you're still welcome to move in with me, and at an affordable rent. I'm barely there anyway. I'm not going to let you live out of your car, Haley."

"I'll think about it," I tell him once more.

"Thanks." He holds my gaze for a few more beats, then closes the door behind him, the sound of his boots crunching on the gravel growing duller as he retreats.

Once I can no longer hear them, I sink into my chair, my brain reeling.

There was a time I would have done anything for him.

But that was a lifetime ago. Before he shut me out. Before he pretended I don't exist.

Can I really marry him and keep my heart intact, knowing when it ends, I'll lose him all over again?

SEVEN

Haley

"Penny for your thoughts?" Parker asks, handing me a cup of coffee and lowering herself onto the bench beside me.

I tear my gaze away from Maggie as she runs around the playground in the kid's area of Parker's ranch.

While Maggie will never miss an opportunity to come here, she particularly loves it during winter when there are so many fun activities — from ice skating, to train rides on a makeshift Polar Express, to ornament making, and everything in between.

I take a sip of the robust coffee, relishing in its warmth. Then my eyes wander back to Maggie, and I watch her with a mixture of love and exhaustion.

"She's so happy. Isn't she?"

"The happiest. But that's to be expected." Parker nudges me. "She's got a great mom."

"I try to be, Parker. But it's definitely not easy, especially lately. Don't get me wrong," I add quickly. "I'm grateful you and Grandma Estelle are always willing to help with her whenever I need it."

"Because we love that little girl. And you."

"I know." I exhale deeply, shaking my head. "But sometimes I feel so alone. Like no matter what I do, it's not good enough."

Parker wraps an arm around me and gives me a comforting squeeze. It's moments like this that make me grateful for our friendship. I don't know what I'd do without her. It's a surprising thought, considering we barely knew each other a few years ago. I didn't grow up in Sycamore Falls like Beckham and Parker did. My parents live in Lake Tahoe. The only reason I knew Beckham at all is because my nanny was good friends with his mother and would arrange play dates together.

Still, I fell in love with the small town feel here. When Maggie was born, there was only one place I wanted her to grow up. I wanted her to have the childhood I always wished I could have had. The childhood Beckham was lucky enough to have.

"I talked to him," I announce after several protracted seconds.

Parker darts her eyes to mine, her brow furrowed. "Who?"

"Beckham. I asked about renting his townhouse."

"What did he say?"

"What I expected him to. That his place is booked solid with all the snow bunnies coming here to ski. But then…"

"Yes?" Her gaze brims with anticipation.

I steal a glance at Maggie to make sure she's not paying me any attention. Thankfully, she's preoccupied with the other kids playing.

Leaning in even closer, I drop my voice. "He asked me to marry him."

"He…*what*?" she shrieks.

I hush her, especially when several pairs of eyes look our way. Thankfully, most of the people are tourists with no interest in our conversation.

"Took me by surprise, too."

"Aren't people supposed to date before a proposal? At the very least, they have a hot and heavy one-night stand, then plan to never see each other again until those two little lines appear on a pregnancy test, at which point he proposes." Her eyes widening, she sucks in a gasp. "Oh, my god. Did you sleep together? Are you pregnant?"

"Of course not!" I reply, hoping my face doesn't betray me. "I haven't slept with anyone since I learned I was pregnant with Maggie."

"And you were giving me shit for not dating." She rolls her eyes.

"It's not that I don't want to date. I just have other things to take into consideration now."

"And yet you're considering marrying Beckham Lawrence?" She arches a perfectly manicured eyebrow.

"No. Hell, I don't know…" I push out a sigh.

"Why does he want to marry you?"

"He doesn't *want* to marry me."

"But you said——"

"Grady is planning to sell the vineyard. Beckham made an offer, but Grady's worried he'll make the vineyard his life if he sold it to him." I give her a knowing look, considering Parker can be accused of doing the same thing.

Since her parents passed away several years ago, she's made Holley Ridge her life. Sunk all the life insurance money and her savings into transforming the barn into a wedding venue and building a luxurious inn to accommodate overnight guests. And then there's the annual Christmas festival she puts on. I doubt she's taken a single day off since her father died.

"So he wants him to get married?"

I shrug. "It appears so."

"What are your thoughts on his proposition?"

"It's definitely an attractive offer. Not only will he give me a place to live, but he'll cover all my bills and put Maggie and me on his health insurance. I won't have to worry about anything, so all the money I make——"

"You can use to focus on your cake business."

"Exactly."

"And how long would this fake marriage last?"

"He'd like to stay married for at least six months after the sale is finalized so Grady doesn't feel like he was tricked or lied to. We *would* be tricking him, but it's for a good purpose, I suppose."

"And Maggie?"

I shift my gaze forward, watching her pump her little legs as she swings back and forth, her auburn pigtails flying behind her.

"I can't tell her the truth. She'd blab it all over the county. I probably shouldn't even tell you, since this only works if the entire town believes we're madly in love."

"That won't be a problem," she snorts. "Pretty sure there's a pool going for how much longer it'll take before the two of you just bang it out already. You'd have to be blind not to see the chemistry between you two."

"Maggie's where it gets sticky," I say, ignoring her remark. "It's one thing if we only have to pretend to be married in public, but since I have a four-year-old, I can't have her telling everyone that mommy's only married so her fake husband can buy the winery. Which means she needs to believe it's real. Which also means—"

"She'll believe it's real when you split."

I nod gravely. "The reason I didn't go after paternity or support from her sperm donor is because I didn't want Maggie to deal with that kind of rejection or abandonment. I'm not sure if I can put her through that."

"Is it Maggie you're worried about?" Parker narrows her gaze on me. "Or yourself?"

I should have known she'd see through my lies and uncover the truth I've been trying to hide for years.

That I've been trying to forget about for years.

Because she's right.

It's not only Maggie I'm worried about.

It's me.

Or, more accurately, my heart.

EIGHT

Haley

"I hate it here," I mutter under my breath as I place my tray on the serving station, waiting for the bartender to finish pouring the drinks I just punched into the register.

Despite it being Christmas Eve, the casino is packed with entitled and obnoxious assholes. I don't think I've ever been hit on or propositioned as many times as I have during this shift.

And I've only been here an hour.

It's the last place I want to be right now. I'd much rather be celebrating Christmas Eve with Maggie. I *should* be celebrating Christmas Eve with Maggie.

Instead, Frank threatened to fire me if I didn't show

up for my shift. Claimed he needed all hands on deck with the hotel at full occupancy.

I'm pretty sure he scheduled me as punishment for all the times I've been late for my shift, considering he knows I have a daughter. Being here on Christmas Eve is definitely making me give serious consideration to Beckham's proposal. But can I really marry him and survive with my heart intact, knowing the power he once held over me?

The power I fear he still holds.

"It's a jungle out there tonight, isn't it?" Ivy exhales as she joins me at the serving station. "At least the tips make working on a holiday worth it." She takes a few bills off her tray and shoves them into the top of her dress.

"I'd rather be home, to hell with the tips."

"Why are you working?" She fully faces me. "Shouldn't you be home with your kid?"

"Frank said he'd fire me if I called out. And since I'm on the verge of being homeless as it is, I had no choice but to come in."

"What a prick."

"Tell me about it." I roll my eyes as I set my drink order on my tray. "Not only do I have to miss out on reading *The Night Before Christmas* to Maggie and listen to her excitedly talk about Santa, I won't get home until four, so I'll probably only be able to sleep for a few hours before she'll be up." I push out a breath. "I'd love to quit this job."

"You just need to find a sugar daddy to pay all your bills." She playfully nudges me. "There's a casino full of prospective applicants, if you know what I mean."

"Tempting, but no."

"Suit yourself," Ivy shoots back. "But if agreeing to be some rich dude's mistress means I don't have to work, I'd jump on that in a heartbeat. But you do you."

"I always do," I sing as I carefully balance my tray and head back into "the suck", as I call the casino floor.

Machines whirl and clang as excited voices bellow through the space, the only evidence of it being Christmas Eve the decorations and pop remakes of carols being piped in through the sound system.

With a congenial expression plastered on my face, I skirt through the crowd toward the blackjack tables and drop off drinks for the men spending their evening gambling instead of with their families. After removing several abandoned glasses, some still full, I head toward the next table, where a bunch of rowdy men gamble.

"Can I get you gentlemen anything to drink?" I ask in a sweet voice after the dealer finishes a round.

Their eyes shift from the cards to me, their gazes lingering on my body like predators sizing up their prey.

"Are *you* on the menu?" a tall blond slurs with a suggestive waggle of his brow.

"I'll come back when you know what you'd like to order," I reply with forced patience, ignoring his comment. I start to turn, but his voice stops me.

"How about an Irish redhead?" he asks, as if it's the first time I've heard that.

I should be used to this by now. After all, these assholes are no different from all the other men I've dealt with since taking this job.

But tonight, it hits differently. Maybe it's because I should be home with Maggie, setting all the presents beneath the tree. Or because Frank's a prick for scheduling me to work when I requested the night off months ago. Or because I can't stop thinking about Beckham's proposal.

Whatever the reason, I'm more irritated than usual tonight, dangerously close to snapping.

"No. That's not it. Not in the mood for that." The heat of his eyes creeping over every inch of my body makes my stomach churn. "How about a redhead in bed? Think you can get me that?"

With every word he speaks, my smile fades, my grip on my tray tightening. Especially when his friends only seem to encourage his behavior, not a single decent one among them.

"Nope. Nope. That's not it, either. As much as I'd love a redhead in bed, I think I'm in the mood for something different." All the amusement disappears from his tone as he moves toward me.

I abruptly step back, my eyes briefly locking with the dealer, who raises a brow in question. I shake my head, telling him I can handle myself. No doubt Frank would find my inability to handle an unruly customer as another reason to fire me.

"Do you know what would make my Christmas *really* memorable?" He glances back at his friends, his smirk growing. Then he returns his gaze to mine. "A redheaded slut." He licks his lips as he rakes his stare down my frame. "From where I'm standing, you most definitely fit the bill."

My heartbeat echoes in my ears as every muscle in my body goes rigid with anger. Normally, I'd walk away and let security know about a problem customer. That's what I'm *supposed* to do.

But I've seen how these situations go. Nine times out of ten, they're given a warning and continue their entitled behavior, hitting on more cocktail waitresses as if it's their right. I'm so sick of everyone thinking they're better than me. Of being taken advantage of. Of not standing up for myself.

I'm so tired of this fucking job.

When he runs a finger down my arm, all my self-control flies out the window. Without hesitation, I grab one of the full glasses off my tray and fling its contents onto his smug face.

All traces of his pompous attitude instantly disappear and he glowers at me.

"You… Do you have any idea who I am?"

"You're a fucking asshole. That's who," I snap back, adrenaline coursing through my veins. "You have no right to touch me or anyone else."

He laughs dismissively, wiping the liquor out of his eyes. "Get off your high horse. You honestly think I'm going to buy that? I'm more than aware of how all you girls supplement your income by spreading your legs for the right price. So tell me… What's yours?"

My blood boiling, I reel back, delivering a harsh slap across his face with my open palm. "Fuck you."

The seconds stretch as he stares at the carpet, massaging his cheek. Then he turns his malice-filled eyes on me. "You'll regret this."

"Actually, I don't think I will. Because that felt really good." I spin on my heels and hurry away, feeling everyone's stare burning my skin as I go, the casino floor seeming unusually silent.

Probably because the thunderous beating of my heart is infinitely louder.

I've never done anything like this before. Up until now, I've just let these assholes get away with doing and saying whatever they want so I could keep this shitty job. Not anymore.

As I approach the serving area, Frank barrels down the hallway like an enraged bull, his dark eyes on fire and face so red I'm convinced he's about to keel over and have a heart attack.

"Haley!" he roars, pointing an accusatory finger at me. "My office. Now!"

"That won't be necessary." I shove my tray at him, a surge of defiance washing over me. "I quit."

His gaze widens. "You…what?"

"Isn't that what you threatened me with if I didn't come in tonight? Well, I'm done with this shitty job. Done letting asshole men ogle and grab at me, which your actions seem to encourage. Done with your sexist comments. So fuck off, Frank."

I storm past him, my entire body vibrating with fury as I hurry into the break room and quickly collect all of my things.

It's not until I'm driving away that the reality of what I just did hits me.

I quit my job.

I quit the job that provides the majority of my income.

I quit my job when I'm on the brink of having nowhere to live.

As I come to a stoplight, I glance into the rearview mirror, the lights of the casino visible. For a split second, I debate turning around and begging for my job back.

But I hate that job. Have been wanting to quit for a while now.

As skeptical as I am about the whole manifestation thing, I can't help but wonder if the universe had something to do with my actions tonight.

I asked the universe for a solution to my problem. Seconds later, Beckham Lawrence knocked on my door with a proposition that would solve both of our problems.

Maybe this is the universe giving me a push in that direction.

NINE

Beckham

"How are things at the vineyard?" Jude asks as I lean against the counter in my mom's kitchen, the scent of freshly baked cookies and pine from the Christmas tree surrounding me.

Its twinkling lights cast a warm glow over the open living area, but my mind keeps drifting to the tiny fake tree in Haley's cramped apartment.

Seeing where she's been living hit me harder than I thought it would.

I'm more than aware she hasn't had it easy these past few years, but I didn't realize just how bad things have gotten. How much she's been struggling. It's why I offered her a place to live, even if she doesn't agree to marry me.

It was rash, considering our complicated history, but I can't just let her live out of her car.

"Things are good," I tell Jude, although I know he's not asking to find out about the vines or the different formulas I've been testing.

He's asking to see if I've given any thought to his suggestion.

My eyes scan the crowded living room, ensuring no one can overhear us. With my four siblings here to celebrate Christmas Eve, the noise level is practically deafening. I haven't seen my mother this happy in a while. It's been years since all five of her kids have been in the same place at the same time. Probably since before Dad passed away.

Before I was sent to prison.

Still, it's nice to have everyone together again, especially my older brother, Hayden, and his two kids.

Even if the reason he left his hospital job in Chicago and moved back home is due to his wife's unexpected death.

"I took your advice," I tell Jude in a soft voice, sipping on my wine. "About the vineyard. And Haley."

"You did?" His eyebrows shoot up in surprise. "You actually asked Haley McBride to marry you?"

Hushing him, I glance toward my mother, convinced she heard him. When we were kids, she always had an uncanny ability to hear things she wasn't supposed to, especially when we were doing things we shouldn't.

Thankfully, she's preoccupied with little nine-month-old Jeremiah and six-year-old Presley, both of them playing with all their new toys. We may have gone overboard with presents for them, but considering this is their first Christmas without their mom, it's warranted.

"I did," I confirm.

"And?" He takes a swig of his beer, leaning against the kitchen counter beside me.

"She asked to think about it. She has a kid to consider. I'm not really holding my breath, though, which sucks since Grady's met with a few people interested in buying the vineyard." My phone buzzes in my pocket and I pull it out. "But unless a miracle happens and—"

I stop short as my eyes fall on the screen, Haley's name prominent.

There was once a time it was a normal occurrence for my cell to buzz with an incoming text from her.

I don't think I've received a text from her in years.

Not since I went away.

"Maybe you'll get your miracle after all." Jude chuckles, glancing at my phone.

"Maybe," I murmur as I click on her message.

HALEY:

Are you at your mom's?

ME:

I am. Why?

HALEY:

Can you come outside? I need to talk
to you.

"Is everything okay?" Jude asks.

I rush toward the window over the sink and peek through the blinds, finding Haley's car parked on the street in front of my mother's house. My mind reels about why she might be here, especially on Christmas Eve.

"I'll be right back." Setting my glass on the counter, I hurry out of the house before Jude can ask any more questions.

Or the rest of my nosy family.

As I step off the porch and jog down the walkway, Haley climbs out of her car, tugging her coat close to her body. Based on the copious amount of makeup plastered on her face and the fact that the only things visible beneath her thigh-length pea coat are her nylon-clad legs and black heels, I assume she came straight from work.

"I'll do it," she blurts out before I have a chance to utter a single syllable.

"Do what?" I ask cautiously, trying not to get my hopes up.

"What we discussed last week." She holds her head high. "I'll marry you."

"You will?" My eyes widen in surprise.

"Considering I just quit my job at the casino after a guy...well, it—"

"After a guy, what?" I grind out, my jaw clenching.

"It doesn't matter. But since I'm now minus a job, I figure maybe it's the universe pushing me toward you. Well, not you in that sense. But us. This." She gestures between our bodies. "Accepting your proposal and all that. As long as you don't mind I'm down to just my dog walking job."

"I hated you working in that casino anyway."

"The money was good," she argues, as if that makes enduring hours of wandering hands and rude comments worth it.

"I can talk to Grady. Get you a job in the tasting room."

"You're already doing enough for me."

"I don't mind."

"And I appreciate it."

She gives me a soft smile, and I'd be lying if that small gesture doesn't cause a crack in the wall I built around my heart. At least when it comes to Haley McBride.

"Just like losing my job is the universe pushing me to help you, maybe it's also the universe telling me to finally follow my dreams. Without having to work at the casino, I'll have more time to experiment with cakes and build up my social media presence. Even without a physical bakery, I can still make cakes."

"Yes, you can." I shove my hands into the pockets of my jeans, locking my gaze on hers to stop myself from checking out her legs.

"Well, I just wanted to let you know. I guess I could have texted you, but I wanted to see you first. Make sure…" She shakes her head.

"Make sure you don't mind spending the better part of the next year with me?" I blow out a nervous laugh.

She pulls her coat tighter. "Something like that." Her gaze drifts up to mine.

I step toward her, drawn into her eyes just like I have been most of my life, even when I knew it was a lost cause. Knew her parents would never approve of me. My heart never seemed to get the message. It still doesn't.

"You should get back to your family," she says, tearing her gaze from me and increasing the distance between us.

"Would you like to join us? Mom made enough food to feed all of Sycamore Falls. As usual. She'd love to see you."

"I need to get home to Maggie. Santa's coming tonight."

"Right. Of course. Well, thanks for doing this for me."

"I'm not doing it for you. I'm doing it for Maggie. And me."

"Regardless, I still appreciate it."

She nods, then starts to turn. "Merry Christmas, Beckham."

"Merry Christmas, Haley."

I watch as she retreats, her heels clicking on the

pavement. She only makes it a few feet before I call out, "Haley, wait!"

I jog toward my truck and open the back door, retrieving an oversized box wrapped in penguin-covered paper.

"What's that?" she asks, warily eyeing the box as I approach her. "Is that—"

"I was going to drop it off after I left here," I interrupt. It's obvious by the size and shape of the box she knows exactly what it is. The Barbie camper Maggie asked for. "There's no tag so you can tell her it's from Santa."

"Beckham, you didn't have to do that."

"I wanted to."

"She's not your responsibility. She—"

"I know she's not. But it's Christmas, and I wanted to do something nice for you and your daughter. Okay?"

My voice seems to echo in the stillness of the air. I glance back at the house. When I do, I notice the curtains immediately shift, confirming that someone's definitely been watching us.

Most likely my sister, Dylan. Probably my mom, too.

Hell, probably my entire family.

It's not often they see me talking to another girl, especially Haley McBride.

"I just don't like to depend on other people for what I should be able to give my daughter on my own."

"If you're going to be my wife, I'm going to take care of both you and Maggie."

"Fake wife," she reminds me, although I'm not sure if it's for my benefit or hers. "It won't be real."

"True, but we'll need to make everyone think it's real. Can you do that?"

"I spent the past several years pretending I like delivering drinks to drunk men while they try to get in my pants. I'll be just fine. It's you I'm worried about."

"Me?" I scoff, pushing down the renewed anger bubbling to the surface at the idea of anyone trying to get into Haley's pants, especially the assholes at the casino.

"Yeah." She places a hand on her hip. "You've got your work cut out for you with that brooding persona you've had going on the past few years. You won't be able to get away with being your normal, charming self. You'll have to act like you don't hate me. And it will have to be believable, Beckham."

In a heartbeat, I advance on her, barely a whisper separating us. She inhales a sharp breath, her gaze locking with mine. Fire heats my veins, my hunger for her just as strong as it once was. I can't remember the last time I've been this close to her. Probably since the night I lost control.

As I lean closer, I inhale her scent. She smells like she did all those years ago. Lavender. Powder. And fresh air.

Her chest rises and falls, her breathing increasing

with every inch I erase between us until my lips almost skim the spot beneath her earlobe.

The spot that once drove her crazy.

Does it still make her moan? Still send a rush of desire through her veins? Still make her burn for me?

A subtle tremble shakes her body as she whimpers. If I weren't so close, I probably wouldn't have heard it.

But I did. And damn if it doesn't make me want to haul her into my arms and kiss her. Find out if she still tastes the same. If her body still fits mine like it once did.

"I think I can make it look convincing," I murmur, lingering near her ear for several protracted moments.

It's a test in extreme restraint to be this close and not dart out my tongue to taste her.

But restraint is one of the things I had no choice but to learn over the past several years. My lack of restraint is what nearly cost Haley her life. What sent me to prison. It's not a mistake I can afford to make again.

With that sobering reminder, I increase the space between us.

"Merry Christmas, Haley," I say softly before jogging back toward the house.

After climbing up the front porch, I pause, if for no other reason than to give my erection a chance to go down before having to face the barrage of questions I'm sure my mother is desperate to ask.

I glance over my shoulder as Haley carefully slides

into her car on unsteady legs, just as affected by me as I am by her.

One thing is certain. The next several months will be a test in self-control.

But it's one I refuse to fail.

Not when I live with a constant reminder of what happened the last time I did.

TEN

Haley

"Are you sure you don't mind watching her tonight?" I ask Parker through the mirror in her living room as I check my reflection one last time.

"Of course not." She hugs Maggie against her and tickles her stomach, eliciting excited squeals. "Miss Magpie and I are going to have an awesome time. We're going to order a pizza, watch a movie, and roast some marshmallows for s'mores."

"I love s'mores!" Maggie responds enthusiastically.

"Me, too." Parker nuzzles her nose against Maggie's, then stands, moving toward me. "Seriously, Hales. Don't worry. Enjoy your night. And if you want, Maggie can always sleep here."

"It's not that kind of date," I say in a low voice so Maggie can't hear. Thankfully, her attention is now back on the *Bluey* episode currently playing on the TV. "It's more of a business meeting than anything."

Parker gives me a knowing look. "I seem to remember having a similar conversation a few weeks ago, although the roles were reversed. I tried to tell you the same thing when I was going to dinner with Callum."

"That was different," I argue, remembering all too clearly how I encouraged her to leave her options open with the sexy man who showed up with an offer to buy her property, since she was on the brink of foreclosure. She resisted at first, but eventually fell for the man she swore was her arch nemesis.

But neither could deny the attraction, and Callum Reed ended up being the Christmas miracle Parker needed. He not only gave her a reason to open her heart again but also helped save her beloved ranch.

"You and Callum have insane chemistry. I saw it the night you tricked him into swing dance lessons. It was straight fire."

"And you and Beckham don't have chemistry?" She crosses her arms in front of her chest and arches a disbelieving brow.

"It's…complicated."

"So what? That doesn't mean anything."

"It means everything. I'm only doing this for Maggie. And because I stupidly quit my job."

"It was a crappy job."

"That was responsible for the majority of my income."

"I'll hire you when we reopen after all the renovations are finished."

"I appreciate it." I squeeze her hand. "But maybe this entire situation — quitting my job and Beckham's proposal — is the universe telling me it's time to turn my dreams into reality. If I have to suffer through a short marriage so I can finally fulfill those dreams and make sure Maggie's provided for, so be it. But that's the only reason I'm doing this." I shift my gaze to my daughter, my heart warming with a love I didn't think possible a few years ago. "For her."

"Whatever you say," Parker sings. "Just answer me this."

I take one last sip of wine, smoothing a hand down my dress. I wasn't sure what to wear tonight. I didn't want to seem like I was putting in too much effort, but as a single mom who spends most of my free time taking care of my precocious four-year-old, I don't often have a reason to dress up.

So I went with a staple of every woman's wardrobe — a little black dress.

"What's that?"

"Did you shave?" Parker waggles her brows.

I pin her with a fiery stare for using my question against me. I asked her the same thing when she was getting ready for her "business meeting" with Callum. It may have started out as a business meeting, but when they got snowed in together and the hotel only had one room with one bed available, things got interesting.

But things are different between Parker and Callum. For one, they don't have a shared history to complicate things. Not like Beckham and I do.

"That's what I thought," Parker says with a smirk when I refuse to answer.

The truth is, I *did* shave. Quite extensively, too. There's nothing wrong with a little self-care once in a while.

"I'll let you know if I'll be any later than nine." I walk toward Maggie and give her a big squeeze. "You be good for Auntie Parker, okay?"

"Yes, Mama," she says, barely looking away from *Bluey*.

"I love you."

"Love you, too."

I give her one last hug, then make my way out of Parker's apartment that's attached to her inn, the plush carpeting in the hallway cushioning my heels until I step onto the hardwood floor of the lobby.

It's still decked out for the holidays, even though Christmas is over. Parker keeps the decorations up through the second weekend of January to allow any last-minute stragglers to come see it all.

Waving at Claire at the front desk, I continue farther into the lobby, searching the cozy space for

Beckham. A fire crackles in the hearth, Christmas music playing in the background as a few patrons sit at the lobby bar, enjoying a drink.

But there's still no sign of Beckham.

Until I zero in on the tall man in dark jeans and a crisp black button-down shirt with the sleeves rolled up strolling toward me.

I blink repeatedly, convinced I'm seeing things. The man has Beckham's dark eyes and the tattoos visible on his forearms are an identical match, but the rest of him looks different.

I can't remember the last time I saw him wear something other than dirty jeans and work boots. Hell, even when I stopped by his mother's house on Christmas Eve, he looked like he just came from the vineyard.

But tonight, he's wearing a shirt without stains and jeans that fit his body so perfectly it should be criminal. His hair is neatly styled, albeit in a sexy, disheveled kind of way. He even trimmed his beard.

"Who died?" I ask as he approaches.

"Died?" He stops abruptly, giving me a quizzical look.

"I'm just not used to seeing you in something without mud and grime. I figured there must be some sort of explanation, and a funeral seems the most logical."

He leans down, his lips a breath from my skin,

reminding me of Christmas Eve. My heart hadn't raced so hard in years.

Probably since the summer I lost him.

"I guess you could call it a funeral," he says in a husky voice I feel deep in my core. "I *am* marrying you, after all." He pulls back and shoots me a mischievous look.

"It was your idea," I remind him. "I can leave right now and we'll forget the entire thing."

"And miss being able to irritate the piss out of you every day for the next few months? Baby, I'm just getting warmed up."

"Why did I agree to this?" I mutter under my breath, although I'm secretly grateful for the comfortable banter.

To be fair, I'm somewhat surprised by his sudden easy-going attitude toward me. It reminds me of how things once were between us. I'll happily take this over the heated glares and clipped responses any day.

He places his hand on the small of my back and steers me toward the restaurant. I try to ignore the warmth spreading through me from the innocent touch, but there's no denying the way my body reacts.

We approach the host stand, and he doesn't even need to give his name. Everyone around here knows Beckham. As we follow the hostess through the restaurant, several locals look our way and whisper amongst themselves. No doubt this will be front-page news tomorrow, especially given our past.

"I had Parker reserve us a more secluded table," he says once the hostess has left us alone at a table overlooking the lake, the entire property twinkling with thousands of lights. "This way, we don't have to worry about anyone hearing something they shouldn't. Or worry about people looking at us."

"They still haven't forgotten, have they?" I absentmindedly muse as I place my napkin on my lap and grab my menu.

"Have you?"

I dart my eyes toward his. "Of course not. I just… I figured people would get over it. Find something else to talk about."

"Not sure this town has had another juicy story since then. It's not every day the rich beauty queen is sent to the hospital by the town delinquent."

"It wasn't your fault. Plus, you weren't a delinquent. Your dad was sick."

He stares at me for several long moments, a response seemingly on the tip of his tongue. But instead of talking about it, he closes up, grabbing a large binder the hostess left.

"Red or white?" Beckham asks as he flips through the pages.

"You're the expert," I say around a sigh.

If we're to spend the next several months together, I may as well get used to him being purposefully evasive about our past. Maybe some things are better left unsaid or forgotten.

"What are you thinking of ordering for your meal? If you want seafood, I'll order white."

"I don't mind drinking red with fish."

His jaw drops, a look of horror and disgust filling his expression. "You can't seriously be okay pairing a full-bodied cabernet with a flaky white fish."

"What's wrong with that?" I feign confusion.

I'd never do that, but I need to do something to pull him out of his funk. To cut through the tension of the past lingering between us.

"Everything, Haley. Everything is wrong with it." His voice is firm, determined. "The flavors, the texture. It's all wrong. Just…" He trails off when he sees the smile I struggle to hide. "You're fucking with me. Aren't you?"

I pinch my lips together. "Maybe."

"You're going to regret that."

His threat shouldn't send a shiver of anticipation down my spine, but it does, especially as my sex-deprived libido considers all the ways he might exact his punishment.

Does Beckham like it rough in the bedroom? When we were together all those years ago, we were teenagers. Sex was new to both of us. At least to me. We weren't sure what we were doing, but we figured it out together. I can only imagine he's gotten better with age.

"Parker's chef makes a fantastic filet," I suggest in an effort to take my mind off Beckham's proclivities in the bedroom. Then I inhale a sharp breath when I realize it's one of the more expensive dishes on the menu. "I don't have to get the filet. It's kind of pricey. I'll just get—"

"Order whatever you want," he interjects.

"It's fine. I don't—"

"Get the goddamn filet, Haley. If you don't, I'm going to order it for you anyway, so you may as well just do it yourself."

I bring my eyes toward his and softly say, "Thanks."

He gives a subtle nod as our server approaches. "What can I get you to drink? Will you be having one of your bottles, Beck?"

"I drink enough of it at work. We'll have a bottle of the Grgich Hills cabernet."

"I'll go grab it, then come back to take your order."

"Are you ever able to enjoy it?" I ask once we're alone.

"What's that?"

"Wine. Can you ever enjoy a glass without it reminding you of work?"

"It's not work for me. Sure, the tedious process of checking the soil and vines can feel like it. But tasting someone else's finished product, knowing all the effort they put into making it…" He shakes his head. "There's nothing better."

My lips curve slightly in the corners as I take in the excitement in his expression. I don't think I've ever heard him speak so passionately or animatedly about anything before.

"You love it, don't you?"

"I couldn't imagine doing anything else. I wouldn't *want* to do anything else."

"Then I'm glad I can help." I reach across the table and cover his hand with mine.

The instant our skin makes contact, he darts his gaze toward our joined hands, his Adam's apple bobbing up and down.

This might be the first time I've felt his skin in years. Sure, he teased me the other night as he leaned into the crook of my neck, torturing me with the heat of his breath. But it's been years since I actually felt the warmth of his touch.

And damn him for scrambling my insides even more.

"Here you go," our server sings as she approaches our table, carrying a bottle of wine and two glasses.

I quickly pull my hand away and straighten in my chair, acting as if Beckham's touch hasn't left me completely breathless.

I keep my eyes averted as she expertly removes the cork and pours a small amount of red liquid into a glass for Beckham to taste. After he approves, she pours more into both glasses, then gives us some privacy.

"To the future," Beckham says, raising his glass.

"The future," I repeat, clinking my glass with his before bringing it to my lips and taking a sip, savoring the delicious wine.

Once I return my glass to the table, Beckham peers at me expectantly. "What do you think?"

"I don't know what the big deal is. This would go fine with tilapia."

Beckham's jaw tenses as a subtle growl tumbles from his throat, sending my girly bits aflutter once more.

ELEVEN

Beckham

"Where should we start?" Haley asks after our server has taken our dinner orders.

As I expected, she tried to order pork, but all it took was one harsh glare from me, and she changed her order to the filet.

Years ago, I never could have imagined I'd be the one telling her to order the expensive meal at a nice restaurant. Haley grew up in one of the wealthiest neighborhoods in Lake Tahoe. To say she comes from a different world than me is an understatement. A fact I was forced to learn when I was eighteen, despite foolishly thinking it didn't matter.

I was wrong.

And she paid the price.

"Start?" I repeat, taking another sip of wine.

"The whole getting married thing. Aren't we here to make sure our stories line up?"

"Right. Of course." I clear my throat, attempting to act as normal as possible.

Except there's nothing normal about the way my body's been reacting to Haley lately, especially tonight when I saw her round the corner into the lobby wearing a slim-fit black dress that has me wanting to gouge out the eyes of every man who looks at her any longer than I deem appropriate.

"We should probably start at the beginning," she suggests, taking charge. "When was our first date?"

"A party at Kaplan Farm comes to mind."

"So we're doing that?"

"What?"

"Telling the truth," she replies pointedly.

"It's better than coming up with some lame story. Hell, the reason I asked you in the first place is because of our…history."

She fidgets with her wine glass, not looking directly at me. "So we're just going to tell people we had a secret fling years ago and are now getting married?"

"It's a second chance love story. Don't people love that shit?"

She gives me a quizzical look. "Have you been spending time with Grandma Estelle?"

"Why do you say that?"

"She's an avid romance reader and second chance is a favorite. Along with monster romance."

"Monster romance? You mean…"

"Exactly like it sounds."

I chuckle, shaking my head. "It doesn't matter how long I've known that woman. She still manages to surprise me every day."

"Me, too." A smile teases her mouth before her expression turns serious. "But let's get back to our story. I just—"

"Haley." I place my hand over hers, the warmth of her flesh on mine sending desire spiraling through me.

I tell myself the only reason I'm brushing my thumb along her knuckles is to sell the idea of us as a couple. Not because I actually want to feel her skin on mine.

But it's hard to ignore the rush of memories the feel of her hand against mine brings back — memories of the summer our paths crossed after years of not seeing each other. We spent every free minute we could together, often sneaking out in the middle of the night. And not simply so I could get laid. While I certainly loved that, too, I was just as happy holding her hand as we gazed at the stars together.

With the rest of my life feeling like it was falling apart around me, Haley was the one good thing in it.

Until I ruined that, too.

"Let's not make this more complicated than it has to be," I continue. "We've known each other since we were kids. You used to piss the shit out of me with your uppity attitude. And I irritated the hell out of you by constantly arguing with you, even when I knew you were right. Over the years, I continued picking arguments with you, not to prove something, but because I thought it was the only way I could get you to talk to me. Then I tricked you into giving me your first kiss because I hated the idea of you giving it to someone from that stuck-up private school you went to, so I said you could practice on me."

I stare into the distance as I recall that particular day. I should have known once I had my first taste of Haley, nothing else would ever satisfy me again.

And nothing else has.

"I didn't think you'd ever go for it," I say around a chuckle, bringing my gaze back to her. "But you did. And that's just one chapter of our story. Do you see what I'm saying? The truth is enough. It may not be pretty or full of heartfelt declarations. But I'll take real over a bunch of lies any day."

"Except this *isn't* real," Haley reminds me, pulling me back to reality.

I blink, suddenly aware of my hand still caressing hers, as if second nature. As if the last fourteen years never happened.

"I just mean our *story* is already real." I pull my hand away. "No need to make this more confusing than it has to be."

She nods, a furrow creasing her brow, as if deep in thought. I'm convinced she's about to reveal some earth-shattering truth or ask a question I don't want to answer. Then she shakes it off, the same practiced smile I remember from her teenage years pulling on her lips, all poise and grace.

"What are your thoughts on the wedding?"

"At first, I was going to suggest Reno."

Haley's nose wrinkles in obvious disapproval, and I chuckle at her response.

"But I figured you wouldn't like that idea," I continue, "so I was thinking something small at the vineyard. Nothing flashy. If we want Grady to believe this is real, we should do something other than a quickie wedding at some cheesy chapel."

"Agreed. Plus, if I'm only going to have one wedding, it may as well be something I can enjoy."

I raise an eyebrow. "Why would you only have one wedding? If all goes according to plan, you'll be free of me in around nine months. If Grady still doesn't want to sell to me even after we're married, you can be free of me in just a few weeks."

The idea makes my stomach twist, but I remind myself it's for the best. I may have convinced Haley to marry me, but it's a marriage in name only. Nothing more. Hell, I keep waiting for her father to show up and remind me I'm not good enough for his daughter. That I'll ruin her life.

Then again, he'd have to actually care about her.

I doubt he ever has.

"Most guys my age are looking to start their own family. Not have to settle for a used model, so to speak."

"Guys your age are fucking idiots."

"*You're* my age," she reminds me.

"Exactly. I'm a fucking idiot."

"They say admitting it is the first step." She winks.

"Then I'm on my way to recovery."

A brief silence falls over the table, and I hesitate before asking the question that's been on my mind since she accepted my offer.

"Have you told your parents?"

"No."

"Are you going to?"

"Eventually. Maybe. I don't know."

"Don't you think they'll find out? It's a small town."

"They don't live here. They're in their own privileged world in Tahoe. Plus, I don't really talk to them much. Apparently, having an unwed mother for a daughter looks bad on them, even though I was twenty-seven when I got pregnant. It's not like I was fifteen or something. Still, they kept going on and on about what everyone would think, not even caring about what I was going through. All they cared about was how it might affect them."

"Well, your parents are fucking idiots, too."

This earns me a small laugh.

"What about your mom?" she asks after taking a sip of her wine. "And your brothers and sister?"

"What about them?"

"Do they know this isn't real?"

"No. And they won't. Except Jude. He knows."

"And Parker's the only one I told."

"We should probably keep it this way. The fewer people who know, the better, especially with the way the gossip mill in this town works."

"And you're okay lying to your mom?" she asks. "Making her think this is real?"

"I don't love it, but at least she'll finally stop attempting to set me up with every woman who comes into the salon."

Something flickers in Haley's eyes, her mouth forming a tight line, but it only lasts a second before she fixes her expression once more.

"When should we plan to have the wedding?"

"You need to be out of your place by the end of January, right?"

She nods.

"We'll need to do it before then. What's your availability?"

"Now that I'm no longer working at the casino, I have more flexibility. I've picked up a few more dog walking clients from Angie, but I'm sure she'll give me the day off for my wedding."

"Okay." I pull out my cell and navigate to my calendar. "The twenty-eighth might cut it close. What do you think about the twenty-first? We could start moving your stuff out sooner if you'd rather wait until the twenty-eighth. I don't—"

"No sense in waiting. May as well get it over with. The twenty-first is fine."

"Okay," I reply, although the way she makes it sound like she's going in for some uncomfortable medical procedure stings.

But this is what we agreed to. A marriage in name only. Nothing more.

The more we act as if it's merely a business transaction, the better off we'll both be in the end.

And anytime I fool myself into thinking maybe it can be real, all I'll have to do is look at her leg and see the scar that still runs the length of her thigh.

All because of me.

TWELVE

Haley

"You can do this," I tell myself as I study my reflection in the floor-length mirror in Grady's office on the second floor of the tasting room. "It's not real. And it will be over in nine months at most, at which point you'll hopefully have had enough time to make your cake business profitable."

I've given myself this same pep talk countless times over the past few weeks, especially as we neared January twenty-first.

When we set this date, it seemed so far off, but it arrived practically overnight. Now, I'm mere minutes away from becoming Beckham Lawrence's wife.

When I told Maggie last week, I nearly called it off

after I saw how excited she was. Because I'll eventually have to break her heart when we end this charade.

Then I reminded myself why I'm doing this. To give her the life she deserves. So we no longer have to worry about where we'll live or whether I'll make enough tips to buy groceries.

"Are you decent, Haley?" Parker's voice sounds from the other side of the door, along with a gentle knock.

"You can come in." I refocus my attention on the mirror, smoothing my hands down the satin material of my dress as she slips inside.

"Oh, Haley," she sighs, walking toward me and wrapping me in her embrace. "You look beautiful."

"It's not real," I say, unsure if it's for her benefit or mine.

As I went through the motions of getting ready this morning, from having Beckham's mom style my hair in a classic chignon, then having my makeup profession-ally done by one of the other girls at the salon, I've had to remind myself of that more and more.

This has been the hardest thing about this entire ordeal. I'm forced to make everyone believe our story is the sort of fairytale romance people love to read about in books or see on the big screen. That we were childhood friends who eventually fell in love. That we never forgot about each other, even when life tore us apart. That we eventually found our way back to each other.

That we've been waiting for this day for years and

don't want to wait another second, which is why we're getting married right away.

So far, not a single person has questioned the story. Probably because it's true… Mostly, anyway.

"The marriage may not be, but you still look gorgeous," Parker says with all the sincerity I've come to expect from my best friend.

"You don't think it's too much?"

Since I was short on time, I went with a non-traditional dress. I didn't feel right spending Beckham's money on anything extravagant. Luckily, I found a retro-style cream dress with three-quarter sleeves that's fit to my waist before flaring out, stopping at my knee. I added a fifties-inspired hat with a birdcage veil to complete the look. Couple the dress with my hair and bright red lips, and I've never felt so glamorous.

Never felt so beautiful.

"It's perfect. Trust me." With her hands on my biceps, Parker forces me to face her. "When Beckham sees you, he's going to want to find somewhere private so he can consummate your marriage."

"Highly doubtful." I roll my eyes, pushing out of her hold. "Let's just get this over with. The sooner we're married, the sooner we can divorce."

"If you say so," Parker sings as I open the door and slip onto the second floor landing.

The instant I do, Maggie runs toward me, stopping just short of me to do a twirl in her white dress with a full tulle skirt. "Look, Mama! I'm a princess."

I crouch down to give her a tight hug. "Yes, you are. But even without the pretty dress, you're always a princess to me."

"But you like my dress, right?"

"Of course." I press a soft kiss to her forehead. "Do you remember what you're supposed to do?"

She nods, her expression becoming serious. "I'm supposed to put flower petals down for you."

"Perfect. Are you ready?"

"Yes." She beams, then furrows her tiny brows. "Does this mean Mr. Beck is my daddy now?"

"No, sweetie. He's not. He can be *like* a daddy, but he's not your real father."

Although I'm not sure I should even give her sperm donor the courtesy of referring to him as her father.

"Then who *is* my real daddy?"

I glance nervously at Parker, who discreetly steps away, allowing me the chance to talk to Maggie in private. I knew she'd eventually ask these questions, especially now that she's around other kids and sees them play with their fathers.

When I chose to keep Maggie, I promised myself I wouldn't do or say anything that would make her feel like she wasn't wanted. Which is exactly what telling her about her sperm donor might do.

After all, his solution to my surprise pregnancy was to throw money at me and tell me to make it go away.

Make *her* go away.

That was the last time I saw or spoke to him. I

didn't even bother reaching out when Maggie was born. I grew up with parents who acted like I was nothing more than a giant inconvenience. At least when they weren't bossing me around and dictating my life for me. I swore I'd never put Maggie in a similar situation.

"Your daddy is someone I knew a long time ago who's no longer in our lives."

"Is he under the stones?"

"The stones?"

"Yeah. Like where people get buried when they go to haven."

I laugh at the way her innocent brain processes things.

"No. Your father isn't in heaven. He's alive."

Confusion wrinkles her brows. "But if he's alive, then—"

"Some mommies don't need daddies to help raise their kids. Sometimes mommies are better off without the daddy."

"And you're better off?"

"*We're* better off."

She contemplates this for several moments. Then she gives a curt nod. "Okay. When are we having the cake you made?"

I pull myself to my full height. "After lunch, sweetie."

With her hand clutched tightly in mine, we make our way down the stairs and into the back hallway of the tasting room. While I hate the idea that Grady closed down just for us, especially on a Sunday, he wouldn't hear otherwise. Said we deserved to get married with the stunning backdrop of the vineyard behind us. And the view from the floor-to-ceiling windows in the main hall is more than just stunning. It's breathtaking.

"Ready?" Parker asks once she sees me.

I take a calming breath and nod.

"Okay." She peeks her head out of the hallway and signals Grady to start the music. Once he does, Parker takes Maggie's hand and walks out with her.

I close my eyes, taking a few seconds to calm my breathing. I give serious consideration to running out the back door, especially when I hear the music change, my cue to head down the aisle. I'm not sure how many seconds pass before I finally move, but it's probably enough to make people nervous.

"This is for Maggie," I say softly as I take the first step into the main hall.

The handful of guests immediately stand, everyone turning to look at me. Including Beckham's mother, who has tears in her eyes. If I felt guilty about deceiving her earlier as she was going on and on about how she always imagined we'd get married, even after everything fell apart, I feel even worse about it now.

I do my best to remain steady on my heels as I make my way down the aisle, trying not to look at his mother for fear the guilt will become too much and I'll blurt out the truth.

After what feels like an eternity, I finally reach Beckham. I'm momentarily caught breathless by how handsome he looks. I didn't really take a moment to appreciate him as I walked down the aisle, too uneasy about the prospect of being married in mere minutes.

But now that I'm standing in front of him, it's impossible to ignore.

I thought he looked handsome when we went out to dinner all those weeks ago. But that's nothing compared to how he looks in his gray suit. Being who he is, he kept it casual by foregoing the tie. But he still looks good. Hell, he looks better than good. He looks good enough to eat.

Based on the way his hungry eyes skate over my frame, I get the feeling he's thinking the same thing about me.

"You look beautiful," he says softly as he takes my hands in his, his warm skin sending a delicious shiver down my spine.

I resist the urge to remind him he doesn't need to say that to me. But several pairs of eyes are on us, including Grady's as he stands mere inches away, about to marry us.

It's better than having a minister perform the ceremony. I need as many karma chips as I can get, and I'd rather not get on God's bad side any more than I already am.

"So do you," I tell him, my voice trembling from

nerves. "I mean, you don't look beautiful. But you look good. Better than good, really."

"Ah, young love," Grady remarks, which earns a laugh from everyone.

I look away from Beckham and smile at our guests.

Like we agreed, we kept the guest list small. Just Beckham's immediate family, as well as Parker and Grandma Estelle. Not surprisingly, my parents didn't show up. I sent them an invite as a courtesy, but I didn't expect them to be here. They didn't approve of Beckham all those years ago. They certainly don't now, as evidenced by my mother's scathing phone call last week. It doesn't matter how successful he is. How much he's overcome. How much he's changed since high school.

He'll always be the boy who tried to corrupt their daughter.

"Friends and family, we're gathered here today to celebrate the long-awaited marriage of Beckham Lawrence to Haley McBride," Grady begins, pulling my attention back to him.

Beckham squeezes my hands, and my eyes lock on his as I listen to Grady go through the short ceremony we insisted on. It's probably for the best, considering the longer I stand up here, the more I fear someone will take one look at my expression and realize the truth. Beckham always teased me about having a terrible poker face. That hasn't changed with time.

"It's my honor to be the first to announce you

husband and wife," Grady proclaims a short while later, finally bringing the ceremony to an end. "You may now kiss your beautiful bride."

Over the past several weeks, Beckham and I have spent as much free time together as possible to make everyone believe we're a real couple. Thankfully, Maggie was often with us, which proved beneficial for cutting through the tension between us. But even when she wasn't, the one thing neither of us thought to discuss was the inevitability of having to kiss at the end of our wedding ceremony. Aside from a few pecks on my cheek when we were in public, he's barely touched me. If my knee somehow grazed his, he'd immediately increase the distance between us.

Now that we're here, I have no idea what I'm supposed to do.

Well, I know what I'm *supposed* to do. We're supposed to kiss. I just don't know if I'm ready to feel Beckham's lips on mine again. Not ready to experience all the emotions I've fought to bury for the past fourteen years.

It's just one kiss. We'll get it over with, then never have to do it again, and I can keep pretending I feel nothing for him.

With painfully slow movements, Beckham licks his lips and curves toward me. My heart thunders in my chest as I hoist myself onto my toes to meet his height and close my eyes. The seconds tick by, yet his mouth still doesn't touch mine.

I'm about to open my eyes to see what he's doing when his lips finally brush against mine. His kiss is firm and stilted, lasting less than a second. It's even more awkward than our first kiss was.

"Is that the best you can do?" Grady jests, slapping Beckham's back. "You're married, son. Kiss your wife like you mean it."

"My wife," Beckham muses, almost bewildered by the term. As if he's just realized the reality of what we've done.

By the furrowed expression on his brow, I half expect him to tell everyone the truth. Then his eyes darken and he loops an arm around my waist, tugging my body against his, his eyes focused on my lips.

I inhale a sharp breath, caught off guard by his sudden motion, my pulse kicking up when I peer into his lust-filled eyes.

"My wife," he growls again before pressing his mouth more firmly against mine.

This time, his kiss isn't even remotely awkward. And certainly nothing like our first kiss. Instead, he takes total command of my body, coaxing my lips to part, our tongues tangling briefly. His kiss is warm. Firm. Intoxicating. So much so that a tiny whimper falls from my throat, my veins heating.

There's something familiar yet different about his kiss. I lost count of the number of times Beckham kissed me during our short-lived summer fling. But kissing him as an adult is much different than when we were teens. It's much more charged. The way he explores my mouth as if he's uncovered a priceless artifact turns me to putty. I thought I'd be able to control myself better. Thought I could separate the lies from reality.

Instead, nothing seems to stop me from unraveling in response to his expert kiss.

"Now *that's* how you kiss your wife," Grady says once Beckham brings our kiss to an end, his hand on my hip the only thing keeping me upright.

"My wife," Beckham repeats, his eyes flaming as they remain locked on mine.

And for a moment, a part of me can't help but think *he* wishes this were real, too.

THIRTEEN

Beckham

"Is this where we're going to live now, Mama?" Maggie asks as Haley leads her up the front porch of my house on the vineyard later that afternoon. The setting sun casts a golden hue over the property, giving the vines a vibrant glow.

With the strange hours I work, it's more convenient to live out here so I can tend to the vines if anything comes up. Even so, I kept my townhouse in the historic district, as well, since it's in a highly desirable area, especially for tourists.

Although once Grady told me his plans, I stopped taking bookings. I hope I don't have to move out of the place that's been my home since Grady refurbished this house and suggested I live here after routinely finding me asleep on the couch in my office.

I haven't spoken to him about rethinking his stance now that I'm married. I figured if I brought it up at our mini-reception this afternoon, he might get suspicious. While I know he's been in discussions with a few interested parties, he hasn't signed any deals yet. I'm hoping I have a little time before I need to raise the subject.

"Do you like it?" Haley asks her daughter.

Maggie's eyes widen as she takes in the wraparound porch. "There's a swing on the front porch! I've always wanted a swing."

"You swing all the time at the park."

"But I can swing any time I want here."

"Once it gets a little warmer and the ground has thawed some, I'll put in a playscape for you," I offer.

Provided I convince Grady to sell to me.

"For real life?" Maggie asks, her expression lighting up.

"You don't have to do that," Haley says quietly, an edge to her voice.

"I don't have to do anything. I *want* to," I tell her, fighting to keep from staring at her mouth, something that's proving increasingly difficult.

As if it isn't bad enough that her lips are painted a deep crimson, in stark contrast to her fair skin, all I've been able to think about is that damn kiss.

I'd like to say the only reason I kissed her like I did was to convince everyone this is real. But when I heard

Grady call her my wife, something primal and protective stirred inside me. Before I knew it, I crushed my mouth against hers, wanting to claim her as mine, for once and for all.

"She'll be fine going to the park," Haley insists, giving me a pointed look. "No sense going to the trouble."

I can hear what she doesn't say. That there's no reason for me to put in a playscape when Maggie won't be around to enjoy it for more than a few months.

"Come on. Let's get settled," I say, not wanting to start our marriage by arguing, even if we're good at it.

It might be the one thing we *are* good at.

Well, that's not entirely accurate. There's another thing we were damn good at, too, even as teenagers. I can only imagine how incredible it would be now.

Which is the last thing I should be thinking about, considering I'm about to share my bed with her for the foreseeable future.

"Great." Her response comes out at a slightly higher pitch than normal, evidencing her nerves about the prospect of living under the same roof.

I'd be lying if I said I wasn't uneasy about it, too. Just a few months ago, we barely acknowledged each other. Now we'll be living together. And not just in the same house, but also sharing the same room. The same bed.

I'll have to fall asleep next to her, knowing how sweet she tastes, how incredible she feels, and not be able to do anything about it. I shouldn't *want* to do anything about it. But my brain and my body seem to be on two different wavelengths when it comes to Haley.

"Is this really my new house?" Maggie asks excitedly as I open the door and they step inside.

"It's really your new house," Haley replies.

Monte wastes no time in bounding down the hall toward us, his nails clacking on the hardwood floors. When he sees Maggie, he barks excitedly.

"Is this really my new dog?"

I chuckle as he licks her face. "It's really your new dog."

Maggie wraps her arms around Monte, showering him with love and affection. "I've always wanted a doggie."

I steal a glimpse at Haley. I can't quite read her expression. It's happiness, but mixed with sorrow. I know her well enough to know she's probably already thinking about how Maggie's going to react when it ends.

I can't blame her.

I'm already thinking about it, too.

"Do you want to see your room?" I ask Maggie.

Her entire face brightens. "I get my own room?"

"Sure do."

"I've never had my own room before."

My heart squeezes.

I know Haley hasn't had an easy time the past few

years. I don't know the details about her relationship with Maggie's father, but I do know he's not in her life. Our differences aside, I certainly admire Haley for everything she's done for her daughter. And for having the strength to keep her in the first place.

"Let's go see it." I scoop Maggie up in my arms, and her excited squeals fill my house with life. Something I never thought I'd hear within these four walls.

Monte follows as we make our way up the stairs, Haley bringing up the rear. When I reach the door to her room, I set Maggie back down on her feet.

"I know you're used to sharing a room with your mom, but she'll be right across the hall." I point toward our door. "Okay?"

"Okay. Can I see my room now?"

I nod, pushing the door open. When I do, her eyes go wider than I've ever seen them, her jaw dropping.

"Is this really my room?" she all but shrieks as her gaze darts around the space that was once all drab walls and lackluster furniture.

Now three of the walls are painted pink with the wall behind her bed an accent of teal. I asked my younger sister, Dylan, for a recommendation on what kinds of toys and books she might like, since she's been taking care of my niece and nephew to help out my brother. Thankfully, she came through with a long list of things Maggie might like.

I wasn't sure what books or toys she already had, but I wanted to do something to make this transition as easy as possible. I filled a small bookcase with books, and got her some stuffed animals, as well as a few Barbies to go with the four-foot dollhouse in the corner.

But she doesn't give any of that stuff a second glance. Instead, all of her attention is focused on the exact bed I noticed described on Haley's pad the night I went over to ask her to marry me — a loft bed with a slide and club house underneath.

"Is this really my bed?" Maggie asks, barely able to contain her excitement.

"It is."

She whirls toward me and flings her arms around my waist, the sudden gesture taking me by surprise. I'm not used to this kind of attention from kids.

"Thank you, Mr. Beck."

I gently pat her back, overwhelmed by how trusting this little girl is. How easily she hugs me.

After a few moments, she drops her arms and goes to her mom, giving her a tight squeeze. "Thank you, Mama. Can I slide?"

"Of course, sweetie."

Without a moment's hesitation, Maggie darts toward the bed and tries to climb up the ladder.

"Careful," I caution, my heart caught in my throat when she slips on the first step. It's an odd reaction, considering she's not even my kid. I still hate the idea of any harm coming to her, no matter how small.

"Why don't you take off your shoes?" Haley suggests.

"Okay, Mama."

Maggie sits on the floor and removes her black Mary Janes before yanking off her socks. This time, when she climbs up the step ladder, she doesn't slip, successfully reaching the mattress. She scoots toward the head of the bed, then whooshes down the slide with a look of pure joy on her face.

"This. Is. Awesome!"

"I'm glad you like it."

"I don't just like it. I *love* it. It's the bestest bed ever made." She shifts her bright eyes toward her mother. "Can I put on my pajamas and play in my new bed?"

"Sure." Haley looks around, probably for the suitcase I grabbed from her place earlier this morning.

"It's all unpacked," I tell her. "Pajamas are in the top drawer."

"Thanks."

"I'll let you have some privacy." I retreat, closing the door behind me before heading across the hall, whistling for Monte to follow. I don't waste any time in toeing out of my shoes and shrugging off my jacket. After ridding myself of my shirt and pants, I find a pair of gray sweatpants in the drawer and tug them on. I open another drawer and start to rummage through it for a t-shirt just when I notice a motion out of the corner of my eye.

I look up as Haley comes to an abrupt stop just over the threshold, her gaze wide and mouth agape.

"Sorry. I didn't know… The door was open and—"

"It's okay." I grab a t-shirt and yank it on. It doesn't escape my notice that Haley watches me with rapt attention, her skin flushing. Thanks to her light complexion, it's even more noticeable when she's embarrassed.

Or turned on.

Based on past experience, it's most likely the latter.

Or maybe I *want* it to be the latter.

"I'm not used to having other people in the house." I laugh slightly to cut through the tension. "I'll try to remember to close the door from now on."

"Probably a good idea."

"I'll let you get changed," I offer, although it's the last thing I want, considering how stunning she looks in her dress.

"Hey, Beckham?" Haley calls out just as I'm about to slip into the hallway.

I pause, my eyes locking with hers.

She steps toward me. "I appreciate everything you've done for Maggie, but you don't need to go over-board. We're not your responsibility."

"I just wanted to make the transition easier. Not only is she in a strange place, but she's living with a strange person." I shrug. "I saw your wish list and figured giving her the room of her dreams might make it easier on her."

"But it won't make it easier on her. Not in the long run."

"What do you mean?" I give her a quizzical look.

"In a matter of months, this marriage will end," she whispers. "I'm just trying to manage her expectations so it's not as hard on her."

I shake my head. "I didn't consider that."

"Because it's not your responsibility to consider that. It's mine. It won't be easy on her when it ends. Not if you keep doing these sort of things for her. Things I may never be able to give her on my own. So please. Do what you can to soften the blow, so to speak."

Exhaling a long sigh, I run my fingers through my hair. "I'm sorry. I'll make sure to discuss anything involving Maggie with you going forward."

"Thank you."

I nod, then turn back around and head down the hallway, unable to shake the feeling she's not just concerned about softening the blow for her daughter when it ends.

But also for herself.

FOURTEEN

Haley

I can't remember the last time I've been so tired. If this was any other Sunday, I would have been in bed hours ago. Hell, I probably would have been asleep mere minutes after Maggie had gone to bed.

But it's nearly midnight and I'm still awake, even though I barely slept last night, too riddled with nerves about whether I could really marry Beckham. I made it through most of the day on pure adrenaline.

Thankfully, Maggie was asleep before seven. It took a lot of convincing to get her to leave her new bed to eat dinner, which consisted of a pizza Beckham ordered. I've never seen my little girl as happy as she was when she saw her bed. Normally, bedtime can be a bit of a struggle. Not tonight. She was bouncing with excitement over the idea of sleeping in her brand new "big girl bed", as she calls it.

As much as I want to be upset with Beckham, I can't deny it warms my heart how he went out of his way to make her comfortable here. Still, I have to keep in mind what's best for Maggie in the long run.

"Do you want to head up to bed?"

I snap my eyes open and glance at the opposite end of the couch where Beckham and I have been lounging the past few hours.

I didn't get a chance to appreciate his house when we first walked in, since Maggie was so excited about seeing her room. It's exactly the kind of place I pictured for him. White walls with dark trim, complete with exposed wood beams lining the open space of the living, dining, and kitchen areas. The decor is what I'd describe as vineyard chic with obvious inspiration from Tuscany, especially in the art pieces adorning the walls.

"We can watch another episode if you want. I'm not tired," I say, fighting a yawn.

"Haley…" He narrows his gaze on me with a teasing glint in his eyes. "Are you only staying awake because you're nervous about your wedding night?" He waggles his brows suggestively. "The first time can be scary, but I promise to make it good for you."

I throw a pillow at him. "You're such a jackass," I retort, trying to suppress memories of just how good he made my first time.

It's the last thing I need to think about, considering

I'll be sharing a bed with him for the next few months. After feeling his lips against mine again earlier today, it's nearly impossible not to let my mind wander to what could have been.

Which won't do either of us any good.

"I just really like this show."

It's not a complete lie. *Schitt's Creek* is one of my favorite series. But I'd be lying if I said I wasn't purposefully staying awake to delay slipping into bed with Beckham.

"This episode is one of the best ones, too," I continue. "The whole 'fold in the cheese' bit is hysterical." Another yawn fights to be set free, and this time, I can't hold it back.

"Okay, sleepy head." Beckham grabs the remote and turns off the TV.

"I was watching that," I attempt to protest as another yawn escapes.

"You're done watching it."

Standing, he grabs my hand and pulls me up from the couch, his grip on my hip holding me steady.

"You're being unusually bossy." My words come out somewhat slurred, despite only drinking one glass of wine tonight.

"Trust me, Haley…" A devious smile teases his lips. "You haven't seen bossy."

His voice is a low growl that sends shivers through my body. It makes me wonder just how bossy he might be in the bedroom now that he's older and more experienced. Based on his kiss earlier, he's definitely a man who likes to take charge. I was more than happy to give up control to experience the bliss filling me from his expert kiss.

My insides ignite from the memory, my gaze drawn to his lips, full and tempting. A part of me wouldn't mind feeling them again, and this time without an audience forcing us to keep things PG-rated. As his eyes trace over my mouth, I get the feeling he's thinking the same thing.

He leans closer, his hand on my hip tightening as a combination of desire and restraint dances in his dark gaze.

We're standing on a landmine, waiting for one wrong move to set off an explosion.

Or one *right* move.

"Come on," Beckham says around a sigh, releasing his hold on me, leaving a tingling sensation in its wake. "You need to sleep."

"Right. Sleep." I swallow down any disappointment that he didn't kiss me. I'm not supposed to want him to kiss me.

Do I actually want him to kiss me?

Or has it just been so long since I've had the attention of another man that I'm doing things I normally wouldn't?

I try to convince myself it's the latter, but deep down, I know it's not the case. Not with the way my body always buzzes to life in his presence, even after he ignored me and pretended I meant nothing to him. The passing of years hasn't dulled this feeling. If anything, it's even stronger now.

"Is there a side you prefer?" Beckham asks once we step into his bedroom.

I refuse to call it *our* bedroom.

The room is dimly lit with warm hues emanating from a lamp on the nightstand by the far side of the bed. Pieces of him are scattered throughout the space — a guitar in the corner, a pile of books on the dresser, even an old record player on a stand against the far wall.

"It's your bed. I've been sleeping on a couch the past few years."

His jaw twitches, something he does whenever he's upset or angry.

"I'll sleep on this side then." He nods to the one closest to the door.

"Is that where you usually sleep?"

"No." His eyes lock with mine. "This way, in the unlikely event of an intruder, they'll have to go through me to get to you."

"Oh." I ignore the butterflies that take flight in my stomach from the protectiveness in his voice.

Then he spins and disappears into the en-suite bathroom.

The sound of running water fills the silence as I blow out a long breath and move to my side of the bed, pulling back the fluffy duvet before slipping underneath.

It's even more comfortable than I imagined.

And to make matters worse, his sheets smell like him. Leather. Bergamot. And raw earth. When he was ripped from my life, I found myself craving his scent, needing it to feel any sort of comfort.

Now, as I bask in it once more, I feel more at ease than I have in years, so much so that I start to succumb to sleep within seconds.

But not before sensing the bed shift as Beckham crawls onto the other side.

"'Night, Haley." He touches a soft kiss to my temple.

"'Night, Beck," is my barely audible response.

Then he rolls over, placing a pillow between us.

I'm not sure if it's for my benefit or his, but a part of me wishes it wasn't there.

FIFTEEN

Haley

A sweltering heat rouses me from sleep, the glimpse of sunlight peeking into the room indicating it's morning. I can't remember the last time I've slept this well without tossing and turning. Probably because I finally slept on an actual bed instead of the couch. I would have most likely still been sleeping if I weren't so damn hot. It's like a sauna in here.

But as the fog of sleep clears, I come to realize it's not the temperature that's making me burn up. It's something else.

Or perhaps I should say some*one* else.

Beckham's arms are wrapped around me, his warm and solid chest pressed against my back. The pillow he placed between us last night is gone, not so much as a whisper separating us, a single leg around my waist locking me in place.

And that's not all.

There's something poking me.

Something hard and thick.

And incredibly tempting.

My cheeks flush as I push down the urge to turn around, to feel him between my legs. This man has a way of making every inch of my body react with just one look. One touch.

And I can't touch.

"Beckham," I say somewhat hesitantly.

A low, guttural moan escapes his lips, sending a rush of desire through me. He pulls me closer, not yet fully awake but clearly responding to my proximity.

"Beckham," I say again, this time with a bit more edge.

And again, his only response is a moan.

Which sends another shock straight to my girly bits. My libido does a few warmup stretches, thinking she's about to finally get some action after a five-year dry spell.

But definitely not today.

And definitely not with Beckham, despite how much my mouth waters at the prospect.

When he pulses against me, I know I need to change tactics before I throw caution to the wind and succumb to him. Instead, I elbow him in his stomach.

He jerks upright, nearly pushing me off the bed from the sudden movement.

"What was that for?" he barks, blinking his tired eyes open.

"You were poking me with your..." I whistle as my gaze darts down to his waist.

Which I definitely shouldn't have done, since his impressive erection is still straining against his pajama bottoms.

"Shit." He grabs the pillow that should have been separating us and covers himself. "I'm sorry. I didn't realize. I—"

"Mama," Maggie's sleepy voice interrupts, followed by a soft knock on the door.

I haul ass out of bed, not wanting her to come in here and see Beckham with a raging hard on.

As a mom, I've learned how to handle my fair share of difficult questions.

I'm not ready for my daughter to ask why Beckham has a pole in his pants.

A hard, long, thick pole that has the ability to bring me to orgasm more times than should be possible.

"Good morning, sweetheart," I say in a chipper voice as I step into the hallway, making sure to close the door behind me. "Are you hungry?"

She rubs her eyes and nods.

"Let's get some breakfast in you so you have lots of energy for preschool."

I take her hand in mine and lead her down the

stairs. I'm not sure what kind of food I'll find in Beckham's kitchen, but when I start going through his cabinets, I'm surprised to find them well-stocked. He even bought all of Maggie's favorite snacks — apple sauce, fruit chews, granola bars. I have no idea how he knew exactly what flavor and brand she likes, but he did.

"Do you want pancakes?"

Maggie's eyes light up. "Yes!"

I collect the ingredients and mix them together, then fire up the gas on the griddle section of Beckham's stove.

"Mr. Beck! Mama's making pancakes!"

I whirl around and meet Beckham's stare as he casually strolls through the kitchen to let Monte outside. A shiver of awareness trickles down my spine from the memory of waking up wrapped in his arms.

With his dick pressing against my back.

And the way my body responded.

Hell, the way my body is *still* responding.

At least his erection has gone down and he threw on a t-shirt. Although, I'm not sure it makes much of a difference, considering his muscles seem to be stretching the material.

"Something interest you, Haley?"

I inhale a sharp breath and blink repeatedly. I didn't even realize I was staring at him.

Then again, I'm not sure that's the appropriate word for what I was just doing to Beckham.

Ogling is probably more appropriate.

Mentally undressing.

Wondering if the way he fucks has matured with age like his kisses have.

"Not at all. I… Coffee," I finally blurt out. "I was just looking for your coffee maker."

Arching a disbelieving brow, he slowly stalks toward me. His dark eyes remain locked on mine as he leans closer, trapping me against the counter. Despite his proximity, not a single inch of his body touches mine, remaining painfully out of reach.

I swear I'm about to combust from the sexual tension filling me, my body throbbing with a craving to feel his skin on mine.

With calculated movements, he reaches past me, and the familiar sound of a one-cup brewer whirring to life fills the space. But even once it's powered on, he doesn't move, invading my space as if he owns it.

Owns *me*.

"Is this what you were looking for?" His voice is low and teasing, accompanied by a sly smirk on his stupid yet kissable lips.

Goddamn him for being so ridiculously attractive.

And for smelling so good.

And for making me forget every reason this is a terrible idea with just one hypnotic look.

One thing is certain… This man is going to destroy me. If my daughter weren't sitting mere feet away, I'd probably slam my lips to his. Tug him against me. Wrap my legs around his waist and treat myself to the kind of mind-erasing orgasm only Beckham has been able to give me.

"Are you guys doing crush business?" Maggie's sweet voice interjects, cutting through the charged atmosphere.

Slowly, Beckham tears his gaze from mine, but he doesn't step back, keeping me caged in his strong arms.

"Crush business?" he asks with a single brow arched.

"Yeah." She looks up from her coloring book splayed in front of her on the large island. "Kissing and stuff."

"Do you mind if we do crush business?"

A contemplative look crosses her expression. But before I let her answer, I push against Beckham and duck under his arm.

"Why don't we focus on some pancake business instead?"

I hastily pour the batter onto the hot griddle, determined to ignore the electricity crackling in air. And how much I like crush business with Beckham.

"Here." Beckham approaches with a steaming mug, handing it to me. "Oat milk and stevia."

"Thanks."

I take a sip, mindful not to ask how he knows the way I take my coffee in front of Maggie. Did I tell him? Was it one of the things we discussed in the weeks leading up to the wedding? If anything, I may have prepared a cup of coffee for myself in his presence. I didn't think Beckham would be observant enough to watch how I liked my coffee.

"There's a boy at school who has crush business with me," Maggie says proudly.

"Is that right?" I ask, adding some chocolate chips to the pancakes before flipping them.

"Yup. He chases me during recess."

"What's this boy's name?" Beckham asks in a stern voice as he heads to the French doors to let Monte back inside before returning to the kitchen.

"Christian."

"And what are Christian's intentions?" His gaze narrows in concern as he widens his stance, crossing his arms in front of his chest.

"His…what?" Her tiny brows scrunch in confusion.

"Is he nice to you?"

Maggie nods excitedly. "He always lets me catch him when we play *What Time is it Mr. Fox*."

Beckham chuckles, the raspy sound jumpstarting my libido yet again.

As if the old girl had time to cool down in the last few minutes.

"I suppose that's all that matters." He adds a scoop of kibble to Monte's bowl, and his dog gobbles it up like it's his last meal. "I'm going to jump in the shower," he tells me before moving toward Maggie. "If I don't see you, have a good day at school." He gives her hair a quick tousle, then retreats up the stairs.

As soon as his footsteps fade away, I push out a long

breath, praying this situation will get easier over time. If all our mornings are like this, I'm not sure if I'll survive the next few months. I have a feeling my vibrator will be getting quite the workout in the weeks to come.

"Okay, sweet pea. Eat up." I place a plate of pancakes in front of her, then set down her cup of water. "Will you be okay for a few minutes while I get changed?"

"Yup," she says around a mouthful of food.

"And don't feed the dog any of those." I point to her plate, watching as Monte circles her like a hawk, waiting for her to drop even the smallest morsel. "There are chocolate chips in there. Remember what I told you about dogs and chocolate?"

She nods gravely. "It can make them very sick."

"Exactly." I press a kiss to the top of her head, then dash up the stairs, coming to an abrupt stop when I see the door is closed. Of course it is. Beckham just said he was going to take a shower. It didn't dawn on me until now I'd need to get into the bedroom. I'm so used to it being Maggie and me the thought never even crossed my mind.

"Beckham, are you decent?" I call out as I knock. "I just need to grab some clothes."

I wait for a few seconds, but no response comes.

I press my ear up to the cool wood and listen, able to make out the sound of water running. The last thing I want to do is walk in on a naked Beckham, but I need to get dressed.

All I can do is hope he remembered to also close the door to the bathroom.

Placing my palm on the door, I hesitantly push it open, relieved when there's no sign of Beckham.

I make a beeline toward my suitcase and pull out the first decent outfit I find — a pair of leggings and a tunic. After dressing, I check my reflection in the floor-length mirror and arrange my hair into a messy bun on the top of my head.

It's innocent enough.

Except my reflection isn't the only thing I see. Just behind me, the bathroom door is open, giving me the perfect view of the shower as I gaze into the mirror.

The shower where Beckham stands.

But he's not washing his hair.

He's giving a certain body part quite a bit of attention.

I should leave. Forget I saw him. Make an effort to learn his schedule so we don't have to be in the bedroom at the same time.

But I'm mesmerized, unable to look away, even though that's precisely what I should do. What I *need* to do.

He's even bigger and more built than he was during our teenage years, every inch of him hard panes and defined ridges. Even his thighs are a sight to behold. And don't get me started on the tattoos covering his arms and chest like the work of art he is.

But what has me completely captivated is the way

he leans a forearm against the tile wall as he works his erection. The raw desire etched on his face causes a renewed wave of lust to crash over me, forcing me to steady myself with a hand on the dresser.

This is so wrong on so many levels, not to mention a massive invasion of his privacy. But as he jerks himself with increasing desperation, I can't find the strength to put one foot in front of the other or look anywhere but at his reflection in the mirror. The harder he yanks, the faster my own breathing becomes.

Finally, a hungry growl rips through the space, the sound practically deafening.

But when he snaps his eyes open and catches mine through the mirror, I realize he wasn't the only one who made a sound. I did, too, the ghost of my wanton moan still intermingling with the symphony of his release.

I'm frozen for a beat, at a loss for words. What can I say? Sorry I watched you jerk off, but it was one of the hottest things I've witnessed in a long time and I just couldn't look away?

I doubt that would go over well.

Instead, I spin on my heels and hurry out of the room, contemplating the likelihood of never seeing Beckham again for the duration of our marriage.

SIXTEEN

Haley

"There's the newlywed," Parker sings as I walk into the kitchen of her inn after dropping Maggie off at preschool.

My original plan was to do some baking in order to start boosting my social media presence before having to get to my mid-day dog-walking clients. The last thing I want to do right now is be in the same vicinity as Beckham Lawrence, even if he's probably at work by now.

I don't want to take the chance.

Instead, I decided to spend some time with Parker, something I don't get much of these days.

"Don't remind me," I mutter, heading toward the canteen of coffee on the serving station. The inn may be closed for renovations, but she still keeps the coffee nice and fresh, probably for all the construction workers currently swarming the grounds.

"Is the hanky-panky that bad?" Grandma Estelle asks from her perch on a barstool in front of the windows overlooking the vast lake.

It barely resembles how it looked mere weeks ago during the height of the Christmas season. Now, with Callum's help, Parker's finally able to turn Holley Ridge into the luxurious wedding destination her parents always dreamed of. But it's going to take a lot of time and effort to do that.

And a lot of construction workers, who currently have Grandma Estelle's attention, her eyes glued to a pair of binoculars as she checks out a few of the more attractive ones.

"That honestly surprises me," she continues, not even looking my way. "I thought that man would have you walking bow-legged for the next week with the way he was eye-fucking you yesterday."

"Grandma Estelle!" I exclaim, although I shouldn't be surprised.

The octogenarian, who's as much of a fixture at Parker's inn as is the towering Norwegian Spruce she decorates every Christmas, has absolutely no brain-to-mouth filter. She speaks her mind, to hell with what anyone might think. After over eighty years on the planet, she's earned that right.

Regardless, I doubt I'll ever get used to hearing her talk about fucking and walking bow-legged.

"It's an honest question, Haley dear. I'm surprised you're only realizing he's not any good in the sack now. Even in my day we took the car for a test drive before we drove it off the lot."

"I…"

"Grandma Estelle," Parker interjects, saving me from having to come up with a plausible excuse.

Because therein lies the problem.

I *did* take Beckham out for a test drive. He was my first test drive, but only a few people know that.

"Why don't you go check on the crew? See if they'd like some fresh coffee or pastries."

"Are you kicking me out?" Grandma Estelle lowers her binoculars long enough to give Parker a heated glare.

"Not at all." She skirts around one of the steel prep tables, placing a variety of pastries and muffins into a large bakery box. "Just giving you an excuse to check out all those hotties from a better spot. And maybe get the number of the silver fox you keep drooling over."

Grandma Estelle doesn't respond for several seconds, and I'm waiting for her to pry about why Parker needs to talk to me in private. Or, more accurately, why *I* need to talk to her. While I adore Grandma Estelle, she's not known for her ability to keep secrets.

"Fine," she finally says with a huff, climbing down

from her stool, taking a moment to smooth her pixie-cut silver hair. "I'll leave. But only because one of them boys is wearing a really tight pair of jeans and I've only gotten a view of his backside today. I'd love to know if the front looks just as good."

"Make sure to report back." Parker winks as she hands Grandma Estelle the box.

"You know I will." She waggles her brows, then pushes through the swinging door of the kitchen, making her way onto the back veranda. The instant she does, I hear a muffled chorus of men shouting her name.

One thing is certain. Everyone loves that woman.

"Where's Callum?" I ask once we're alone. "Did he go back to San Francisco already?"

While they're committed to making their relationship work, Callum is still the head of a successful real estate development firm. For now, he's splitting his time between the city and here. According to Parker, he doesn't mind. He always traveled a lot for work before. Now Parker is his reason for being away from the city.

"Not yet." She brings her coffee mug to her lips, a blush building on her face as her eyes focus on one of the construction workers.

I follow her line of sight, realizing he's not a construction worker at all, but Callum Reed in a hardhat and tool belt.

It's a far cry from the stiff in a suit who first walked onto Parker's property almost two months ago.

"So what's going on?" Parker asks, forcing my attention back to her. "Obviously something happened."

I collapse onto a nearby barstool. "This morning as I was getting dressed, I saw Beckham in the shower."

"You were bound to have a few awkward run-ins at some point."

"No, Parker. I *saw* him in the shower," I say again, hoping she picks up what I'm trying to tell her without having to spell it out.

"Okay," she draws out, confusion wrinkling her brow. Then her eyes widen. "Was he—"

"Yup. Sure was. Was really going to town on it, too."

Her eyes light up as if this is the juiciest piece of gossip she's heard since I told her about my fake marriage.

It probably is.

"And what did you do?"

"I wasn't thinking clearly. This whole thing has me out of sorts. First, he gives Maggie her dream bedroom. Then he says he wants to sleep on the side of the bed closest to the door so anyone who breaks in has to go through him first. Then I wake up with his dick against my back. We won't even talk about the extreme restraint I displayed when I didn't rub my ass against it.

"Then he turns the goddamn smolder up to eleven when I was making pancakes, which made me want to climb him like a fucking tree. And then, seconds later, I walk into the bedroom to get dressed and he has the bathroom door open. And he's jerking off in the shower. And my god, Parker…" I sigh. "It was fucking glorious."

"Then what's the problem? He *is* your husband after all."

"The problem?" I shoot back, pushing down the renewed heat coursing through me from the memory of watching Beckham this morning. I've never seen anything so magnificent. So scintillating. So damn erotic. "The problem is this isn't real. And he keeps doing things that make me wish it were. Like giving Maggie her dream bedroom and being nice."

"The nerve of him. How dare he actually be a decent human."

"See!" I slam my hands on the table. "You get it. It's just…" I expel a long breath, rubbing my temples. "This is a lot more complicated than I thought it would be. I thought we'd live under the same roof but wouldn't spend much time around each other. I certainly didn't plan on there being any of this…other stuff."

"And there *is* other stuff?" She arches a brow.

"Yes. No. I don't know." I take another sip of coffee, contemplating adding a splash of whiskey to it.

While she may know Beckham and I spent a lot of time together as kids, she doesn't know the full story. All she knows is what most people do. That Beckham was a notorious hothead who physically assaulted the guy I was supposedly dating, and when I intervened, I suffered several major injuries to my hip and leg.

It's not even close to the full story.

Beckham seemed adamant about leaving the past in the past. Maybe I need to, as well. Talking about it won't change what happened, even if it might give everyone a better understanding.

"What did you two discuss regarding the 'other stuff'?" Parker asks, pulling me out of my thoughts.

"What do you mean?"

"What kind of parameters have you established?" She eyes me over her coffee cup. "You *have* set up guidelines, right?"

"Not really." I shrug. "We were more focused on planning the wedding and making sure we had our stories straight."

"Haley! What were you thinking? That's, like, fake relationship 101! Have you never read a fake dating romance?"

"I've been on a monster romance kick lately, thanks to Grandma Estelle."

"Okay. Well, in all good fake dating romances, the two parties typically sit down and iron out some ground rules so lines don't get crossed. They always do, which is my favorite part. I just love when they reach their breaking point and go at each other like animals in heat."

"You won't have to worry about us crossing any

lines. And we certainly won't be going after each other like a bunch of horny animals."

She crosses her arms in front of her chest. "We'll see about that. I already told Jude I give it a month."

I widen my eyes. "What?"

"We made a little wager yesterday." She takes a sip of her coffee. "You should be happy I'm giving you two a month. Jude said he'd be surprised if you lasted the week."

"I already told you. That will never happen with Beckham and me."

"Famous last words," she sings. "Trust me on this, Haley. You put two people who have always had amazing chemistry in the same space for any amount of time, and you eventually cave. I can't wait to hear all about it when you do."

"Some friend you are," I retort playfully.

"Just keeping it real."

SEVENTEEN

Beckham

I navigate my truck along the winding dirt path leading to the outskirts of the vineyard, darkness enveloping me. The sun set hours ago, leaving behind a serene stillness that only seems to grow as I approach my house.

While I usually work from early morning to long past sunset, I can't do that if I hope to convince Grady to sell to me. Even though I left at a reasonable hour, I wasn't ready to face Haley just yet, not after this morning. Instead, I stopped by Jude's brewery for a beer, where I proceeded to tell him all about my night.

And my morning.

As expected, he got a kick out of it.

Apparently, he and Parker have a bet on how long

Haley and I will last before we sleep together. The asshole gave us until the end of the week. Parker was a bit more realistic with her prediction of a month. I can only assume it's because she doesn't know everything that occurred between Haley and me all those years ago. At least, that's the impression Jude got from her.

I shouldn't be surprised Haley never told her. As close as she is to Parker now, Haley didn't grow up in Sycamore Falls. Once she no longer needed a nanny, I didn't think I'd ever see her again.

Until I looked across the pasture during a party at Kaplan Farm and saw a pair of familiar green eyes staring back. She looked so out of place in her designer dress and shoes, but I knew it was all a façade. A mask she wore so no one could see the real Haley McBride.

But I saw her for who she was. A miserable woman desperate to break free.

Pulling my truck to a stop in front of my house, I kill the ignition and hop down, Monte following behind me. When I step into the dimly lit house, I expect Haley to be asleep since it's almost midnight.

Instead, she's perched on a stool by the kitchen island, a notepad and a glass of wine in front of her. Monte wags his tail excitedly as he hurries inside, no longer giving a shit about the person who rescued him from certain death years ago. With Haley around, he only has eyes for her, sitting obediently at her feet as she scratches his head.

Her hair is piled on the top of her head in a messy

bun, a few strands escaping to frame her face. She's dressed in an oversized t-shirt and a pair of gym shorts that barely cover her ass. Even in casual attire, there's a sensuality about her that causes a stirring in my pants.

It doesn't help that I can tell she's not wearing a bra.

And it also doesn't help that I can't seem to look away from the faint outline of her nipples hardening against the fabric of her t-shirt.

"I need you to sign this," she announces in a firm tone, forcing my eyes away from her chest.

"Is this the paperwork from Maggie's preschool?"

She mentioned I'd need to sign a few forms to transfer the billing over to me.

"It's a contract, more or less."

I arch a brow. "A…contract?"

"Yes." She squares her shoulders and holds her head high. "After this morning, I thought it best we spell out our expectations, so there are no more…surprises."

"Surprises? Like you watching me in the shower like a peeping tom?" I cross my arms in front of my chest, unable to stop myself from teasing her.

If I'm going to survive this marriage, I can't take anything too seriously.

Including the way my heart still races every time her eyes find mine, as if the past fourteen years never happened.

But all I have to do is look at the faint scar still visible on Haley's leg to remind myself they did happen. And there's nothing I can do to change that.

"I was just surprised. That's all." She swallows a gulp of wine, her face turning a shade of red that might rival her hair.

"Didn't look like it." I grab a glass from the cabinet and pour myself some of the pinot noir she'd opened. "It looked like you quite enjoyed yourself." I fully face her. "It *sounded* like you quite enjoyed yourself."

I take a sip of the light-bodied wine, savoring the hints of cherry and oak that dance on my tongue.

"I… That doesn't matter," she stammers, obviously flustered. "That's why we need this contract. To avoid incidents like this in the future. We should have done this before we got married, but I was so focused on moving it never crossed my mind to set forth any expectations and…limitations."

"Listen, Haley…" I assume the barstool beside her.

When my leg brushes hers, a buzz of electricity shoots through me. She sucks in a sharp breath, but quickly adjusts her position, scooting as far away as she can.

"We don't need a contract to tell us what we should and shouldn't do," I continue. "I knew going into this there might be a few growing pains along the way. That we'd both have to make a few sacrifices."

"And you're okay with that? Have you thought about what you'll have to give up to convince people this marriage is real?"

"Like what?" I bring my wine glass to my lips, studying her from over the rim before taking a sip.

"You know." She gives me a pointed look.

Setting my glass onto the island, I feign confusion. "I don't."

"Sex, Beckham. You'll have to give up sex."

I give her a nonchalant shrug of my shoulders. "I know."

"And you're okay with being celibate for the next six-plus months?"

"I'll survive." I hesitate, then ask. "Will *you* be okay?"

I hold my breath, unsure I'm ready for her answer. I know she's been with men since me. Hell, she has a four-year-old daughter. But I'm not sure I can stand hearing the details without wanting to fly into a jealous rage.

"You don't need to worry about me. I haven't slept with anyone since I got pregnant. I'll be just fine."

"Are you serious?"

While her answer fills me with a certain level of ease, I can't mask my surprised reaction. And I thought I'd set some sort of record by going on six months.

"I have a kid," she reminds me, as if it's the only explanation I need.

"Still. You haven't been with anyone since then?"

"Why do you sound so surprised?" she snips back. "Don't tell me you believe what some of the other preschool moms say. That because I used to work as a cocktail waitress at the casino, I probably supplemented my income by spreading my legs, since so many of the other girls do it."

"No," I answer quickly. "Not at all. I…" I trail off, my stomach churning over the idea of anyone thinking that of her.

A surge of protectiveness builds inside of me, making me want to go to school drop-off in the morning and give some of those women a piece of my mind. Tell them about the Haley McBride I once knew so intimately.

"Is that what they really say?" I ask softly.

She lowers her head, fidgeting with the hem of her t-shirt.

"Maybe not to my face, but I hear them talking. I know it wasn't the most respectable job, especially for a mom, but it paid better than most other part-time jobs. *Without* having to spread my legs."

"I'd never think that of you, Haley."

On instinct, I grab her hand in mine and brush my thumb along her knuckles. I'm not sure if it's more for her or me.

"They really did a number on you, didn't they?"

She darts her gaze up to mine. "Who?"

"Your parents."

She doesn't agree. But she doesn't defend them, either.

I saw how they treated her when she was younger. How they always demanded the world of her. Expected her to be content with the life they planned for her without a single care for what she wanted.

"Forget about them. If they can't see what an incredible woman you are, it's their fucking loss. Because you are so much more than a cocktail waitress or a mother or a dog walker or anything else. So fuck them. Fuck them all."

It's the same thing I used to tell her whenever she gave me one of her excuses about why we needed to keep our relationship quiet. After all, her parents would never approve of their daughter dating some kid from Sycamore Falls who'd already been arrested on more than one occasion. Not when they had big plans for her that included her marrying the son of a respectable politician.

That still didn't stop me from pursuing something with her.

From sneaking into her bedroom every chance I got.

From falling in love with her.

Until my love nearly sent her to the morgue.

Her brilliant eyes lock onto mine, her lips parting slightly as she leans closer.

I move my hands to her cheeks, even though this is probably one of those limitations she mentioned. I don't care about that right now. All I do care about is making her realize she matters. That she's enough. That she's perfect just the way she is.

I curve toward her, our breaths intermingling as I trace my eyes over her face. From her emerald green eyes, to the delicate curve of her button nose, to the plump lips I've fantasized about feeling again an unhealthy number of times since kissing her yesterday.

I've also fantasized about seeing them on other parts of my body an unhealthy number of times.

It's what I was thinking about when she saw me in the shower this morning.

I inch closer, her mouth so close I can practically taste her. But before I can, she abruptly pulls back and jumps off the barstool. Her chest rises and falls with each heavy breath as she looks at me with confusion and perhaps a bit of fear.

"Just sign the contract, Beckham," she orders before spinning on her heels and hurrying up the stairs.

I don't move until I hear the door to the bedroom close behind her.

When I do, I expel a deep sigh, then take a sip of wine as I read over the so-called contract she drew up.

Sure enough. Number one on her list is no unauthorized touching.

And I definitely almost did more than just touch her.

A chuckle escapes when I read number two, though.

Always disinfect the shower after extracurricular use.

EIGHTEEN

Beckham

The tires of my truck crunch on the gravel as I park in front of the tasting room building after spending the day de-budding vines. Now that it's March and we're in the middle of the time of year referred to as "bud burst", my focus is doing everything to ensure flavorful grapes, including removing certain buds to further concentrate the flavor.

The sun still glimmers bright and warm in the sky, though it's beginning its descent toward the west. A year ago, I'd still be in the fields or my lab, despite having already worked eight hours. These days, though, I've been stopping work earlier and earlier.

As much as I thought the idea of Haley's contract was ridiculous, it's actually been good for us. With established boundaries, she seems more relaxed around me.

In fact, over the past six weeks, we've been spending a lot more time together than I imagined when I proposed this arrangement. My once empty house now feels cozy and inviting, Maggie always greeting me at the door with an enthusiastic hug as she recounts her day at preschool, complete with details about who got into trouble and who she played with during recess.

It's become the highlight of my day.

I hate the idea that there will come a time when I'll walk into my house and she won't be there. Neither of them will.

Jude claims that's the real reason I still haven't approached Grady about buying the vineyard. That I'm worried the answer will still be no and we'll have done all of this for nothing.

That Haley and Maggie will no longer have a reason to stay.

Which is crazy.

I like having them around, but I want this vineyard more than anything. I don't want Grady to become suspicious of my sudden nuptials.

That's all.

Jude's just bitter Haley and I didn't sleep together within the first week, like he predicted. He knows our history. He knows better than anyone exactly why that will never happen.

I've already ruined her life once. I won't do it again.

"Hey, Beck," Gretchen calls out from behind the bar when I walk into the cavernous tasting room.

The floors are repurposed wood, crafted from old wine barrels, while the walls are exposed stone, except for the far wall, which is made up of floor-to-ceiling windows overlooking acres upon acres of budding vines.

I'm immediately reminded of marrying Haley in that exact spot. Of her appearing at the end of the aisle and my heart stopping as I took in how beautiful she was. In that split-second, a part of me wished her breathtaking smile wasn't just for show — an act to convince my friends and family we're madly in love. Instead, I wished it was because she couldn't wait to spend the rest of her life with me.

"Hey, Gretch." I move toward the long, polished bar where several tasting stations are set up.

It's a Thursday afternoon, so it's not too busy, but there are still a few people here.

"How's the response to the Syrah blend been?"

Last week, we were able to bottle a new varietal I've been working on over the past several years. I've always loved a good Syrah, and the climate a few years ago was perfect for cultivating those grapes.

"It's a hit. I might be taking bigger tastes than necessary when opening a fresh bottle."

"Nothing wrong with that. Is Grady upstairs?"

"Sure is."

"Great. Thanks."

I head down the long hallway and make my way up

to the second-floor landing, slowing my steps when I hear raised voices through the closed door of Grady's office.

"You can't do this," a stern voice I don't recognize seethes. "We had a deal."

"We were *working* on a deal," Grady corrects, his tone calm despite the other man's obvious frustration. "Neither one of us has yet to sign anything. You've been in this business long enough to know nothing's definite until the ink is dry."

"Do you want more money? I'll raise my offer to fifteen million."

I have to suppress my cough. There's no way he'll turn down that much money. He deserves it after the years he's spent turning this land into a profitable vineyard.

And after everything he's done for me.

"It's not about the money," Grady responds. "You could offer me twice the amount. Hell, ten times, and it still won't be enough to change my mind."

"You saw the plans. We'll maintain the spirit of the vineyard, will still cultivate the grapes and make wine. We'll just be building a hotel on the property, as well, which will allow more people to come and appreciate everything you've built here."

"While I like the concept, my answer is still no. And final."

It's silent for several tense seconds. I may not be able to see them, but I can picture Grady's calm demeanor, a contrast to the anger radiating from the other gentleman.

"This isn't over," the man says, his voice low and threatening. "You can be damn sure you'll be hearing from our lawyers."

"I look forward to it," Grady replies flippantly.

The door flies open and a man dressed in a designer suit complete with monogrammed cufflinks storms out. It's probably a good thing Grady declined his offer. A real winemaker wouldn't be caught dead in a suit like that. Hell, I didn't even own a suit until a few days before I married Haley.

I meet the man's irate gaze, a sneer plastered on his face. Then he storms past me and down the stairs. My eyes follow him until he disappears from view. Then I approach Grady's office and peek my head inside.

"Ah, Beckham." He slowly stands and skirts around his desk to greet me, keeping his hand on the surface for support. "You're here early."

"I figured I'd get home so I can spend some time with Haley and Maggie before bedtime."

"Good for you." He gives me a brief hug and pats my back. "Married life looks good on you. I didn't think there'd ever come a time you'd go home while the sun was still shining."

"I like being around them."

"I have to admit," Grady continues, making his way back to his chair. "I was doubtful at first."

"You were?" I sit opposite him, attempting to remain cool and genuinely curious.

"I thought maybe you only married her because of what I said."

I feign surprise, despite my pulse steadily increasing over the prospect he saw through our ruse, regardless of our best efforts.

Does this mean it's all been for nothing? Is he about to tell me he has no plans to sell to me, like he did the man who just left?

"But I've been watching you these past several weeks." A gentle smile tugs on his mouth, crinkling the lines around his eyes. "There's been a change in you, Beckham. It's obvious you love her and her little girl. Which is why I'm happy to tell you I've decided to accept your offer."

My eyes widen, his statement nearly stealing my breath. "You… You have?"

"Yes. As long as it's still on the table."

"It is. Definitely. You know how much I love this place."

"I certainly do."

"But are you sure, Grady? I overheard your conversation with the stiff suit." I drop my voice. "I heard what he was offering. I can't come remotely close to that."

He waves me off. "I'm seventy-six years old. What would I possibly do with all that money this late in the game? I'd much rather know this land is taken care of."

"You know it will be," I assure him.

"Then as long as everything checks out, the vineyard will be yours at the end of the harvest."

I blink repeatedly, his statement catching me off guard. "The harvest?"

"Call me a sentimental fool. This upcoming harvest will be my thirtieth on this land. I'd like to go out on an even number."

"Of course. Sorry. I guess I'm just excited."

"It's understandable." Grady pulls himself up to stand and I do the same, moving toward him as he wraps me in a hug. "I'm proud of you, son." He gives my back a pat before pulling away and meeting my eyes. "Your dad would be proud of the man — the *husband* — you've become. You didn't let your past mistakes dictate the rest of your life. Instead, you made something of yourself."

"All thanks to you." I swallow the ball of guilt gnawing at my stomach.

This is what I wanted, why I married Haley. But now that the wheels are in motion, I can't help but feel like shit for deceiving the man who's been like a second father to me.

The man who took me under his wing and taught me all his winemaking secrets when no one else would hire me.

Worse, I'm not sure how Haley's going to respond to the changed timeline. I told her we'd probably only need to stay married for nine months. Three months to give me enough time to convince Grady to sell and get all the paperwork in order, then six months after the sale goes through so he won't become suspicious.

Harvest goes from late August through October. I'll be asking her to stay married until next April.

While I can't ignore the relief filling me at the prospect of being able to come home to them every day through April, I worry how Haley will react.

Will she want to stay married until then?

Or will she want to cut bait now?

NINETEEN

Haley

Maggie's excited squeals echo as she swings back and forth on the playscape Beckham put in for her a few weeks ago. The sight of her auburn curls flying through the air and her chubby cheeks warms my heart. The happiness she exudes is everything I imagined for us the night I sat with my notepad, worried if I was going to find a place to live.

Never in my wildest dreams could I have anticipated I'd find a home with Beckham Lawrence. Even more surprising, it hasn't been nearly as awkward as I expected it would be, considering our tumultuous past.

At first, I was reticent about the idea of him spoiling her more than necessary. But now that we live a good fifteen minutes from Maggie's favorite park, I caved and let Beckham put in a play area for her. I told myself it was just out of convenience, but I'd be lying if I didn't tear up a bit from the look on Maggie's face when she saw the new playscape.

Beckham even took a day off so he could surprise her when she got home from preschool, going so far as to enlist the help of his brothers, Jude and Finn. Since Finn's on the fire department, he had all the guys who weren't on shift help, too. What would have taken one person several days to put together was constructed in a matter of hours.

When I hear the familiar sound of tires crunching against dirt, I glance into the distance as Beckham's truck navigates up the country road toward the house. I do my best to temper the butterflies wanting to take flight in my stomach, something they've been doing more and more lately whenever I'm in his presence, despite the rules I put in place.

It doesn't matter how much I avoid touching him. How much I tell myself this isn't real. How much I remind myself he hurt me. My feelings for him are just as strong as they were all those years ago.

Maybe even stronger now that I've seen how amazing he is with Maggie. How he treats her as if she were his own.

"Beck! Beck!" Maggie says excitedly, jumping from the swing and running toward him as he heads our way, Monte following close behind, as always.

"Hey, squirt." He scoops her into his arms and gives her a kiss on the forehead. "How was school today?"

"Good," Maggie chirps.

"No one gave you any trouble?"

"Nope."

"You'll let me know if they do?" He arches a brow.

She gives him an exaggerated roll of her eyes. "Yes, Beck."

"That's my girl."

He gives her another kiss, then sets her on the ground. In a flash, she runs around the yard, Monte chasing after her.

"How was your day?" Beckham asks, pulling my attention to him.

"Good. I finished and delivered another cake." I beam.

Over the past six weeks, I've been able to devote most of my days to experimenting with different cakes and amping up my social media presence.

It's paid off. People love watching time lapse videos of me building and decorating these cakes, so much so that several of my videos have gone viral.

I'm now getting so many orders I've had to give up my dog-walking job.

All because I finally took a risk.

It helps I also have access to a decent kitchen now that I'm living with Beckham.

"That's amazing." He blows out a laugh. "I still

don't know how you make a cake look like the things you do."

"Lots of practice," I reply. "Just like with what you do."

"I guess so." A comfortable silence passes between us as we watch Maggie and Monte play together. Then he says, "I talked to Grady."

I dart my eyes toward him. "You did?"

"Yeah."

His expression falls, and I fully expect for him to tell me it's over. That we went through all of this for nothing.

"He's agreed to sell to me, pending everything checking out. Even pissed off some corporate prick in a suit by refusing to accept his obscene offer."

My entire body relaxes with relief. "That's incredible. I'm so happy for you."

I'm about to wrap my arms around him, but stop myself, remembering the rules we have in place.

But as I survey his demeanor, I sense something's off. He just told me Grady's going to sell him the vineyard, yet he looks like someone just informed him his dog died.

"What's wrong? I thought you'd be over the moon. This is what you've always wanted."

"I know." He briefly squeezes his eyes shut. When he returns them to mine, they're conflicted. "I just… I should have asked him earlier. Or known. But the sale won't be finalized until after this year's harvest, since it's his thirtieth. Harvest goes August through October."

"So that means…"

"If we stick to our original agreement, we'd need to stay married until at least April. Possibly May."

"Oh." My shoulders fall as I peer into the distance, Maggie and Monte zooming around the yard in a blur.

While I feared Beckham was about to tell me it was all over and we got married for nothing, I'm not sure how to feel about this, either. Not sure how to feel about staying married until May. At that point, we'll have been married for over a year.

Over a year of watching him play with Maggie.

Over a year of sharing a bed with him.

Over a year of reminding myself it's not real — even though a part of me still wishes it could be, despite all the past hurt.

"We could end things earlier," Beckham suggests when I don't immediately respond. "I'm worried what Grady might think if we split right after the sale goes through. After everything he did for me, I don't want him to know the truth. I want him to be able to retire thinking I'm happily married."

I bring my eyes back to his. "Then we'll stay married."

"Are you sure?" He narrows his gaze on me.

"What's a few more months? Plus, look on the bright side," I say in a chipper voice. "He's going to sell to you. You're getting the vineyard. If you ask me, that's something worth celebrating."

He studies me for several long moments, his brows furrowed. "How do you do it?" he asks softly, almost as if to himself.

"Do what?"

"Always remain so positive." He glances at my leg, regret and guilt flickering across his features.

I want to tell him what happened all those years ago isn't his fault. That I don't blame him. That I've never blamed him. But we've gone this long without talking about the giant elephant in the room. Why change things now?

"Maybe Parker's influence is rubbing off on me," I respond with a laugh, breaking through the tension. "After all, I manifested a solution to my living situation. While I didn't foresee this exact scenario being the solution, I think it's working out. Being married to you isn't as bad as I thought it would be."

"Likewise, Hales." He gently nudges me.

When he does, a jolt of electricity shoots through me. It's the first time any part of his body has been in contact with any part of mine in over six weeks. Ever since I made him sign that contract, we've both kept our distance, probably obsessively so.

But when I see the flash of desire in his gaze, I can't help but wonder if we're just setting ourselves up for failure by having these rules. If by denying ourselves of any touch, we're making it more inevitable we'll both crack.

And when we do, it'll be with such force I won't be able to put all my pieces back together again.

This is the kind of power Beckham Lawrence has over me.

That he's always had over me, even if I've tried to forget him.

Forget *us*.

"We should go celebrate," I suggest, tearing my gaze from his before I do something I'll regret. "Or you can go celebrate with your brothers. It's not every day you buy a vineyard, after all."

"That's a good idea."

"Great. I'll take care of feeding Monte dinner so you can—"

"I meant us. I'd like for us to celebrate. None of this would have been possible without you. Hell, after the way I've treated you the past several years, you had every right to slam the door in my face when I came to you with my proposal. But I'm grateful you didn't."

He flashes me his panty-melting smile that still affects me like it did when we were reckless teenagers.

"What do you say? Are you up for a night on the town as a family?"

For the first time, I don't remind him we're not a real family. Instead, I respond, "I'd like that."

TWENTY

Haley

The sun warms my face as we sit on the back patio of Jude's brewery in the historic district of downtown Sycamore Falls. Now that it's spring and the weather's warming up, quite a few other people have gotten the same idea. The outside area is filled with locals and tourists trying a few of Jude's microbrews while their kids play on the playground he put in a few years ago.

"To Beckham," Finn says, lifting his pint glass.

"To Beckham." We all join his brother, and I meet Beckham's eyes from across the table.

Despite the fact that he's surrounded by all his siblings, apart from his oldest brother, his eyes are still focused on me. I tell myself it's only an act. That the only reason he's looking at me this way is because we're in public and everyone is supposed to think we're married, especially his mother, Danielle, who also joined us.

He's certainly not looking at me with a heated stare because he *wants* to.

"How are the kids doing, all things considered?" I ask her as I tear my eyes from Beckham and take a long sip from my beer.

With the summer months fast approaching, Jude's been serving some of his fruit-inspired beers, including his signature blueberry lager, which is also my favorite.

"They're adjusting. The baby's a piece of cake."

She nods toward Finn as he bounces Jeremiah in his lap, which has probably caused every woman's ovaries to burst. As if seeing three of the four Lawrence brothers sitting at the same table isn't enough of a sight to behold. One thing is certain. The Lawrence family has incredible genes. But despite how attractive Jude, Finn, and even Hayden are, all of them with similar coloring and build as Beckham, there's something about the second oldest Lawrence brother I'll always be drawn to.

"It's not that he doesn't remember his mother," Danielle continues, "but it's not as difficult for him since he's so young. There are moments you can tell he misses her, but those are becoming fewer as time passes."

"And Presley?"

She blows out a sigh, looking over at the playground

where Maggie is currently playing with the long and lean brunette little girl.

"She still hasn't spoken. I keep telling Hayden he can't avoid this forever." She brings her water up to her mouth and takes a sip. "I understand he needs to work a lot now that he's taking over the medical practice here in town. But it seems like he's putting in more hours than necessary so he doesn't have to face this new reality of life without his wife."

"It can't be easy," I offer.

"I'm not saying it should be," she says sweetly before leaning toward me and dropping her voice. "I think it would help both of them if he were more present. They just lost their mom. And now their father is barely around." She shifts her attention to her granddaughter as she follows Maggie. "But I think Maggie's been good for Presley, especially since they're so close in age."

"She loves making friends," I remark, my heart warming at how kind and accepting Maggie is.

After she first met Presley, she'd asked if she was deaf and that's why she didn't talk. I explained the situation the best I could. Unlike other kids, she didn't get frustrated that Presley wouldn't talk to her. Instead, she shrugged and said maybe she would when she finally had something to say.

"She's been good for Beckham, too," Danielle offers.

"She adores him."

"He hasn't always had it easy, as you know."

I respond with a barely imperceptible nod. I'm more than aware of Beckham's somewhat troubled past.

"His father's diagnosis was especially tough on him," she says as she peers into the distance, a nostalgic gleam in her eyes. "Beckham and Ryan had such a special bond."

"I remember," I say quietly, swallowing hard.

Every time I saw them together when I was a kid, I couldn't help but be jealous. I think it's why I was often standoffish and rude to him as a young girl. My parents never played with me like Beckham's parents did. Most of the time, my parents couldn't be bothered to even acknowledge me, unless it was to order me around.

"When he got sick, Beckham lost part of his spark. Took his anger out on the world, as you remember."

I give her another small nod, the lump in my throat tightening as a phantom ache shoots up my leg.

"For the longest time, I worried he'd let his past mistakes define him. Sure, he may have made some poor decisions, but haven't we all? Don't we all deserve a second chance to make things right?"

As I listen to her, my gaze drifts back toward Beckham, his intense eyes instantly locking on mine, as if drawn to me by some invisible force. It doesn't matter that mere seconds ago, he was involved in an animated conversation with his brothers about the upcoming baseball season. Right now, all his attention is focused solely on me.

"I guess what I'm trying to say is I'm grateful you found it in your heart to give him a second chance."

"He's a good man," I manage to say through the heaviness weighing me down. "He deserves to be happy."

"I couldn't agree more." She gives my hand a squeeze, then clears her throat, her voice turning bright. "Well, enough of this mushy stuff. I'm relieved Beckham found someone he can grow old with. And who will hopefully give me a few more grand-babies." She gives me a playful waggle of her brow.

I laugh with her, but this entire conversation has left me feeling unsettled. Not simply because of the role I'm forced to play in lying and deceiving everyone.

But because there's still a small part of me that hasn't let go of my teenage dream of a happily ever after with Beckham Lawrence.

"Will you excuse me for a minute?" I ask, doing my best to mask the uneasiness in my tone. "I need to run to the ladies' room. Do you mind keeping an eye on Maggie?"

"Of course."

As I push back from the table and hurry inside the industrial-style building. I'm so lost in my thoughts, replaying Danielle's words about growing old with Beckham, that I barely pay attention to my surroundings…

Until I turn the corner toward the restrooms and collide with a suit-clad body.

"I'm so sorry," I begin, darting my eyes up.

When I do, I hitch a breath, a weight settling in my stomach as I'm met with a pair of familiar gray eyes.

Gray eyes that are nearly identical to those belonging to the little girl I've rocked to sleep every night for the past four years.

"Haley?" His voice is hesitant, almost disbelieving, as he repeatedly scans my figure.

This is the last place I ever thought I'd run into Oliver St. John. It's not like I've been actively avoiding him. There's no reason to. He ended things by throwing a wad of cash at me when I revealed I was pregnant. After all, he had a brand new wife at home, much to my surprise.

As the memories of our relationship return to the surface after nearly five years, the reality of Oliver being in the same place as Maggie sets in.

Protecting her from learning the truth is all I can focus on, and I whirl around, not giving him another moment of my time, even when he calls my name.

With quick steps, I rush toward the patio, barely acknowledging any of the locals I pass on the way. Their voices fade into the background as I emerge outside, met with the sound of children happily playing and boisterous conversation.

My eyes immediately find Beckham as he laughs

with his brothers. But when he sees me, his expression drops. In a heartbeat, he's on his feet, closing the distance between us.

"What's wrong? What happened?" There's a protective edge to his voice as his concerned gaze sweeps over me, looking for what could have caused my distress.

"I need to go," I say urgently. "You can stay, but I need to take Maggie home. Can I have your keys?" I nervously shift from foot to foot.

"Hey. Slow down. What's—"

"I just ran into Maggie's father," I hiss under my breath. "He doesn't know about her, and I'd like to keep it that way. So please just give me your keys."

Without another word, he turns from me and bends to whisper something into Jude's ear. His eyes briefly widen, then he gives Beckham a small nod before offering me an encouraging smile.

"I'll get her," Beckham tells me.

"What do you mean? I just need your keys. You don't—"

"I'm driving you home." The finality in his voice makes it clear this isn't up for discussion.

I'm not sure I have it in me to argue with him right now anyway. Instead, I grab my purse as he scoops Maggie up from the playground and hoists her onto his shoulders.

Just as we're about to turn the corner away from the

brewery, I glance over my shoulder to see Oliver watching us with interest, his eyes trained on the little girl who bears an uncanny resemblance to him.

TWENTY-ONE

Beckham

The car is quiet on the ride home, apart from Maggie's occasional chatter about whatever pops into her head. Normally, Haley is involved in the conversation. Today, she barely acknowledges what she's saying, her expression pensive as her eyes remain trained out the window.

I don't know the story about Maggie's birth father, other than the fact that Haley has seemingly gone to great lengths to keep her from him. I can only assume if Haley doesn't want him in their life, there must be a damn good reason.

Which is why giving her my keys so I could stay and have a few drinks with my friends and family wasn't an option. Haley needed me, even if she'd never admit it.

Or maybe I just need to be here for her right now. Maybe I don't want her to be alone.

Once we're back at the house and Maggie's preoccupied with an episode of *Bluey*, I head into the kitchen and pour an oversized glass of chardonnay for Haley. When I hand it to her, she takes a large gulp.

"I didn't think I'd see him again," she says, breaking the silence. "Especially here, of all places."

"What happened between you?" I ask guardedly as I pour myself a glass of wine.

I'm not sure I want to hear the answer. Don't want to listen to her talk about how she fell head over heels in love with some guy who wore expensive suits.

I didn't get a good look at him, but he appears to be much more Haley's type. Then again, my knowledge of Haley's type is relegated to what I knew of her when we were teenagers.

"We met on one of my routes when I was working as a flight attendant. At first, we kept things professional, but one night, he was staying at the same hotel and we connected over a bottle of really good wine.

"Throughout the next year, we saw each other as much as we could. He often flew out at a moment's notice to be on one of my routes, especially if it was to Hawaii. Or Miami. Or even Europe.

"I thought everything was going great. That all changed when I learned I was pregnant. We were safe," she adds quickly. "I always insisted on him using a condom. They're not lying when they say it's not a hundred percent effective." She rolls her eyes, taking a long sip from her wine.

"What did he do?"

"Turns out I wasn't the only woman in his life. He was married."

"Jesus."

"When I told him, he threw a pile of cash at me, instructed me to 'take care of the problem'," she says, using air quotes. "Then he warned me never to contact him again or he'd have me fired from the airline for fraternizing with a customer." She scoffs, bringing her wine back to her lips. "He did that anyway, most likely to make sure I had no choice but to terminate. Without a job, how could I take care of a baby?"

"What an asshole," I grind out, clenching and unclenching my fists. "You should have gone after him for child support, at least."

I don't even know this guy, but the more she talks, the more I want to hunt him down and break every bone in his body for the way he treated her.

"I didn't want to give him that kind of control over me. After everything my parents did…" she trails off, taking a moment to push down her emotions. "Well, it took me years to finally get out from under their thumb. Longer than it should have." Her mouth twists into a sad smile.

I know better than most just how much her parents tried to control her. It had been a huge bone of contention throughout our relationship. Why she felt the need to keep what we had a secret. Even when I promised to take care of her and give her the life she deserved, she was still reluctant to take that risk.

"So when I finally did, I swore I'd never let anyone have a say in my life again. Never let anyone control me again. Not after everything I lost the last time I did that." She slowly lifts her eyes to mine, so many unspoken regrets filling the space between us.

This is the first time in months either of us has made a passing reference to what happened all those years ago. While a part of me knew it would eventually come up, another part secretly hoped it wouldn't.

Hoped I wouldn't have to be reminded of everything I stole from her.

"I…" I shake my head, trying to find the right words. But none seem adequate. "I really want to give you a hug right now, but I don't want to break rule number one."

She chokes out a laugh, a lone tear trickling down her cheek, a crack in the wall she built around herself to shield her from anyone who could hurt her again.

Myself included.

"I could really use a hug," she admits.

"Does this mean I have your permission to break rule number one?" I arch a brow.

Swiping at her cheek, she nods. "You can break rule number one."

"It's about damn time," I exhale, not wasting a second in pulling her against me.

The moment our bodies come into contact, we both release a simultaneous sigh of relief.

"This feels really fucking good," Haley whispers as she draws in a breath.

"Yes, it does."

I press a gentle kiss to the top of her head. I don't ask if it's okay. Right now, I don't care. All I do care about is giving her the comfort she needs.

The comfort she's been deprived of her entire life.

The comfort *I* need, too.

"Ewe. Crush business," Maggie's innocent voice interjects.

Neither one of us moves for several moments.

Then Haley throws her head back and laughs.

And not just any laugh.

A full-bodied, enthusiastic laugh.

I can't remember the last time I've heard her laugh like this. Even when Maggie has done something silly, it's tempered, as if the weight she's been carrying for too long prevents her from being truly happy. But right now, I see the girl I once knew.

The girl I fell in love with all those years ago.

The girl I might be falling in love with all over again.

"Why don't you go upstairs and draw yourself a bath?" I suggest once her laughter dies down.

"I can't. I need to—"

"You don't need to do anything right now except

take care of yourself," I admonish, running my hands down her arms.

I expect her to step out of my hold, tell me the no-touching rule is back in force. Thankfully, she doesn't.

"How can you expect to take care of a little human if you don't take care of yourself first?"

She opens her mouth to argue yet again, but I cut her off.

"If I have to carry you up those stairs and throw you in the bath myself, I will." A hint of playfulness creeps into my tone as I waggle my brows suggestively. "Then again, maybe you should fight me on this. I'd actually enjoy it."

"Of course you would, you ogre." She playfully pushes against my chest, but I don't miss the growing smile tugging on her lips, erasing all traces of her earlier unease and trepidation.

With her wine glass in hand, she turns, but only makes it a few steps before facing me again.

"What do you think about amending our contract to allow for touching?" She chews on her bottom lip as she peers at me with hope in her eyes.

"I'll have my lawyers get right on it." I beam.

"Good."

Turning, she makes her way toward the stairs. Just as she's about to disappear, I call out.

"Hey, Haley?"

"Yes?" Her eyes meet mine.

I open and close my mouth several times, unsure what I even want to tell her. Why I called her name.

Actually, I know why. I just don't know if I can finally say the words after so long.

"I'm sorry," I finally tell her.

"It's not your fault. I—"

"I'm not talking about your douche of an ex," I interject. "I'm talking about us."

She swallows hard. "Us?" Her voice trembles.

"Yeah." I run my fingers through my hair. "I'm sorry for anything I may have done that made you feel…unwanted."

She pushes out a long breath. When she returns her eyes to mine, she almost looks lighter.

"Me, too."

TWENTY-TWO

Haley

I lean my head against the cool porcelain of the claw-foot tub in Beckham's bathroom as I relish in the warmth of the water enveloping me. The aroma of lavender wafts through the air, making me feel more relaxed than I have in a while.

I can't remember the last time I've slowed down enough to just soak in a tub. Since Maggie was born, I've had no choice but to dedicate every waking minute to working and finding a way to provide for her.

But Beckham's right.

How can I expect to take care of Maggie if I don't take care of myself first?

And after today's unexpected encounter with Oliver, this is exactly what I need.

Noticing my fingertips beginning to prune, I reluctantly get out of the bath and wrap myself in a plush towel from the warmer Beckham installed after he saw me throw a towel in the dryer before jumping in the shower one day.

It's just one of the many things he's done for me over the past few weeks.

But he doesn't do them for the fanfare or in expectation of anything. He does them because he *wants* to.

After toweling off, I slip into a halter dress and cardigan, pausing to apply a fresh coat of eyeliner and lip gloss before making my way back downstairs. I tell myself the only reason I put on a dress is because of the gorgeous weather.

Not because I love the way Beckham looks at me whenever I wear one.

When I emerge into the kitchen, my heart melts at the scene that greets me. Beckham and Maggie stand by the counter, Maggie on her step stool as she helps Beckham prepare a marinade.

"That's it. Just a little more brown sugar," he encourages.

Despite his towering height, he bends down to Maggie's level, gently guiding her small hands as she scoops a spoonful into the mixing bowl.

"Like this?" Maggie asks.

"Perfect. Are you sure you're not a trained chef?"

My daughter's infectious giggles echo in the space. I lean against the wall, watching them interact with ease, as if Beckham Lawrence cooking dinner with my daughter is a normal occurrence. He's always been so good to her, even when he couldn't stand the sight of me. Now that he's softened up, it makes me want all the things I have no right wanting.

Especially after everything he lost because of me.

"I'm too young to have a job, Beck!" Maggie says through her laughter.

"What? Aren't you eighteen?"

"I'm only four." She holds up her hand, demonstrating how many she is.

"Are you serious? Only four? Wow." He shakes his head in amazement. "You could have fooled me. I thought you were much older than four."

"Stop trying to wish time away," I interrupt, moving toward them. "You've already grown up faster than I like."

"Mama!" Maggie jumps down from her stool and runs toward me, giving me a hug. "We're making you dinner!"

"Is that right?" I look from her toward Beckham, meeting his dark eyes.

"Yup." Maggie answers enthusiastically. "I just finished making the marinade for the ahi."

"You're making ahi?"

"Seared, if that's okay," Beckham says softly.

"I love seared ahi."

"I know." He flashes me a grin I feel deep in my

soul. Then he wipes his hands on a dishtowel and pours some red wine into a glass, handing it to me.

"Red wine with fish? Are you feeling okay?"

"Ahi is a substantial fish. If it were a flaky white fish, this would be a sauvignon blanc or chardonnay. But ahi works well with a light red, like a pinot noir. And this one from the Santa Barbara Valley is one of my favorites."

He tilts his glass toward mine, and I clink with him before bringing the wine to my mouth, taking a sip. I can see how it would pair well with ahi. It's not too heavy, but not too light, either. The perfect medium-bodied red.

"You look better," Beckham remarks after a beat. "Not that you looked bad," he adds quickly. "I don't think it's possible for you to look bad. But—"

"I feel better," I interject as heat rushes over my face.

Why does it feel like that one summer all over again? We were awkward around each other then, too. At least when I realized my feelings for him went deeper than him merely being a boy I once knew as a child.

"What can I help with?" I ask, needing to do something to distract myself from the mounting tension between us.

"My sous chef and I have everything covered in here. Why don't you go relax outside? Enjoy the sunset."

"I'll show you to your table!" Maggie offers, looking at Beckham and giving him an exaggerated wink.

"What are you two up to?" I ask suspiciously.

"Just play along," Beckham whispers.

Maggie grabs my hand and pulls me through the living area and onto the back patio. A few strands of twinkling lights hang overhead as soft jazz music sounds from the speakers. There's a slight chill in the air now that the sun has started to go down, but Beckham lit the space heaters, as well as the nearby fire pit.

"How many?" Maggie faces me, playing the perfect hostess.

I look at the table to see it's already set for dinner, a hand-drawn menu placed on each plate.

"Three."

"I have the perfect table! This way, please."

She whirls around, her curls springing with her movements, and walks the few steps toward the long wooden table, gesturing toward a chair for me to sit.

Once I do, she retrieves a small notepad and pencil from the pocket of her apron.

"What would you like for dinner?"

I open the menu and laugh to myself when I see there's only one thing written in her shaky handwriting.

"I'll have the ahi."

"Excellent choice."

She spins around and heads back inside, hurrying into the kitchen to tell Beckham my order. Then she climbs back onto her step stool and Beckham moves behind her, wrapping his hand over hers as he helps her whisk the marinade.

Just like I do whenever we bake together.

As if sensing my eyes on him, Beckham glances up and treats me to a smile so sexy it should be illegal. When he returns his attention to Maggie, I shift my gaze forward, admiring the acres upon acres of vines in the distance, tiny buds starting to appear on them.

Over the past several weeks, I've learned more about the process of making wine than I ever thought possible, mostly from Maggie asking Beckham questions about the "juice" he makes.

According to Beckham, this time of year when the buds form on all the vines is referred to as "bud burst" or "bud break". He mentioned it's one of the most difficult times of year, aside from right before the harvest. Because of the dips in temperature at night, he has to monitor everything closely, often turning on giant fans overnight to protect the budding vines from falling victim to frost.

I never thought much about the technical knowledge required to do what Beckham does, but it's impressive. Makes me appreciate him even more. The amount of care with which he's tended to this land over the past several years is nothing short of remarkable.

His job is so much more than just mixing ingredients together. As he says, his work starts with the vine. He can't make good wine without good grapes. He can't expect good grapes unless he takes care of the vines.

And soon, this will all be his.

He's really come a long way from the boy I knew all those years ago.

"Here we are," Beckham's voice cuts through, pulling my attention to him as he sets a plate in front of me, the scent of garlic and ginger invading my senses. "Seared ahi with Asian slaw."

"This looks incredible," I tell him.

And I mean it. It looks like something I'd order at a nice restaurant. Certainly not something I'd expect Beckham to cook for me.

"You deserve it." He assumes the chair beside me as Maggie sits on the other side.

Her plate consists of a few bites of fully cooked ahi, but also some chicken nuggets and apple slices.

While she's pretty good at trying new foods, she's still only four and likes to stick to what most kids her age like.

"*Bon Appetit.*" Beckham lifts his glass, and both Maggie and I do the same, all of us clinking our drinks together.

If I could choose any moment to freeze time, it would be this precise instant, the three of us enjoying dinner like we're a real family.

Because there will eventually come a time when it'll just be Maggie and me once more.

Weeks ago, I looked forward to that day.

Now, I hate the idea of never experiencing this again… Whatever *this* may be.

TWENTY-THREE

Beckham

"Okay, peanut. Time for bed," Haley says several hours later, the sun having set a while ago.

But we still didn't make any move to go inside, the three of us sitting on the back patio as we talked about everything that popped into Maggie's head.

She's definitely an inquisitive little girl. All throughout dinner, she peppered me with questions about the different things she noticed in the vineyard.

I told her all about the owl and bird boxes that keep pests away. I also taught her the flowers between the rows of vines she saw in the winter are cover crops, and are used to nourish the vines during dormancy. I also told her the rose bushes planted at the end of each row aren't there to make everything look pretty but to detect disease brought on by louses eating the vines.

Maggie wasn't the only one fascinated by everything I shared. I could tell Haley was also impressed.

"But I'm not tired, Mama," Maggie says around a yawn, her head drooping.

"Sure you aren't." Haley pushes back from her chair. "Come on. Time for bed."

When she starts to stand, I place a hand on her shoulder, stopping her. "I can read to her."

She meets my gaze. "You don't have to. She's not—"

"If you're about to tell me she's not my responsibility again, I'm going to stop you right now. She may not be my responsibility, but I can still help with her. I still *want* to help with her. So please. Let me read to her."

She stares at me for several long moments. I half expect her to refuse, like she typically does.

At first, I thought her reticence to accept help was due to her stubbornness. But I get it now. Hell, I should have understood it long before now. I saw firsthand how controlling her parents were. It's understandable she'd avoid any scenario that would give anyone power over her.

Knowing what I do now, it's a miracle she even agreed to our fake marriage.

"Thanks, Beckham," she finally says.

"Anytime." I squeeze her arm, then move toward

Maggie. "Come on, pipsqueak. You're with me tonight."

"You're going to read to me?"

"Yup." I lift her off her chair and place her feet on the ground, making sure she's steady before I release her. "Go on up and change into your pajamas." I arch a brow. "You don't need help, do you?"

She rolls her eyes dramatically, placing her hands on her hips. "I'm four," she replies with the attitude of a fourteen-year-old. "I know how to put on my pajamas. I can even brush my teeth." She marches inside and runs up the stairs, her heavy footfalls echoing even out here.

"I have a feeling we'll have our hands full with her when she's a teenager," I muse absentmindedly, not having realized what I said until Haley darts her wide eyes toward me, her breath hitching.

It's not the subject of the statement that catches her by surprise, but that one word… *We.*

"I mean, you," I correct. "*You'll* have your hands full."

"I certainly will," she says with a smile, although it doesn't reach her eyes.

I grab our dinner plates and bring them inside, placing them in the sink. Haley follows with a few glasses.

"You don't have to do that," I tell her as she turns on the faucet and starts to scrub the dishes. "I can clean it up."

"I don't *have* to do anything," she throws my words back at me. "I *want* to do it."

"Touché, Haley." I playfully nudge her.

God, I love being able to touch her again. I hope the no-touching rule remains permanently erased. I doubt I'll ever be able to go back to not touching her, even if all reason tells me it's probably best for both of us.

"Anything I should know about reading to her?"

She turns off the faucet and faces me. "She only gets three books. Otherwise, she'll have you read every one she owns. Twice. She's a bit of a bookworm."

"Three books. Got it." I wipe my hands on a dishtowel, then start up the stairs.

"Thanks, Beckham," Haley calls after me.

I glance over my shoulder and meet her gaze. "Anytime, Haley. I mean it."

She gives a slight nod, then turns around, continuing to clean the kitchen.

I head up the stairs and pause outside Maggie's door that's slightly ajar. "Maggie?" I knock softly. "Are you ready?"

"Yup!"

I push the door open, smiling as she slides down her bed. With a blanket and her favorite stuffed elephant in her hands, she heads toward the oversized chaise lounge I bought after I noticed Haley standing beside Maggie's bed to read to her. This way, they can snuggle together on the chair before Maggie climbs up into her bed.

"What do you think you're doing?" I ask as Maggie sits in front of the bookcase, pulling book after book out of it and stacking them in a lopsided pile.

"Picking out the books I want you to read!"

I narrow my gaze at her, crossing my arms over my chest. "Your mom said you have a three-book limit."

She gives me a pleading look to rival the puppy-dog eyes Monte reserves for when he wants a treat. "Please, Beck. You never read to me. And I want you to read all these books."

"I tell you what, squirt." I crouch down to her level. "I'll talk to your mom and ask if we can take turns reading to you at night. How does that sound?"

Her expression lights up. "For real life?"

I chuckle, pressing a soft kiss to her head. "For real life. Now pick three."

She scowls, but it only lasts a second before she has three books picked out. And they're three books I bought for her upon my sister's recommendation.

I climb into the chaise lounge and arrange Maggie beside me, my heart expanding when she rests her little head on my chest. I've spent the past few months living with this little human, but I've never held her like this. There's something so innocent and pure about it.

And something absolutely terrifying, too.

It makes me appreciate everything Haley's sacrificed for her even more. I'm not sure I would have had the strength to do what she did — continue her pregnancy with no support. It's further proof of how tough she is.

How much she's changed since everything fell apart. She's no longer the scared teenager who refused to stand up to her parents and fight for what she wanted.

She's already done that.

It's more than I can say for myself.

I snuggle Maggie closer to me as I read her a story about a farting dog who ends up saving his family from a bunch of burglars, thanks to his putrid gas problem.

When Dylan recommended it to me, I questioned whether a book about a farting dog would be appropriate for a four-year-old. But I can't ignore the message inside — to accept everyone, even if they're not perfect.

Noticing a movement out of the corner of my eye, I look up and meet Haley's gaze as she leans against the doorjamb, a heartwarming smile pulling on her lips. I return her smile before continuing to read to Maggie. Even though she's already asleep, I'm in no rush to finish, savoring the warmth of her in my arms.

When I finally reach the end of the book and place it on top of the pile, Haley starts toward us.

"I got her," I whisper so as to not wake Maggie.

I can't help but laugh at the fact that she initially wanted me to read every book she owned, yet she couldn't even manage to stay awake for the first one.

Carefully arranging her in my arms, I stand and carry her to her bed, easily hoisting her over the railing and onto her mattress. After covering her with blankets, I smooth her auburn curls out of her face and touch a gentle kiss to her temple.

"Sweet dreams, pipsqueak."

I move toward the lamp in the corner, but Haley stops me. "She sleeps with it on. It's like a nightlight for her."

"Right. Sorry."

I leave the light on and follow Haley into the hallway, closing the door gently behind us.

"She's a great kid," I say, still keeping my voice low.

She glances at the artwork adorning Maggie's door. Hell, there's even random drawings now taped to the walls in practically every room, including a sign on the door to my office advertising a nail polish store.

"Yes, she is."

"But it's to be expected. She's got an amazing mom."

Her cheeks flush with a hint of pink and she averts her gaze. "Thanks, Beckham."

"I mean it, Haley. She's lucky to have you." I lick my lips, then add, "We both are."

She lifts her eyes to mine. "Both?"

"Yes, Haley." I step toward her, only a fraction of an inch separating us. "I'm lucky to have you, too."

She searches my eyes for several moments, as if trying to unravel some complicated mystery that's eluded her for years.

Then she clutches my cheeks and her lips collide with mine.

I still, momentarily surprised.

After six weeks of purposefully avoiding any kind of

physical contact, the last thing I anticipated was for her to kiss me.

And my god, it feels incredible.

Her lips are just as intoxicating as they were on our wedding day.

As they were all those years ago.

Since the first time I kissed her, I knew her lips were dangerous. Knew they'd eventually be my undoing.

I never could have predicted to what extent.

"Sorry." She quickly pulls back when I remain frozen. "I don't know what came over me. I just… It won't happen again."

Spinning around, she hurries into the bedroom. She's about to close the door behind her, but before she can, I press my palm on it. She snaps her wide eyes to mine, surprise and confusion swirling within as we stare at each other for what feels like an eternity.

I know this is a bad idea. Know nothing good could come out of this.

But right now, I don't care about any of the possible ramifications.

All I do care about is finally succumbing to the desire that's been building since I watched her walk down the aisle to become my wife.

My jaw set in a determined line, I erase the remaining space between us and yank her against me, her body fitting mine like the lost piece of a puzzle.

"Beckham, what are—"

"If we're going to get rid of the no-touching rule, may as well make it count. Don't you think?"

I don't give her a chance to respond before I slam my lips against hers.

TWENTY-FOUR

Haley

I have no idea what came over me. Why I kissed Beckham.

I went into this sham of a marriage certain nothing he did or said would make me bend my rules. Not after the way he cut me out of his life as if I didn't exist.

As if I were just another notch on his belt, like my mother warned me.

But after everything he did for me tonight — from forcing me to take time for myself, to cooking me dinner, to reading to Maggie — I've seen a different side of Beckham yet again.

And when he swipes his tongue against mine, tilting my head to allow him better access, all my defenses crumble. The heat of his kiss ignites a wildfire within me, awakening every desire I've struggled to suppress since our wedding day.

I convinced myself this was the only way. That depriving myself of his touch was necessary for me to keep my heart intact. After all, losing him all those years ago absolutely ruined me.

But as he pushes me farther into the room, his hands roaming my body, I *want* him to ruin me. Want everything he'll give me, regardless of what kind of devastation he'll leave in his wake.

He breaks his mouth from mine, his heavy breaths filling the room as he peppers rough kisses along my jawline. When he takes my earlobe between his teeth, a moan slips from my throat.

"Beckham," I whimper.

I'm running hotter than I have in years, an inferno scalding my veins. I don't know how much more of this torture I can handle, every inch of my body throbbing with need. I haven't been with another man since Oliver. I'd resigned myself to a life of no attachments. I had to think about Maggie, put her first, even if it meant sacrificing my own needs.

But now, I want nothing more than to lose myself in Beckham. Pick up where we left off all those years ago.

He *did* tell me to start putting my needs first.

And right now, I need him. More than I do my next breath.

"What do you need, Haley?" he rasps, his husky tone sending electric currents through me. "Whatever it is, it's yours." His eyes lock with mine as he grips my cheeks, not allowing me to escape. "Tell me what you want."

I wrap an arm around his neck. "I want you, Beckham." I hoist myself onto my toes, but he keeps his mouth just out of reach.

"You can do better than that, Haley. Tell me exactly what you want from me."

"I want…" My words trail off as his lips leave a fiery path down my neck.

I close my eyes, losing myself in the feel of his arousal pressing against my stomach.

"I want," I whimper again.

"Tell me."

"I want you to take off my dress."

He pulls back. "I thought you'd never ask." He slams his lips against mine, his tongue plunging into my mouth.

I thought Beckham's kiss when we got married was hot. The way he owned me in that moment turned me on more than I thought possible. But right now, as his desperate hands explore my body, his erection pressing against me, it makes one thing abundantly clear.

This isn't just a kiss.

It's a claiming.

And I'm more than happy for him to own me in every way possible.

Too soon, Beckham tears his lips from mine and abruptly spins me around. I stare at our reflection in the mirror and he meets my gaze, arching a single brow in question. I don't hesitate, quickly nodding my permission.

The seconds stretch as he laboriously tugs at the tie securing my dress around my neck, allowing the halter straps to fall to the side. When he touches his lips to my shoulder blades, a delicious tremor courses through me. His eyes focused on mine through the mirror, he pushes the dress down the rest of my body, leaving me in just a pair of lacy white panties.

"Beautiful."

His hand roams my bare stomach, the stretch marks I haven't been able to get rid of over the past four years still visible. I avert my gaze, starting to feel somewhat self-conscious. While Beckham's body has become more defined and muscular since we were teenagers, I haven't had the same luxury, my curves displaying the unmistakable signs of pregnancy.

But before I can attempt to hide from him, he whirls me around, holding my face in his hands.

"You are so fucking beautiful, Haley. Don't ever doubt that." He covers my mouth with his once more, his kiss consuming me as he walks me back toward the bed and lowers me onto the soft sheets.

"Tell me what you want," he repeats as he settles between my legs and nuzzles my neck.

"I already did." I try to force his lips back to mine, but he doesn't let me.

"You've spent your entire life following the demands

of others. Tonight, I'm putting you first. You're in charge. You hold all the power. You call the shots. You do what makes you happy." He sensually circles his hips, his erection hitting the spot between my legs where I'm desperate to feel him. "Tell me what will make you happy."

"If my memory serves, your mouth makes me *very* happy. At least when it's not talking."

He throws his head back, his sexy laugh echoing against the walls.

"Then give me something better to do with it. Where would you like it?" He dares me with his suggestive gaze.

My pulse kicking up, I touch a single finger to my lips, indicating my desire. He responds with a subtle nod before erasing the space between us. Pressing his lips to mine, he cradles my head in his hands as he takes control of the kiss. His tongue explores my mouth like a man who's just discovered a one-of-a kind treasure, handling me with immense care and attention.

"Where else?" he asks after bringing the kiss to an end.

I tilt my head slightly, revealing the spot where my earlobe meets my neck.

"One of my favorites, too," he hums in appreciation before lowering his mouth toward to the sensitive area, teasing it with his tongue and causing me to let out a soft moan.

I wrap my legs around his waist, pulsing against

him, his hard length on my clit driving me wild. And we still have the barrier of his jeans and my panties. I can only imagine how I'll react when there's nothing between us.

"Where else?" Beckham asks again.

This time, his voice is no longer cool and seductive. It's needy, his breathing ragged, jaw tight.

"Between my legs, Beckham. My god, I need your mouth on me so bad."

"As you wish." He presses a full but brief kiss to my lips. "But first…"

He slowly inches down my frame, leaving a path of kisses in his wake. Then his eyes meet mine.

"I can't ignore the rest of this incredible body."

He circles my nipple with his tongue, the warmth of his mouth causing the pebbled bud to harden. As he wraps his lips around it and gently nibbles, I struggle to hold back my scream. Not because it hurts. While it's painful at first, it pales in comparison to the raw pleasure filling me, moisture pooling between my thighs.

Nothing has ever felt so damn incredible. I knew it would be different than when we were teens. But I didn't think it would feel this good. Didn't think it was possible.

Beckham continues his exploration of my body, giving my other nipple the same treatment before snaking down my torso. When he reaches my stomach, I instinctively tense up. My stretch marks aren't nearly as pronounced as they once were, but they're still there, as well as a tiny pouch below my stomach that wasn't there the last time we did this.

"Beautiful," he murmurs like he did when he first removed my dress.

His lips worship me as they scrape against each bump and ridge. When he finally settles between my thighs, I lift my hips, expecting him to take off my panties.

He doesn't.

Instead, he presses his hand to my stomach, gluing me to the bed. Then he covers my center with his mouth.

"Beckham, please," I pant and buck against him, out of my mind with lust.

"Please what?"

"You're killing me."

"This is what you asked for. You said you wanted my mouth between your legs. This is between your legs."

"That's not what I meant," I whine. "I need your mouth on me. On my pussy. Not on my panties. I need your fingers inside me. Need your tongue on my clit."

"That's my girl."

He grips my panties and slides them down my legs before returning to me, his eyes meeting mine.

"That's my *wife*," he growls in the seconds before he drags his tongue up my center.

I moan, all the tension that's been building between us over the past several weeks, hell... years, evaporating as his tongue traces patterns against my clit.

"Goddamn, Haley. You're even more delicious than I remember. I fucking love the taste of your pussy. Can't get enough of it."

I tug on his silky hair, grinding against him as he eases a finger inside, pleasure flooding through my veins.

"Tell me what you need now," he pants. "My mouth is on you. My fingers are inside you." He slips in another finger as he increases his rhythm, the sound of my slickness filling the space. "What do you need next?"

"I need you to make me come. I need to come so damn bad, Beckham."

"And I need to make you come so damn bad. Been fantasizing how you'd feel for too long now."

"Then what are you waiting for? Make me come, Beckham. And don't you dare stop until you do."

"Yes, ma'am." He returns his mouth to me, his tongue circling my clit with the perfect amount of pressure.

When he twists his fingers to hit the spot that only he's found, I detonate around him, my body convulsing through the most intense orgasm, leaving me gasping and shaking. But he doesn't stop, savoring every drop of pleasure while I writhe beneath him.

As my tremors slowly subside, he drags himself back up my body and crashes his mouth against mine in a heated frenzy before pulling back and panting.

"This doesn't seem fair," I whine once I catch my breath.

"What's doesn't?"

"I'm naked."

He bites his lower lip, his eyes flaming with lust. "And I love that about you."

"But you're not."

"You *have* already seen the goods."

"True." I curve toward him, dragging my tongue down his neck. "But I haven't touched the goods. Not in years. And Beckham?"

"Yes?" His voice cracks.

I run my fingers through his hair, my nails digging into his scalp. "I *really* want to touch. I need to touch. Need to feel you inside me. Need to watch you lose control." I grab his face and force his eyes to mine. "I need you to fuck your wife."

"My wife," he growls, the animalistic tone causing a primal hunger to stir inside of me.

A hunger for this man to claim me. To own me. To possess me.

"Yes, Beckham. Your wife."

TWENTY-FIVE

Beckham

I slam my lips against Haley's, hearing her refer to herself as my wife making me forget all the reasons I've kept my distance. I swore I wasn't going to cross this line with her. Swore I'd be stronger than this, knowing what's at stake.

But when a tiny whimper escapes her throat, that's the last thing on my mind.

The only thing that *is* on my mind is giving Haley everything she's been deprived of for too long.

And everything I've deprived myself of for too long.

With a growl, I tear my mouth from hers and stand, ripping my t-shirt over my head in one swift motion. As I drop it onto the floor, her appreciative gaze sweeps over every inch of my physique. I guess one good thing to come from prison followed by years of manual labor is it's forced me to stay in shape.

I keep my eyes glued to hers as I slowly unfasten my belt and pull it from the loops with a sharp jerk. The sound echoes in the room, drowning out our heavy breaths as I lower the zipper on my jeans and push them down along with my boxer briefs.

She's not shy about staring at my erection, especially when I begin to stroke myself. I just pray I don't explode the second I'm inside her, something that's entirely possible with the way she's currently sliding her tongue along her lips like I'm a rare delicacy she's dying to devour.

"What's the verdict?" I playfully waggle my brows. "As good as you remember?"

Smirking, she climbs off the bed and saunters toward me with a hypnotic sway in her hips.

"Definitely not." Her hand glides down my torso, my muscles tightening as she moves closer to my waist.

Her lips graze my neck and I struggle to remain in control as she replaces my hand with hers.

"It's so much better."

"Goddamn, Haley."

"What were you thinking of?" she purrs as she strokes me. "The day I watched you in the shower, what had you all worked up?"

"You," I answer without hesitation.

It's not a lie. I *was* thinking about her. Hell, she's all I've thought about since I first laid eyes on her when we were kids. Even when I tried to convince myself the best thing I could do for her was stay away, I still couldn't erase her from my mind.

Or my heart.

I doubt I'll ever be able to.

"What about me?" Her words come out in a throaty whisper, deep and sensual. "What was I doing?"

"You were on your knees."

"Is that right?" She slows her motions to a near stop. I'm both frustrated yet grateful at the same time, not wanting this to be over too soon. "And what was I doing on my knees? Was I praying?"

"Fuck no."

"Then why don't you show me?" She releases my erection from her grasp, several protracted seconds passing as we stare at each other.

Then she sinks to her knees in front of me.

This is the last thing I expected for her to do. Hell, I can't believe we're doing this in the first place. But I never expected for her to ask me to show her exactly what I was fantasizing about the morning she caught me jerking off in the shower.

And practically every day since then.

Sometimes twice.

"Open for me," I tell her as I fist my cock.

She does as I request, eagerly parting her lips as she peers up at me with her captivating green eyes. Every touch, every look between us is a battle of restraint.

One I fear I'll lose before the night is over, especially

when I bring my erection up to her mouth and she swipes her tongue along the tip.

"Jesus," I hiss, the subtle touch sending my pulse skyrocketing. I cup her head as I guide my arousal past her lips, her mouth widening to take me. "That's it," I encourage. "Relax your jaw."

She does as I instruct, allowing me to ease inside her mouth. With every inch, her eyes widen even more, her tongue teasing and torturing me.

"God, that feels incredible." I run my free hand along the curve of her jaw, encouraging her to relax, not breaking my gaze from hers. "You should see yourself right now, Haley. See how good you take my cock."

She moans, attempting to bob against me.

"Mmm. You like that, don't you? Like when I tell you how good you are."

She doesn't respond. She can't, not with her mouth full. Instead, she just looks innocently up at me. But I can see the response in her eyes. That she absolutely loves it.

"My wife has a praise kink, doesn't she?" I grind out, my breathing increasing as desire heats my veins. "You're so fucking beautiful right now. Taking my cock like a good girl."

Another moan falls from her and she grabs my ass, pulling me even closer, my dick easily hitting the back of her throat. I tighten my grip on her head as I thrust harder and faster. When I notice her squeeze her thighs together, I abruptly step back, pulling my erection from her mouth.

"Spread your legs," I order through my heavy breaths.

She furrows her brow. "Wha—"

"I don't want you doing anything that's going to dull the hunger building inside you right now. That includes squeezing your thighs together. So if you want me to get you off again…" I narrow my gaze on her, "Spread. Your. Legs."

Her gaze meets mine in a challenge, but her body betrays her as she slowly adjusts her position and parts her legs. I can see the fight in her, though, the stubbornness that's always drawn me to her.

"Wider. I want to see how wet you get from letting me fuck your mouth."

Without saying a word, she obeys me, parting her legs even further until she's wide open for me. Then she surprises me by reaching between her thighs and spreading her slickness around, coating my cock with it before taking me back into her mouth.

"Fucking hell," I hiss, cupping her head again as I push in and out of her, taking control.

And she lets me use her mouth, just like I fantasized about. But it's even better than any of my fantasies because of how much she enjoys letting me do this, the vibrations of her moans propelling me higher until I'm teetering perilously close to the point of no return.

Just when I feel like I'm about to lose my mind, I

pull out and roughly haul her to her feet. My lips crash down on hers, our tongues colliding in a frenzied dance as we fight for control.

"Why did you stop?" she pants when I tear my lips from hers, both of us gasping for air. "I would have let you come in my mouth."

If it were possible to get even harder, I probably would have. As it is, the only thing keeping me from coming in my hand is the idea of dead puppies and a lackluster harvest.

"And I love that about you." I touch my mouth to hers, kissing her softly. "But the first time I come in you after this long, I don't want it to be your mouth." I trail a hand along the curve of her frame, her breath catching as I slip a finger between her legs and ease it inside her. "I want it to be in here."

She whimpers, her breathing increasing as I continue to stretch her, her tight walls pulsing against me.

"Can I do that, Haley?" I scrape my unshaven jawline against her neck, her fair skin reddening under my touch. "Can I come inside you?"

"God, yes."

I stop my ministrations and meet her eyes. "Are you sure?"

"I'm on birth control. I don't exactly trust condoms anyway, considering that's how I ended up with Maggie."

"I'll wear one if it makes you feel better. Double layer of protection and all that."

She hoists herself onto her toes, pulling my mouth toward hers. "I appreciate it, but I need to feel you, Beckham. Nothing between us."

"Nothing between us," I repeat as I press my mouth to hers and walk her backward toward the bed, carefully lowering her onto the surface.

Crawling between her legs, I bring my erection up to her entrance, teasing her. I keep my gaze locked on her and slowly ease inside. Her lips part around a noiseless gasp as I fill her, inch by incredible inch.

And it *is* fucking incredible. There's no other way to describe how she feels around me. Even that feels woefully inadequate for how my body responds to being inside her after so long.

Once I'm fully seated, a shiver rolls through me. I cover her body with mine, not wanting even a whisper separating us. I gradually retreat before pushing back in, keeping my motions slow and measured to get her used to my size, especially since she hasn't done this in five years.

"Beckham," she exhales, moving with the rhythm I set.

"Yeah baby."

"Please," she begs, dragging her nails down my back.

I groan, arching into her touch. I never knew a touch could cause such a visceral reaction. No one has ever made me feel anything remotely close to the carnal urges currently swirling inside me.

All the more reason this is a horrible idea. But an even more horrible idea would be depriving myself of this. Because nothing's ever felt more right than being inside Haley.

"I need you to move. Need to feel you."

"You *do* feel me." I rock my hips even slower. It's taking everything I have not to slam my cock into her. I want to. But I love seeing the effect I have on her more. Love watching her become completely unhinged with desperation.

"I need more." She wraps her legs tightly around my waist, pulling me closer. "Need it deeper. Harder. Faster." She grabs my cheeks in her hands. "I need you to fuck your wife."

I didn't think it was possible to crave this woman even more, but I was wrong. She knows exactly what to say to get what she wants. She always has.

"If I do that, I can't make any guarantees you'll be able to walk tomorrow."

She barks out a laugh. "You really think you can fuck me that good?"

I bite back my smile, my heart warming at the challenge in her words. A reminder of who we are to each other. Who we've always been. For as long as I can remember, Haley challenged me, made me put my money where my mouth was. And my god, I loved proving her wrong.

Or at least *trying* to prove her wrong.

But this is one challenge I refuse to lose. My reputation is at stake.

I lean toward her, taking her bottom lip between my teeth and nibbling. "Do you really think you can stand me fucking you that good?"

She digs her nails into my back and drags them down my spine. "Try me, Lawrence."

"Gladly, McBride."

In one swift move, I pull out of her and flip her onto her stomach.

"Hands and knees," I order.

She follows my command, glancing over her shoulder as she spreads her legs for me.

I kneel behind her, teasing her slit with my erection. "Are you sure you really want this?"

"What's wrong? Worried you won't measure up to the hype?"

I thrust inside of her in one quick motion, the sudden invasion causing her to scream out.

"Does this feel like I won't be able to measure up, Haley?"

She buries her face in the pillow, her chest heaving. When she doesn't immediately answer, I curve over her, taking her ear between my teeth.

"I didn't quite hear you."

"No," she struggles to say.

"What was that?"

"I said, no," she repeats, her voice muffled.

"I'm sorry. One more time."

She pulls her head from the pillow, her fiery eyes meeting mine. "I said no. Your dick definitely measures up. Okay, you cocky bastard?"

"No need to get all worked up over it. If my wife wants to be fucked, I'm happy to oblige. After all, you know what they say, don't you?"

"What's that?"

"Happy wife. Happy life." I slowly pull out of her. "And being inside of you definitely makes me happy."

Gripping her hips, I slam into her, and her cries of pleasure mingle with my labored grunts. But this time, I don't stop. Don't pause. Don't give her a chance to catch her breath. I thrust harder, faster, deeper, driven by an insatiable thirst for her.

But no matter how deep I go, it's still not enough. Still makes me want more. Makes me want to consume every inch of her.

"Beckham," she pants, her breaths coming out with each punishing thrust. "It's too good. Why the hell are you so good at this? It's not fair."

My chest rumbles with a deep laugh as I lean over her body, smoothing my hands down her arms and intertwining our fingers. "Are you seriously complaining that I'm too good at sex? I'll stop if you'd prefer."

"Don't you dare," she shouts, somewhat panicked. "Just… Just keep going."

"Gladly." I straighten, moving my hands back to her hips and picking up the pace once more.

Her moans echo in the room as she moves against me, every whimper and clenching of her muscles sending my body higher, my balls tightening. Finally, she cries out as she spasms around me, her orgasm ravaging through her.

"Fuck, yes," I growl, pistoning into her as she continues to convulse. In mere seconds, I join her, spilling into her in one of the most satisfying orgasms of my life.

Neither one of us moves for several long moments, too overwhelmed with sensation. At least *I'm* too overwhelmed with sensation. I can only hope Haley is, too.

When my tremors finally subside, I pull out of her and carefully help her onto her stomach, peppering soft kisses along her shoulder blades. "Give me a second."

Leaving a kiss on her smooth skin, I jump out of bed and dash toward the bathroom, grabbing a towel. When I return, I pull her against me and part her thighs, cleaning her up before tossing the towel onto the floor and wrapping her in my arms.

"Aren't you forgetting something?" she remarks after several silent moments.

"What's that?"

"The pillow," she says drowsily. "It's in the rules. We're supposed to sleep with a pillow between us."

I pull her even closer, circling my hips against her ass, already getting hard again.

Haley laughs softly as she tries to push me away. "Hey now. Rules are rules."

"True, but if I'm not mistaken, we dispensed with the no-touching rule." I smooth my hand down her stomach, and she eagerly parts her legs for me. "Perhaps I can make it worth your while to get rid of this one, too."

When I slip a finger inside her, her head falls onto my shoulder. "Why do I have a feeling you're going to have me breaking all my rules before our marriage is over?"

I nip at her neck. "Because someone's got to remind you what it feels like to live a little."

Then I ease another finger inside of her and make her come again.

TWENTY-SIX

Haley

Warmth surrounds me as I'm roused from one of the most restful night's sleep I've had in recent memory, my body sore in places that haven't seen action in quite some time. But it's a good sore. A delicious sore. A sore I wouldn't mind experiencing again.

And again.

And again.

Snippets of last night flash before my eyes and a renewed ache settles in my core from the reminder of just how incredible it felt to be with Beckham again. How he catered to every single one of my needs. How he made me feel more beautiful than anyone has in years.

"Mmm," Beckham groans, sending a delicious

shiver through me. "This is infinitely better than waking up next to that damn pillow." He pulls my body further into his, his chest hair tickling my back.

"It was a necessary evil after I woke up with your dick against me."

He rocks against me, his erection slipping between my legs.

"Like this?"

"Exactly like that," I whimper, lust spiraling through me.

"Well then…" He abruptly releases me from his embrace. "I wouldn't want to make you uncomfortable."

I quickly roll over and pull him toward me, hooking my leg around his waist. "Don't you dare, you tease."

"And I thought you liked it when I teased you." He skims his lips against mine as he circles his hips. When his arousal hits my clit, sparks shoot through me, and I throw my head back.

"Do I ever."

"And I really like teasing you." He pushes me onto my back. "So damn much," he murmurs, burying his face in the crook of my neck as he drives inside of me.

I release a noiseless gasp at the sudden invasion, my muscles clenching as a myriad of sensations fill me. I didn't think it was possible to feel this much during sex. With most of the other guys I've been with, Oliver included, I couldn't wait for it to be over so I could disappear into the bathroom and take care of my needs.

With Beckham, it's not necessary. He always makes sure I'm completely satisfied before he allows himself the same pleasure. And not just once, either. The man seems to be on a mission to see how many times he can bring me to orgasm, almost like it's a challenge to him. Like *I'm* a challenge to him.

Then again, isn't that what we've always been to each other?

"You feel so damn good, Haley," he grunts as he fills me. "Love how warm you are. How tight you are." He straightens, pressing his thumb to my clit. "How wet you are."

"Beckham…" I moan, lost to the sensation. "I don't… It's too much. I don't think my body can handle another orgasm."

Chuckling, his lips find mine, his tongue caressing mine in a scintillating kiss I feel from the tips of my fingers all the way down to my toes.

"If you ask me, death by orgasm is a damn good way to go." He slows his motions. "But if you don't think you can handle it, I'll stop." He starts to pull out, but before he can, I wrap my legs around his waist.

"You'd really leave your wife unsatisfied?"

His eyes flame, just like they always do when I refer to myself as his wife.

I didn't think I'd like the reminder of my attachment to him, considering the lengths I've gone to in order to keep the lines as clearly drawn as possible.

I'm pretty sure we eviscerated every single one of those lines last night.

The idea doesn't fill me with unease like I thought it would. How can it when I've been the lucky recipient of several earth-shattering orgasms?

"You said you weren't sure your body could handle any more. Just trying to be a good husband and listen to your needs."

I drag my tongue along his neck, taking his earlobe between my teeth. "You probably wouldn't be able to make me come again anyway."

"I believe my record indicates otherwise. If I'm right, and I usually am, I've given you six orgasms over the past eight hours."

"Seven," I correct.

"What's that?"

"It's seven orgasms. You've given me seven orgasms."

"Seven. That's a good number. But I'm not a fan of odd numbers." He lifts my leg and drapes it onto his shoulder. "Why don't we make it eight?"

Before I can answer, he leans closer and thrusts into me, this position allowing him to go even deeper than before.

"God, Haley," he groans, closing his eyes as pleasure covers his expression. "Why can't I get enough of this? Why can't I get enough of you?"

"I have no idea." I crane my head, chasing his kiss.

"But I don't care. I just need this." I pull him closer. "Need you."

"Oh, god," he whimpers, a visible shiver rolling through him. "I need you to come because I'm about to—"

Before he can utter another syllable, the unmistakable patter of little feet cuts through, followed by the sound of a door opening.

But not just any door.

Our door.

I throw Beckham off me and grab the duvet, covering our bodies in the seconds before Maggie appears by the bed. A furrow creases her brow as she looks between Beckham and me, both of us panting.

"Why was Beck on top of you?"

I shift my gaze toward him, horrified my daughter caught us having sex. He doesn't share in my unease, though. Instead, he wraps an arm around my shoulder and drags my body against his, kissing the top of my head.

"Your mom had an itch I was helping her scratch," he tells her, then flashes me a smirk.

I'd love to wipe it off his face, since he's obviously enjoying this. I can't seem to care though, not when he's happier than he's been in the past few years. *Lighter* than he's been in the past few years.

And I love seeing this side of him. Don't want to do anything to go back to the people we were before we succumbed to our desires, to hell with the past.

"She sometimes helps me scratch my back when I can't reach," Maggie announces.

"Moms are good like that. Aren't they?"

"Yup," she chirps, then looks my way. "Can I have my breakfast?"

"I'll be right there, sweetie."

"Okay." She spins on her heels and runs from the bedroom, sounding like a herd of elephants as she scurries down the stairs.

It's not until I hear her tell Monte he has to wait for his breakfast that I release my breath and pin Beckham with a glare.

"Helping me scratch an itch?"

"It's not a lie." He rolls on top of me, settling between my legs once more. "You *did* have an itch." When he nips at my neck, a renewed wave of desire rushes through me, despite having just been caught by my daughter. "And I'm more than happy to help you scratch that itch whenever you need."

"How charitable of you."

"That's me." He pulses against me, a devious look in his dark eyes. "Extremely giving."

"Beckham…" I push him off me, although it's a test of willpower when every inch of my body still craves his touch.

Regardless of whatever's going on between us, Maggie is and always will be my priority.

"What's wrong?"

"I just scarred my daughter for life. I'd rather not risk her walking in on us yet again."

"It's what you get for being addicted to my cock."

Playfully swatting him, I climb out of bed and move to the dresser, grabbing a fresh pair of panties. "I'm not addicted to your cock."

"That's not what you said last night."

"And what did I say?" I face him, pulling a pair of shorts up my legs after tugging on a t-shirt.

He rests his hands behind his head, a cocky grin lighting up his sinful face. "I may not be quoting verbatim, but it was something along the lines of 'Oh, Beckham. How are you so good at this?'" he says in his best imitation of me.

I shoot him a glare. I can't deny it. I *did* say that.

"'I love your cock. It feels so good inside of me. I'll never get enough of it. You're the god of sex.'"

Rolling my eyes, I grab one of the pillows off the floor and throw it at him. "I did *not* say that."

"Maybe not." He waggles his brows. "But you were thinking it."

"Whatever." I hurry out of the room, Beckham's sexy chuckles following me every step of the way.

I definitely *was* thinking it.

But I'll never admit it.

"Hi, Mama," Maggie says sweetly when I walk into the kitchen.

She's already snuggled up on the couch beside Monte, a coloring book in front of her.

"Hey, sweetie." I walk toward her and kiss the top of her head. Monte looks up at me expectantly, and I give his head a scratch, as well. "What would you like for breakfast?"

The instant I utter that word, Monte jumps off the couch, barking excitedly.

"Not you," I tell him. "It's not your time yet." I turn my attention back to Maggie. "Want some pancakes?"

"Yes, please."

"You got it." I place another kiss on her head, then busy myself with making her breakfast.

As I mix up the batter, Beckham slips into the kitchen and it takes everything in me to subdue my racing heart.

Has he always looked this sexy in the morning? Probably. But today, in his pajama bottoms, white t-shirt that clings to his muscles, revealing his tattooed arms, and disheveled dark hair, he looks good enough to eat.

And I was lucky enough to be treated to a meal of him last night.

"Coffee?" he asks.

"Sure," I respond quickly, uncertain how to act now that we're out of the bedroom.

He walks past me as I finish mixing the batter, the two of us moving around the kitchen like it's a normal day.

Like we didn't spend all night having sex in a variety of different positions.

"Should we talk about it?" Beckham asks in a soft voice, handing me my mug.

"Do we have to?"

He shrugs nonchalantly. "You're the one who had me sign a contract so we could manage expectations. That's all I'm trying to do. Manage expectations. We crossed a line last night. I want to know if we should move the line accordingly or keep it where it was."

"I know. I just…" I push out a long sigh, so many conflicted thoughts and emotions filling me.

"Answer me this," he says, bringing his coffee to his lips. The lips that gave me more pleasure than I thought possible last night. "Did you enjoy yourself?"

My cheeks flame as I pour some batter onto the griddle. "Without a doubt."

"Me, too." He sets his coffee on the counter and steps closer. "Would you like to do it again?"

"Would you?"

"I asked you first."

"What are you? Five?"

"Simply stating the facts, Haley. So tell me. And don't stand there and try to think about what I want to hear or what you should say. Give me an honest answer."

Sometimes I hate how well he knows me. How clearly he still sees me, even all these years later.

He touches my chin, forcing my eyes toward his as he repeats, "Do you want to do it again?"

"Yes," comes my swift reply.

"Me, too."

"But—"

He presses his finger to my lips, silencing my protest. "I get it. There are a thousand reasons this is a bad idea."

I laugh, oddly relieved he understands my hesitation.

"But I could probably come up with twice as many reasons why this might be a good idea. Instead of standing here and dictating what this should or shouldn't be, maybe we just…let it be. We'll take it one day at a time." He pulls me closer as he inches his lips toward mine. "Or one incredible orgasm at a time. How does that sound?"

"Like either a really good idea. Or a really horrible idea," I respond breathily.

"There's only one way to find out. Isn't there?" His mouth hovers over mine, so close I can barely focus on anything other than tasting him.

"There is."

"Then let's find out, Haley."

I draw in a steadying breath, then nod. "Okay."

"Okay," he repeats.

I close my eyes, bracing myself for his kiss.

But it never comes.

Instead, he releases me and spins around.

I watch with a mixture of bewilderment and frustration as he walks out of the kitchen without a single care that he's left me a panting mess of hormones.

Or maybe this was his plan all along.

As he's about to head upstairs, he glances over his shoulder. "Enjoy your day… Wife."

TWENTY-SEVEN

Haley

"Oh, my god."

When I hear Parker's voice, I look up from my sketchpad as she plops down into the chair across from me at a table outside the local coffee shop, a knowing gleam in her blue eyes.

"You've had sex."

I choke on my iced coffee, liquid spewing out of my nose.

"What makes you say that?" I ask once I get my coughing under control.

"You've got that thoroughly fucked glow. I'm right, aren't I?" She takes a sip from her coffee and leans closer, her eyes seeming to focus on my neck. "Because that sure as hell looks like some beard burn. And are those bite marks? I'm guessing you and Beckham finally consummated your marriage."

I smooth my hair in front of my shoulder, trying to fight my smile from just how good Beckham was at consummating our marriage. But it's impossible. The mere mention of it causes my skin to flush, my veins pulsing with heat.

"We did," I finally admit.

"I knew it!" She reaches for her phone and feverishly types at the screen.

"What are you doing?"

"Texting Jude to tell him he owes me a case of beer for winning our bet." After she shoves her cell back into her purse, she places her forearms on the table, her attention fully on me. "So tell me. How was it?"

I shake my head, searching for the words I need.

But I don't think there are adequate words in the English language for how amazing last night was.

"It was some top-notch sex, Parker," I gush. "He'd put some of those two-schlonged aliens in Grandma Estelle's monster romances to shame. And Beckham's only working with the one dick. But the way he works that dick…" My face heats, the reminder causing hunger to build inside me.

Then again, it could be because we were interrupted this morning mere seconds before I was about to come.

At least I have something to look forward to tonight.

Before, I often dreaded night time. It was always the most awkward part of the day.

Not anymore.

"How did this all happen? Was the sexual tension too much for either of you to handle any longer?"

"No. I mean, it *has* been building. But that's not what happened." I lean toward her, dropping my voice. "I saw Oliver yesterday."

Her eyes widen. "What? When? Where?"

"At the brewery. We took Maggie to celebrate Grady agreeing to sell Beckham the vineyard."

"He did?" She perks up at the news. "That's incredible."

"At one point, I excused myself to go to the ladies' room. When I turned the corner into the back hallway, I ran into someone." I give her a knowing look. "It was Oliver."

"What's he doing in Sycamore Falls?" She inhales a sharp breath. "Do you think he tracked you down?"

Pinching my lips, I shake my head. "I doubt it. He made it clear he didn't want anything to do with me or the baby. Still, I wanted to get Maggie out of there. I'm not ready for her to learn the truth. I'm not sure I'll ever be ready."

Parker reaches across the table and gives my hand a reassuring squeeze. "She's better off without that prick." She holds my gaze for a beat, then pulls back. "What happened next?"

I tell her how Beckham didn't hesitate in getting

both of us out of there. How he forced me to take some time for myself. Then how he cooked dinner and even read to Maggie.

"I don't know what came over me, Parker. But when I was watching him with Maggie, especially as he read to her, it was too much."

"Pretty sure every woman's ovaries would explode at the sight of Beckham Lawrence snuggling with a little girl."

"And boy, did they explode."

She twirls a strand of blonde hair around her finger. "What does this mean for the two of you going forward?"

I bring my iced coffee up to my mouth and take a long sip from the straw. "Nothing."

"Nothing?" she repeats, arching a brow.

"We agreed that, all things considered, it's best we don't put unreasonable expectations on ourselves or each other. There's just a lot of…baggage to sort through when it comes to us."

"Like what?"

"For starters, how I'm the reason he spent a year behind bars and has a felony record."

"Why do you say that?"

"Because it's the truth."

She eyes me suspiciously, then sets her coffee cup on the table and squares her shoulders, devoting her full attention to me.

"Okay. What really happened all those years ago? I

heard the rumors, but I never knew what to believe. I wasn't around since I was away at college, but I heard about Beckham's arrest. And how you were injured when you tried to intervene. Is that why you think you're responsible? Because——"

"I didn't intervene. Not like all the reports made it sound."

"Then what happened?"

I draw in a steadying breath, unsure if I'm ready to tell her the entire story. No one knows the truth about the events leading up to me being hospitalized and Beckham being sent to prison. My parents made sure of that.

"It was just supposed to be a summer fling," I finally admit, nervously tapping my fingernails against the black metal table. "Growing up, my nanny was good friends with Beckham's mama. Every so often, she'd take me to their house and we'd play together. Or Beckham's mother would bring all her kids to the lake and we'd play at the beach. He was probably my best friend back then, even if we annoyed the shit out of each other." A nostalgic smile tugs on my lips from the memory.

"When I was older, I didn't need a nanny anymore, so we didn't see each other much. My parents lived in Tahoe and didn't come out this way very often, if at all. Our worlds rarely intersected."

"But they eventually did?" Parker prodded.

"The summer before college."

"What happened?"

"I started to feel suffocated by my parents and how they were dictating everything about my life, from where I went to college to who I should date. When one of my close friends mentioned ditching a stuffy graduation party and sneaking out to Kaplan Farm, I was more than willing to defy my parents, even if I'd pay for it later."

"That had to be culture shock for you," Parker remarks, more than aware of Kaplan Farm's reputation for parties, even to this day.

"It certainly was," I agree with a laugh. "Up until then, the only parties I'd been to had been catered events thrown by my parents or one of their wealthy friends. A party at a cow pasture with kegs and loud music? It was like nothing I'd ever experienced but everything I needed at the same time."

"And that's where you saw Beckham again?" Parker prompts after a beat.

"At first, I didn't even recognize him. He looked so different from the scrawny boy I remembered. And the way he looked at me when he realized who I was..." An unexpected shiver trickles down my spine. "No one had ever looked at me like that. And then..."

"Yes?"

"He asked me a question no one ever had."

"What's that?"

"He asked if I was happy." My voice catches with emotion. "Before that night, I didn't think it mattered.

Thought it was my duty to do whatever my parents asked of me. Just like I rode horses for show, and excelled in fencing, and practiced piano for hours every day. I didn't do any of those things because they made me happy. I did them because it's what my parents expected of me. And I resented Beckham for seeing right through me. How could this man who barely knew me see me so clearly, yet the people who purported to love me couldn't see how miserable I was? I didn't want to admit it to him, though, so I stormed off. But Beckham wouldn't let it go."

Enraptured by my story, Parker leans closer, resting her chin on her hands. "What did he do?"

"He came over to my house in the middle of the night. Threw pebbles at my window. I don't know how he remembered which one was mine, but he did. When I opened the window, he managed to climb a nearby tree and sneak into my room. He apologized for upsetting me. Then we stayed up all night long talking. It was the first of many nights he'd climb through my bedroom window that summer."

"I'm guessing your parents didn't approve."

I snort a laugh. "They didn't even know about him. Or us. They couldn't. Not only was his family poor, at least according to their standards, but Beckham was notorious for getting into fights. I understood it, though. He was going through a rough time with his dad being diagnosed with ALS. At first, he said he was okay sneaking around. We kept things casual since we were both going off to college in the fall. At least, we were supposed to. But as time went on, he got more and more frustrated that he couldn't be seen with me in public. That I refused to stand up for myself."

"You were only eighteen." Parker gives my hand a squeeze.

"If I had, so much could have been avoided."

She tilts her head. "How so?"

"Since I didn't want my parents to find out about Beckham, I compensated by doing whatever they asked of me, like going on dates with the guy they kept shoving at me."

"Let me guess. Chase Longmire."

Parker knew enough from reading reports on the infamous incident to know who I was purported to have been dating. In reality, the only reason I went out with him was to make my parents happy and keep them from becoming suspicious of my relationship with Beckham.

"His father was a member at the same country club as my dad," I explain. "My parents didn't find it the least bit unsettling that a twenty-five-year-old man who just finished grad school was interested in a girl who only turned eighteen a few weeks earlier. All they saw was a man from a wealthy and powerful family looking to settle down and get married, since it would help with his run for state representative."

Parker rolled her eyes. "Fucking politicians."

"Exactly." I smooth a few tendrils of hair behind my

ear. "So I went on the occasional date with Chase, making sure to be home before Beckham would sneak into my bedroom."

"And Beckham was okay with it?" She arches a brow.

"I wouldn't say he was *okay* with it. He understood why it had to be this way for the time being. At least until I went away to college. Then I'd have a bit more freedom. But one night…" I close my eyes, sucking in a shuttering breath, the memories so vivid and sharp it could have happened yesterday instead of fourteen years ago.

"It's okay," Parker reassures me, covering my hand with hers once more. "Take your time."

I give her a grateful look before continuing, "One night, instead of going to dinner or a movie, as we usually did, Chase said he heard about a party he wanted to check out. I was a little nervous about this, considering Beckham mentioned hitting up a party that night, but we'd been careful. I convinced myself there was no way Chase would have found out about us."

"Let me guess. The party Chase wanted to go to was the same party where Beckham was."

I nod. "It wasn't enough for Chase to simply show up with me. He made sure to have his hands all over me whenever Beckham was even remotely close. Especially the more he drank. At one point, I'd had enough of it and said I wanted to leave, then went onto the deck to find Beckham and ask if he'd drive me home since

Chase was too drunk. But Chase followed me. Started screaming at me. Calling me names. Pushed me up against the wall and told me if I wanted to act like a whore, he'd treat me like one."

"Jesus."

"Luckily, I wasn't the only one who was out there."

"Beckham?"

I push out a long exhale. "One second, Chase was lifting up my skirt, the next he was on the deck with a broken nose. And the next still, Beckham was on top of him, blood spraying everywhere. I didn't know what to do. I'm glad he was out there to stop Chase, but I didn't want him to kill him, which is exactly what it looked like he was about to do. So I ran toward him. Tried to get him to stop." I swallow hard. "But he was in a trance and didn't realize it was me. He pushed me away with such force, I broke the railing and fell onto the pavement below. The next thing I knew, I was waking up in a hospital bed with a doctor telling me my hipbone was shattered along with my femur. Said I was lucky I wasn't paralyzed or dead."

"And Beckham?"

"He pled guilty to two counts of aggravated assault and battery in exchange for only serving a year in prison instead of the potential ten-year sentence he was facing."

"But why? He acted in your defense."

"I'm guessing he didn't want to take his chances. It wasn't his first arrest for fighting. His lawyer probably saw the one-year sentence as a gift he'd be crazy to turn down, especially with the influence Chase's parents held in this area."

"And Chase? Did you ever tell anyone the truth about him?"

"I tried to tell my parents."

"What did they say?"

"My mom told me I was just confused about what he was trying to do. I wasn't fucking confused. I knew exactly what he was trying to do. But no one would listen. They were gaslighting me into believing Beckham was the one in the wrong, given everyone thought Chase and I were dating."

"That's fucked."

"Yes, it is."

"And you've been blaming yourself ever since?"

I run my hands down the skirt of my sundress. "I suppose. If I'd just stood up to my parents, none of this would have happened. Instead, Beckham never got to go to college. Missed out on being there during his father's last days."

"Is this why you don't want to get emotionally involved?" She furrows her brows, obviously confused. "Because you blame yourself?"

"There are also the letters."

"Letters?"

"I wrote to him every day. Even recruited one of my nurses to mail my letter without my parents finding out."

"And?"

"He never wrote back. Once I was able to walk without assistance, I tried to visit him. He refused to see me every time."

"It must have been hard on him," Parker says in his defense.

This is one of the reasons I adore her so much. While she will always have my back, she also has no problem looking at all sides of an issue and calling a spade a spade when necessary.

"That's what I kept telling myself. That maybe he just needed to get through his sentence and then everything would be okay. The letters were never returned to me. If he didn't want them, he could have refused delivery. Throughout the next year, that's what gave me hope, as well as the courage to finally stand up to my parents. I started applying for jobs that would give me the freedom I never thought possible. Luckily, I got hired by the airline."

"It wasn't luck. It was the universe giving you what you needed most."

I playfully roll my eyes, but I can't deny she might have a point.

"When I told my parents, they were pissed, threatened to cut me off financially if I followed through. I didn't want their money anymore. Not when I knew the true price of their supposed love. The day before I was scheduled to leave for training was the day Beckham was released from prison."

"Did you go see him?"

I nod slowly.

"And?"

"He didn't even look at me, Parker," I squeak out through the tightness in my throat, tears welling in my eyes. "Up until that moment, I managed to hold on to my hope. But that day, when he walked outside those prison gates and continued past me as if I didn't even exist…it hurt. And then when I moved back here after having Maggie and he could barely look at me…" I shake my head. "I think a part of me will always worry he'll remember everything he lost because of me and start to hate me all over again."

"Have you ever asked him about it?"

I shrug. "Not yet. I mean, he *did* apologize last night. Not for this specifically, but for everything. For the way he treated me."

"If you ask me, that's a step in the right direction. You've both been through a lot. I actually think you're being smart about whatever this is." She waves her hand around.

"You do?"

"You're both coming into this with a fuck ton of baggage. And guilt. If you jumped into something and went full steam ahead, you'd most likely crash and burn. Taking it one day at a time is probably the best thing for you. Just promise me something."

"What?"

"Promise you won't let this guilt you've been

carrying for too long ruin what could be the best thing to ever happen to you. To both of you. I've seen the way you look at him. The way he looks at you. Despite what you may want to believe, this is the real deal. Don't let it slip away because you don't think you deserve to be happy. If there are any two people who *do* deserve to be happy, it's the two of you. So just…trust the process."

"I'll do my best," I assure her.

"That's all any of us can do," she retorts as a chiming cuts through.

Parker snaps her attention to her phone, her expression dropping. "Shit. I need to get back to the inn."

"Go do what you need to do," I reply, grateful for the interruption.

"Are you sure? I don't want you to feel like I'm abandoning you after you drop this huge bombshell. If you want me to stay and flesh this out more, I can. Or if you simply want to gush about your sexy times."

"I'm fine." I assure her, gesturing to my blank sketchpad. "I need to work on a concept for my latest cake request anyway."

"Okay," she draws out. "If you're sure."

"I am. Thanks for listening. And not judging."

"My mama always said when you judge others, what you're really doing is judging yourself." She pauses, allowing her words to sink in before brightening her expression. "Drinks soon?"

"Definitely."

"Good. Love ya, Haley. And I'm happy for you."

"Thanks."

She stands and slings her purse over her shoulder, then spins from me, making her way down the sidewalk.

I relax into my chair, staring into the distance.

I understand why people go to therapy, even if they don't think they need to. Just talking to Parker about everything and clearing the air has done wonders for my soul.

Has allowed me to lift the weight that's been burdening me for too long.

Or maybe it was the sex.

This thing with Beckham may not go anywhere, but like we agreed earlier. We'll just take it one day at a time.

Or one orgasm at a time.

And my god, do I love the orgasms Beckham is capable of giving me.

"Is this seat taken?" a deep voice interjects, snapping me out of my thoughts.

I dart my head up, my expression falling as I peer into a pair of familiar gray eyes.

In an instant, all my happiness and relief turns into dread at the sight of Oliver's imposing frame looming over me.

TWENTY-EIGHT

Haley

A knot forms in the pit of my stomach as Oliver's calculating stare pierces through me like a knife. My mind races with dozens of explanations for why he's here, but deep down I know they all lead back to me and the daughter I've tried to keep from him for the past four years.

"I was just about to leave." I attempt to stand, but he wraps his hand around my arm, his punishing grip keeping me in place.

"If you want to keep custody of my daughter, you'll sit and not leave until I say you can."

Panic surges through me as I peer into his gray eyes that are nearly identical to Maggie's. The gray eyes I once thought were so kind, so compassionate.

Until I told him I was pregnant.

The last thing I want is to give in to his demands. To let him have this kind of power over me. But it's not just me anymore. I need to think about Maggie, too.

Keeping my head held high, I force myself to return to my seat, determined to maintain my composure, despite the nerves threatening to consume me.

"After unexpectedly seeing you yesterday, I asked around about you," he remarks as he unbuttons his crisp suit jacket and casually lowers himself into the chair across from me. "Got to love small towns. Everyone is so friendly. Especially a group of older women I met at the diner, who were more than happy to tell me all about Haley McBride and how she came to town just a little over four years ago with a brand new baby." He leans toward me. "Roughly nine months after our last…meeting. Based on the uncanny resemblance, I can only conclude she's mine."

This is why I wanted to leave as quickly as possible yesterday. Maggie may have my hair, but that's where our similarities end. She has her father's steel-gray eyes, slanted nose, high cheekbones, and brilliant smile.

"Does she have your DNA?" I cross my arms in front of my chest. "Yes. But she's not yours. You gave up the right the second you told me to get rid of the problem."

"And we decided that's exactly what you would do."

"*We?*" I shoot back, incredulous.

Is he really this delusional? Or has he just convinced

himself of this version of events so he wouldn't have to carry the guilt all these years?

"*We* didn't decide anything." I gesture between us. "You decided. You made it quite clear you didn't want to be a part of my life. Or the baby's. I made sure you weren't." I hastily collect my things and shove them into my bag. "I took care of the problem for you. Made her mine and mine alone. I'm more than happy to keep it that way. In fact, I'd *prefer* to keep it that way." I shoot to my feet and pin him with a glare. "Good bye, Oliver."

Spinning, I hurry down the street, but before I can get more than a few feet, a hand wraps around my wrist, forcing me to stop.

"That wasn't your decision to make," Oliver seethes.

I bark out a laugh.

I should have known something like this would happen. It's the story of my life. Just when things are finally looking up, something happens to remind me I'll never have it all.

That I'll never be truly happy.

"This may sound like a radical idea to someone as egotistical as you. My body, my fucking choice. If you'll excuse me…"

I attempt to pull myself free from his grip, but he tightens his hold, causing pain to shoot up my arm. I wince as I struggle against him, venom and disgust swirling in his eyes.

"You don't get to walk away from me, Haley. Not about this. I told you to——"

"If you don't want to end up with every bone in your body broken," a voice thunders in the distance as the sound of heavy footsteps grow close, "you'll take your hand off my wife."

I look away from Oliver to see Beckham storming toward us, fury radiating off him as he clenches and unclenches his fists.

"*Now!*" he bellows when Oliver doesn't immediately comply, as if urging Beckham to make the first move.

Based on the wild look in his eyes, I have no doubt he will, if necessary. And will most certainly carry through on his promise to break every bone in Oliver's body.

While Oliver is tall and somewhat built, he's no match for Beckham. I doubt he's ever done a single day of manual labor. Not like Beckham.

After several protracted moments, Oliver releases his hold on me. Beckham wastes no time in wrapping me in a protective hug, keeping me glued to his body.

"She's your *wife*?" Oliver spits.

"She is." Beckham shifts to stand in front of me like a protective shield. "So if I were you, I'd get in your shiny car and not stop until you're far away from Sycamore Falls. If I hear you've so much as looked at Haley or her little girl again, I'll make you regret the day you ever stepped foot in this town. Got it?"

Oliver glowers at Beckham, the tension growing

with each passing second. Beckham puffs out his chest, the distaste in his expression almost lethal. I certainly wouldn't want to be on the receiving end of his glare.

Finally, Oliver relaxes his posture, purposefully shoving into me as he pushes past.

"She's nothing but a cheap whore anyway," he mutters under his breath, always needing to have the last word.

A dangerous fire flickers in Beckham's eyes, and before I can stop him, he storms after Oliver, slamming him into the exterior brick wall of the coffee shop and wrapping his hands around his throat.

"Say it again," he challenges.

But Oliver can't say anything. Instead, all he can do is claw at Beckham's hands as he struggles for air.

"Beckham," I warn, nervously looking up and down the street as several people watch, some of them reaching for their cell phones.

But like all those years ago, he doesn't hear me, his grip on Oliver's throat growing tighter by the second, despite his best efforts to free himself. I fear if I don't intervene, the past may repeat itself. I'll never be able to live with myself if Beckham is arrested because of me.

Again.

It will only add to the guilt I still struggle with.

"Beckham," I repeat, this time louder and more urgent.

When I touch my hand to his shoulder, he snaps his

wild eyes toward mine. I jump back on instinct, then school my nerves.

"He's not worth it. Please. Let him go."

I can see his indecision as he looks between Oliver and me.

Finally, he pushes out a long sigh and releases Oliver. Relief floods my body, and I grab his hand, pulling him away.

But before we can make our escape, Beckham shakes free and storms back toward Oliver. In one swift motion, he delivers a harsh right hook to his nose. The crack of his nose breaking is deafening above the typical background noise of our quaint Main Street.

Oliver's expression contorts in pain as he covers his face, blood staining his hands. "What the hell was that for?"

"Nobody calls my wife names and gets away with it." Beckham grips his shoulders then gives a quick knee to his groin, causing Oliver to bend over and grab his crotch.

Then Beckham wraps an arm around my shoulder and ushers me away. "Let's get you home."

TWENTY-NINE

Beckham

"Are you okay?" I ask Haley as we sit in the front seat of my parked truck, not making any move to start it just yet.

It was by pure luck I was even downtown this morning. After my conversation with Grady yesterday, I wanted to talk to my lawyer as soon as possible to discuss formulating an official offer to buy the vineyard. It's a bit more involved than buying a house, which I expected, so the sooner I get the ball rolling, the better.

But when I got a text from Layla, the owner of the coffee shop, informing me of some prick in a suit bothering Haley, I walked out on my lawyer. Haley's my priority, not putting in an offer on the vineyard.

It's an odd notion, considering the only reason

Haley's my wife in the first place is so I can buy the vineyard. But after Layla's description, I had a feeling in my gut who it was.

I was right.

"Let me see your arm," I tell her once my anger has waned enough for me to think clearly.

"It's fine." She rubs her wrist, and I can see the makings of a bruise starting to form.

If I didn't already punch him, I'd storm out of this car right now.

"It's not fine, Haley. That asshole hurt you."

I grip the steering wheel, needing it to ground me before I do something I'll regret. Or that might land me in prison yet again. Nothing's off limits right now.

"Has he…" I swallow hard and meet Haley's eyes. "Did he ever touch you like that when you were together?"

"No," she answers, then hesitates. "Well…"

"Well, what?" I seethe, frustration seeping into my voice.

She pulls her lips into a tight line, her indecision evident.

"Please, Haley. I have to know." My voice cracks at the mere notion of this guy harming her.

"Do you promise you won't go after him and do something stupid?"

"Where you're concerned, I can't make any promises."

For a moment, we just stare at each other, everything we've left unsaid over the past fourteen years heavy between us.

"When I told him I was pregnant," she finally admits.

"So let me get this straight…" I lick my lips, my nostrils flaring. "You told him you were pregnant, and he…hit you?" I can barely manage to get the words out, my blood boiling.

"He didn't hit me. Not like that."

"There's no fucking gray area here. He either hit you, or he didn't. Which is it?"

"He…pushed me."

"What kind of push?"

"I'll put it this way. When my back hit the mirror on the wall, it shattered."

"And you were pregnant?" I ask again, as if it'll magically change her answer.

"I was only ten weeks."

"Stop," I bark, probably a bit too harshly, since she flinches at my tone.

I exhale a sigh and take her bruised wrist in mine, caressing the marks. "Stop defending him. He doesn't deserve it."

"I know he doesn't. I just…" She lifts her eyes skyward, and I notice tears welling beneath her lids. "I guess there's a part of me that thought *I* deserved it." She hesitantly drags her gaze to mine. "That I still do."

"Why would you ever think that?"

She doesn't say anything.

She doesn't have to.

I know exactly what she's thinking.

Of course she'd still blame herself for what happened to me.

But I can't have that on my conscience. Not anymore.

"Listen to me, Haley." I cup her cheeks, forcing her eyes toward mine. "It wasn't your fault. And you certainly don't deserve to be treated the way that asshole treated you. Hell, the way *I* treated you, too. I don't care what I have to do to make it up to you, but I'll spend the next year trying to figure it out."

Her intense gaze lingers on mine for several protracted moments, as if searching for something.

Then, with a sudden urgency, she crushes her lips against mine.

The second she does, all thoughts of doing some permanent damage to her ex disappear. All that matters is making her feel good. Giving her what she wants. What she needs.

What *I* need, too.

I grip her hip and pull her toward me. But the damn center console's in the way, preventing me from feeling her. Sensing my frustration, she crawls over it and straddles me, sensually rocking her hips into me.

"What are your plans for the rest of the day?" I pant as I leave a trail of kisses from her jawline to her neck.

"I need to design a cake," she replies, throwing her head back, giving me better access. "You?"

"I was supposed to meet with my lawyer to work on my official offer for Grady."

"Sounds important."

"Very."

My hands roam over her curves, up her thighs, and ghost against her panties. When I feel how wet she is, I clench my jaw, my erection throbbing against my jeans.

"But I have a better idea."

"What's that?" She circles against me harder, and it takes everything in me not to whip out my dick and tell her to ride me.

"We both take the day off and see if I can give you even more orgasms than I did last night."

"Do you think you're up for it?"

I thrust upwards forcefully, showing her just how desperate I am for her.

"I've always enjoyed a challenge." I waggle my brows. "But if I'm being completely honest, being with you isn't a challenge at all." I pull back, meeting her eyes. "It's the most natural thing I've felt in a long time."

"If you keep saying stuff like that, I might actually find you tolerable."

A small chuckle escapes my throat, and I'm grateful to see the playful side of Haley again.

"That would be a shame. I should probably say something to piss you off."

"Probably so."

"Okay then…" I capture her lips in mine once more, my tongue teasing hers. "I can't stand kissing you. It's like kissing a corpse."

"Likewise," she pants, grinding on my growing arousal. "I can't wait until this sham of a marriage is over so I no longer have to suffer through them."

"And your tits are god awful." I grope them roughly through her sundress, relishing in the way she moans and arches into my touch. "I think about them anytime I need to make my erection go down."

As if on cue, she writhes against me with more enthusiasm, her heat searing through the fabric of our clothes. I want nothing more than to rip them off and claim her right here and now.

"And that brings me to this cunt," I rasp as I inch my hand up her thigh, settling on top of her panties. "It does absolutely nothing for me. Hate the taste of it. Hate how it feels against my cock."

I slip my hand beneath her panties and rub her clit with my thumb. Then I lean toward her, scraping my unshaven jawline against the sensitive skin of her neck.

"And I definitely hate how fucking wet I can get you."

"Beckham," she whimpers as I ease a finger inside of her. "I can't. Too much."

"Never, baby. There's no such thing."

She closes her eyes, allowing herself to succumb to the moment, her rhythm increasing in time with me.

"That's it, Haley," I hiss as she moves against me. "Get yourself off on me. Use me. Make yourself come."

"Oh, fuck," she cries out, her body convulsing around me as I slam my lips against hers, swallowing her screams.

I doubt I'll ever tire of feeling her completely unravel. And not because I selfishly like the ego boost of knowing I affect her this way. But because, in these moments of intimacy, she lowers those walls she spent a lifetime building. Allows herself to be vulnerable with me.

Allows me a glimpse of the real Haley. The one she's kept under lock and key for years. I'll do whatever I need in order to bring her back. To make her see that she could never ruin my life. Not when she's always been the one good thing in it.

"So tell me," I say once she's had a moment to catch her breath. "Do you find me intolerable again?"

"Absolutely." She scrapes her mouth against mine. "And if you take me home, I'll show you just how unbearable I think you truly are."

She doesn't have to ask me twice. I practically toss her off me and peel down the street, anxious to get home with my wife.

THIRTY

Haley

"Is that really a cake?" Beckham asks as he enters the kitchen, the familiar sound of Monte's paws against the hardwood floor following him. But I don't look up, keeping my focus on putting the final touches on my latest creation.

"It's really a cake."

I finish applying some of the coloring to it and step back, making sure it looks like a real dinosaur. I've lost count of the number of dinosaurs and unicorns I've done lately. But that's not all. I've successfully managed to complete a cake that looked like a bunch of chicken wings, a fireman's helmet, and even an iguana.

Each one has had their challenges, but I've enjoyed every second. For the first time, I feel like I'm taking control of my life instead of life constantly beating me down. This is what I've always wanted. To have my own business. Not have to depend on someone else for my livelihood.

As much as I didn't want to admit it at first, I have Beckham to thank for it.

Even Oliver's unexpected appearance a few weeks ago hasn't unsettled me like it would have in the past. Instead, Beckham's done everything to make sure he doesn't come near either of us, going so far as coming with me to drop Maggie at preschool in the morning and pick her up in the afternoon.

And every time I watch my little girl run straight into Beckham's arms, I find myself falling for him a little more.

"How does it look?" I ask Beckham, finally glancing his way.

As always seems to be the case lately, my heart races at the sight of him in his dusty jeans and plaid button-down shirt with the sleeves rolled up.

Forget suit porn.

I'm a sucker for forearm porn.

Especially Beckham's forearms. Not only are they tastefully covered in artful tattoos, but I can make out his veins as his muscles flex.

"It's incredible, Haley." He looks at me in awe.

This isn't the first time I've shown him one of my cakes. Over the past few months, he's seen quite a few go from a rough drawing in my sketchpad to a complete cake.

Yet with every one, he acts just as amazed.

"Even up close, it looks so real." He leans toward it. "If this one weren't on your cake stand, I wouldn't be able to tell which is the cake and which is the toy." He looks between the plastic dinosaur I used as a model for my cake. "Think I can book you to make my birthday cake this year?" His expression falls. "Then again, I'm not sure you have a pan big enough to make a life-size version of my cock." He playfully waggles his brows.

"Jackass." I roll my eyes and move through the kitchen to clean up my mess. But just as I grab a dish-towel, he wraps an arm around my waist, pulling me against him.

"Where's my kiss?"

"Why? Miss me?"

"Always," he replies in a low, husky voice that sends a rush of exhilaration through me.

"In that case…" I hoist myself onto my toes and touch my lips to his in a soft kiss, keeping it relatively tame.

But Beckham has other ideas.

He tightens his hold on me as he coaxes my mouth open, his tongue sliding against mine. The familiar taste of him consumes me, and all thoughts of cleaning fade away.

What is it about this man and his kisses? It's only been a few short hours since he kissed me goodbye before heading to work. Yet I kiss him like it's been years since I've felt them.

"Now this is my kind of lunch break." He moves from my mouth, each hot kiss along my jawline making me feel like he's branding me as his, igniting a fire deep inside me.

"Beckham," I whimper when I feel his erection pressing against me.

"I just want to be inside you every damn second of every damn day."

"Think you can last that long?"

He pulls back slightly, his hungry eyes locking on me. "For you, I'll put in my best effort."

Then he slams his mouth back to mine as he reaches for the hem of my t-shirt.

"What about lunch?" I pant as he rips my shirt over my head. "Don't you want to eat first?"

A wicked grin lights up his face. "I'm about to."

His mouth collides with mine, and I hook a finger into his belt loop to yank him closer, making quick work of his belt.

I'm about to push his jeans down his legs when the doorbell rings.

"Expecting anyone?" Beckham asks, sliding his hands underneath my bra and cupping my breasts.

"No." I throw my head back, moaning. "You?"

"Even if I were, they can wait until my wife is satisfied."

He moves the cup of my bra to the side, my breast spilling out. Then he takes my nipple in his mouth, his teeth lightly nibbling.

"Fuck, Beckham." I reach into his boxer briefs and wrap my hand around his erection. "I need you. Now."

"Yes, ma'am." He clutches my hips and lifts me with ease, carrying me toward the couch. Just as he sets me down and crawls between my legs, an incessant knock sounds.

At first, we continue to ignore it, too caught up in each other. Until an urgent voice calls out, breaking through my lust-filled fog.

"Haley McBride? Process server. If you're in there, please answer."

"Process server?" I ask, the words like a bucket of cold water.

Beckham looks between me and the door, his own unease evident. Then he stands, running a hand over his face.

"I'll go talk to him." He presses a soft kiss to my forehead, lingering for several moments as dozens of scenarios fill my mind about why a process server would be standing outside.

And none of them are good.

When he finally pulls away, he adjusts himself, then makes his way into the foyer. I strain to listen as I get dressed, but I can't make out more than a few non-distinct words.

Seconds later, Beckham reappears, his jaw ticking and nostrils flaring. "He needs to see you."

On shaky legs, I walk toward the front door, Beckham's hand never leaving my back. I can physically feel his ire as I open the door and meet the eyes of a lanky man in a dark suit standing on the front porch.

"Haley McBride?"

"Y-yes."

Without another word, he hands me a large envelope, then retreats to his car, leaving me dumfounded and scared about what this envelope may contain.

Although I already have a premonition about what it is.

Since my recent encounter with Oliver, I've worried how he might respond to learning he had a child he didn't know about.

But after the first few days passed, I convinced myself I was just overreacting. After all, he didn't want Maggie in the first place. I figured he'd already forgotten about her.

Or maybe I *hoped* he'd already forgotten about her.

Now I fear he was just biding his time, lulling me into a false sense of security before striking hard and fast.

I make my way back into the house, my hands trembling as I pull the tab on the envelope and remove a stack of legal documents. Dread fills me as my eyes scan the pages, my heart twisting in my chest.

"What is it?" Beckham asks with a hint of trepidation.

"He's filing for joint custody of Maggie," I manage to respond, each word a heavy weight on my tongue. "But the arrangement he's seeking will give him primary physical custody. He questions my fitness as a parent."

"That's bullshit," Beckham spits out, the vein in his neck pulsing. "If anything, the fact you've provided for Maggie without any help for the past four years shows just what an amazing mother you are. Hell, the bastard threw a wad of cash at you and told you to get rid of her."

"That may be so, but he contends this isn't a safe environment to raise a child, citing…" I trail off.

"Citing what?" Beckham demands through a clenched jaw.

I hand him the papers, barely able to breathe through the tightness in my chest. "Your criminal record. As well as your most recent 'violent outburst'," I say using air quotes.

His eyes race over the pages, anger and frustration evident with every strained muscle of his body.

"He can't do this," he murmurs, his voice trembling with panic and fear. "I just… *Fuck*!"

He bends over as if in excruciating pain, his breathing ragged. I can see the weight of this crushing him.

"It'll be okay," he says softly, composing himself and straightening. "I'll give Mark Sellers a call this afternoon. Hell, I'll ambush him in court if that's what it takes so we can start fighting this."

I lift my eyes toward him. "This isn't your fight, Beckham. We're not—"

"If you're about to tell me yet again you're not my responsibility, you can save your breath. There's no fucking way I'm going to stand aside and let you fight this on your own. Not when I got you into this mess."

"No, you didn't."

"I didn't?" he retorts incredulously, waving the papers in front of me. "He's using my past in his argument for why Maggie's better off with him."

"It's just one argument." I take the papers from him. "He also mentioned my unstable job history and the fact that I used to work as a cocktail waitress at the casino. Trust me. Oliver was going to use anything and everything he could against me once he found out I kept Maggie. He doesn't actually care about her. All he does care about is asserting his power back over me. He's just using your past to strengthen his case."

"Possibly, but you can't turn down my help about this. I won't let you. It's one thing to refuse my offer to get Maggie a new bike or put in a trampoline. You can't refuse my help about this. Not when you're my wife."

"Fake wife," I remind him, unsure if it's more for me or him.

"You're also someone I care about." He brings his

hands to my face. "So is Maggie. This may be a strange notion to you, considering your parents, but people who care about each other help each other. So that's what I'm going to do. You can yell at me all you want. Hell, you can hate me if that's what you need to do. But you are not going through this alone."

His grip on my face is firm, almost desperate as he pleads with me. Begs me to let him in. To let him do this for me. For us.

And therein lies the problem. I've never let anyone in before. Not even Beckham all those years ago. I always kept him just out of reach, always protecting myself because I knew I'd never have the strength to fight for him.

"You're making this really hard for me," I admit through the emotion in my throat.

"What? To say no?" He smirks, breaking through the tension. "I have that effect on people."

Normally, I'd laugh or roll my eyes at his joke.

Not right now, though.

"No, Beckham. You're making it really hard to keep you out."

His expression softens as he tips my head back, inching his mouth toward mine. "Then let me in."

"I'm not sure I know how."

A serene look crosses his face. "I'll help you with that, too."

He covers my mouth, his kiss achingly soft.

This isn't how it's supposed to be between us. It's

supposed to be filled with lust and raw need. It's not supposed to be filled with emotion and warmth.

But I can't manage to push him away. Instead, I do what I didn't think I could.

I let him in.

THIRTY-ONE

Beckham

"Watch me, Beck!" Maggie squeals as she flies down the slide on the playscape outside Jude's brewery. The sun warms my skin as I sit on the back patio and sip on a coffee.

Since Haley had to meet with her lawyer this afternoon, she asked me to pick up Maggie from preschool, who then begged to come here and play. I could have told her she could play on her swing set at home, but I know how much she loves being around other little kids, something she can't do at home.

"Good job, kiddo," I call out to her.

Ever since Haley received the custody petition last week, I've looked at Maggie differently. And every time I see how happy she is, no thanks to her pathetic excuse of a sperm donor, I get even more angry over the idea that he's trying to get custody of Maggie.

Then feel even more guilty about the role I've played in all of it.

"I never thought I'd see this," Jude states as he plops down in the chair across from me, throwing a dishtowel onto the table between us.

"What do you mean?" I bring my coffee to my lips and take a sip.

"Playing Dad."

I shrug. "Just trying to help Haley. That's all."

His light expression turns serious. "How's she doing?"

I shift my attention back toward Maggie, fighting to push down the renewed wave of anger that washes over me at the reminder of everything.

"She's hanging in there." I laugh under my breath. "Hell, she's probably handling it better than me."

"And how are *you* handling things?"

I expel a long sigh and run a hand through my hair. "I don't know."

While Haley asked me to keep Oliver's custody petition under wraps for now, since she hasn't told Maggie about any of it yet, she mentioned I could talk to Jude if I wanted. She must have sensed I might need someone to confide in other than her.

"What has her lawyer said?"

"What I expected he would." I steal a glance at Maggie as she climbs up the small rock wall, then lean closer to Jude, keeping my voice low. "If paternity is established — and Haley's not contesting paternity — he has a legal right to custody. It's just a question about what kind of arrangement they can come up with." I swallow hard, feeling suffocated by the thought of Maggie having to spend any time with that prick.

"Mark Sellers is getting ready to prepare Haley's response, and once the court receives it, a hearing date will be set. But it's just a formality, since all the judge will do is refer the matter to mediation in the hopes that the two parties can come to an agreement without the court's intervention."

"And if that doesn't work?"

"It'll go before a judge to decide."

"What are his chances of getting primary custody if that happens?" Jude crosses his arms in front of his black t-shirt bearing a vintage style of his brewery's logo.

"It's anyone's guess. I just…" I squeeze my eyes shut. "It's like that damn summer all over again."

Jude straightens, his brows creased in confusion. "What makes you say that?"

"I let my anger get the better of me back then and it nearly cost Haley her life. I did it again, and now Haley could lose Maggie because of me."

"She won't lose Maggie," Jude tries to assure me. "No judge would take her away from her mother. If that happens, I'll officially lose all faith in the judicial system."

"Join the club," I mutter over the top of my coffee, my throat closing up the longer I think about it. "Maybe her father was right."

"Her father? What do you mean?"

"That summer, he found out about us a week before it went to hell. Came to the vineyard during one of my shifts and pulled me aside. Told me to stay away from his daughter. Reminded me she was better off without me, that by continuing to see her, I'd ruin her life." I laugh to myself. "Turns out he was right."

"Beck, you need to stop blaming yourself for what happened. Need to let go of this insane amount of guilt you've been carrying for too long now. You served your sentence. It's time to move on. Her father's an asshole who saw his control over Haley slipping and was willing to do or say anything to get it back."

"I thought so, too, but now…" I sigh, peering into the distance, a heaviness settling in my chest. "I thought maybe this time would be different. Instead, I'm just ruining her life all over again. And not just hers. Maggie's, too."

"How?" Jude shoots back.

I throw up my hands in frustration. "She's about to be subject to a custody battle, all because I couldn't control my fucking temper. Again."

He rests his calf on his opposite thigh, tenting his fingers in front of him. "Let's table the validity of your argument for the time being, because you know I think it's bullshit."

I open my mouth to argue, but Jude interrupts before I have a chance.

"Look at that little girl." He nods toward where Maggie's swinging, her tiny frame silhouetted against the bright blue sky. Her infectious laughter fills the air, bringing a smile to my face.

"Hiya, Beck! Look at me fly! Think I can reach the moon?"

"You can do anything you want, pipsqueak," I reply through the lump in my throat.

"Doesn't look like a little girl whose had her life ruined," Jude remarks.

"Not yet," I shoot back, but Jude won't hear it.

He can be a pain like that.

"And how about Haley?"

"What about Haley?" I ask cautiously.

"She was able to quit working at the casino because of you."

"No. The only reason she agreed to marry me is *because* she quit the casino and had no other options."

"Semantics." He waves me off. "You never told her she had to find a job to replace it. Instead, you encouraged her to take this time to pursue her passion. Now, her business is thriving, thanks to you."

"She did all the work."

"But she never would have taken that first step if it weren't for you. Do you see what I'm saying?"

"Not really."

"Your mistakes don't define you, so stop letting

them. You're a good person. Maggie sees it. Haley sees it. When are *you* going to see it, too?"

I'm about to renew my argument that I'm still the root cause of Haley's current predicament when a tall blonde saunters up to our table, her tight-fitting tank top bearing the Wicked Hop logo indicating she works here.

But I've never seen her before.

"Hey, Jude? Can you show me how to change the tap again? I'm worried I'll mess it up."

His lips curve up in the corners and he nods. "I'll be right there."

"Thanks."

When she spins and heads back inside, it doesn't escape my notice that Jude's eyes narrow on her short denim skirt as she walks away.

"Who's that?" I ask once she's gone.

He snaps his gaze back to mine. "Just a new hire." His response is dismissive.

"You hired someone to work at a brewery who doesn't know how to change a tap?" I arch a disbelieving brow.

"She needed a job."

"Who is she? I haven't seen her around before." I look through the windows, watching as she wipes down a few recently vacated tables. It's not too busy inside, since it's only a little after four. In a matter of hours, this place will be packed with people, especially since it's Friday.

"She's new in town."

"Wait a second." I dart my wide eyes toward Jude, knowing why she looks familiar now. "Is that…"

He nods.

When I took Maggie out for ice cream last weekend, we drove by a woman being pulled over by our local sheriff. That in itself wasn't unusual. What caught both my and Maggie's attention was the fact that she was in a wedding dress. And not a simple one like Haley wore. This thing had layers upon layers of tulle, or whatever the hell they use to make wedding dresses.

From what I've heard through the famously unreliable Sycamore Falls rumor mill, she'd been pulled over for driving a stolen car, but seeing as it was her now ex-fiancé who reported it as stolen, the sheriff took pity on her and didn't arrest her. But he still had to impound the car.

That doesn't explain how she ended up working for Jude, though.

"You hired the runaway bride?" I ask.

"Yup. And now I need to go help her." He jumps up from his chair.

"You're not getting out of this."

"It's nothing," he says as he hurries inside.

Which makes me think it's not nothing. I love my brother, but he's not the type of person who'd hire someone who can't even change a goddamn tap.

Chuckling to myself, I return my attention to Maggie as she pokes her head out of the clubhouse.

The instant she sees me, she waves enthusiastically. It both warms my heart, yet breaks it at the same time.

How did I get here? How did I go from avoiding all personal attachments to becoming like a father to a precocious four-year-old little girl who I'd do anything for?

"She's a cute kid, if I say so myself."

I whip my head to the left as a man in a suit lowers himself into the chair Jude just vacated. In an instant, all the warmth drains from my body as I glower at Oliver.

"Then again, I might be a little biased."

I shoot to my feet, clenching and unclenching my fists. "What the hell are you doing here? I told you—"

"Ah ah, Mr. Lawrence. I'm not an expert, but I don't think any judge would take too kindly to reports of you attacking an innocent bystander in front of your stepdaughter, especially given your...history." His voice drips with condescension.

"What do you want?" I seethe, hating that he's right.

"I want you to sit down so we can have a little chat." He grins a conniving grin.

"I have nothing to say to you."

"If you don't, I'm happy to go tell that little girl exactly who I am."

I immediately still, sucking in a sharp breath.

"I'm guessing by your reaction, Haley hasn't told her yet."

I don't move for several long moments, my jaw twitching. But he's right. Haley hasn't told her about him yet. She hopes to protect Maggie from this prick for as long as she possibly can. So instead of giving him yet another bloody nose and making things even worse for Haley and Maggie, I return to my seat.

"What do you want?" I hiss out again.

He relaxes in his chair, an air of superiority about him. What I wouldn't give to wipe the cocky look off his face.

"I want you to retract your offer to buy Vivanza."

I blink repeatedly, his words catching me off guard. Why would this asshole care about me buying the vineyard? How would he even know?

But as I study his appearance — coifed blond hair, clean-shaven jawline, and designer suit that makes me question whether he's ever gotten his manicured hands dirty — it finally clicks. Especially when I notice the monogrammed cufflinks.

The man I saw storm out of Grady's office a few weeks ago wore an identical pair.

"You were in talks with Grady," I exhale, realization hitting me like a punch to the gut.

His lips curl into a sinister sneer. Then he shifts his gaze, watching Maggie with immense interest.

It makes me want to break every bone in his body. At least I find some satisfaction over the fact that there's still a subtle bruise around his nose and eye from our last encounter.

"Do you believe in karma, Mr. Lawrence?"

"I do, and you better believe it'll eventually come for you after the way you treated Haley. Unless I get to you first, that is."

He chuckles, brushing off my remark like the condescending prick he is. "I also believe in karma. At first, I wasn't sure how I was going to convince Grady Belanger to change his mind. He seemed so set against accepting my firm's offer to buy his vineyard, even after I offered him substantially more than our initial bid. But after learning it was because he planned to sell to his head winemaker, I worried it was a lost cause. I can't compete with keeping the land in the family." He floats his calculating stare toward me. "Until I realized who his head winemaker is married to."

"That's what this is about?" I shoot back, my ire toward this asshole growing with every second he remains in my presence. "You don't actually want custody of Maggie, do you?"

"How could you say that?" He feigns disbelief. "She's my daughter."

"No, she's not," I growl. "You lost the right to call that little girl your daughter when you threw money at Haley and ordered her to terminate the pregnancy. If you think you can come here and threaten to take her away, you'd better think again. She may not be my daughter, but there's nothing I won't do to keep you as far away from her as possible. From both of them."

"I was hoping you'd say that." His eyes dance in

amusement. "Which is why I'm here with a proposition for you."

"For...me?"

He nods slowly, his steely gaze focused on me. Now that I'm peering at him, I can't help but see the remarkable similarity between him and Maggie. The same angle of their striking gray eyes. The same nose. The same shape of their chin.

"Tell your boss you've changed your mind and you're no longer interested in buying Vivanza. Once you do, I'll have my lawyer withdraw my petition for modification of custody."

From the beginning, I questioned what his motive might be. While Haley seemed adamant it was simply to punish her, I couldn't ignore the feeling in my gut there was more to it than that.

Now, I know what it is.

"He'll never sell to you, especially when he learns why I'm rescinding my offer."

"Oh, but he won't. Not if you want to keep sweet little Maggie from being the center of a long, drawn-out custody battle. Rest assured, I have the funds to do so."

"What about your wife? Are you ready to tell her you had an affair while you were engaged?"

"My relationship with my wife has always been slightly...volatile. There's been quite a bit of on again, off again, even right up to our wedding. I can easily make the argument that any time I spent with Haley was during one of our 'breaks'. Which is what I'll do if it comes to it. Plus, I know my wife. She won't care once she learns this affair helped me get promoted to partner at the firm. And that will only happen if I secure this deal. So it's your choice. Rescind your offer and this all disappears. If you don't, I hope you're ready to explain to Haley how you had the power to stop this and didn't."

I'd give anything to punch the smug look off his face. But I can't. Not when he's already using my past actions as a reason for why Maggie isn't safe with Haley.

"Even if I do as you ask, it doesn't mean Grady will accept your offer. From what I understand, he's had multiple parties interested."

"You do have a great deal of influence over him, don't you?"

"I suppose."

"Then you'd better use your influence. If not, enjoy what little time you have left with Maggie."

"You don't even care about her," I seethe.

"You're right. I don't. But I *do* care about getting this promotion and will do whatever it takes in order to get it."

He levels a glare, making it clear he won't hesitate to turn both Maggie's and Haley's world upside down just to make a point.

"Now, do we have a deal?" With a single brow arched, he extends his hand.

I stare at it for several long seconds, my stomach

churning. I want to refuse on principle. Fight him tooth and nail.

But that would mean putting Maggie through a custody battle. Would mean uprooting her from the life she's always known. Even if he doesn't get full custody, he still has a right to spend time with her. I have a chance to make it so that doesn't happen. To protect them both.

After all, it's my fault she's in this mess. This is the least I can do to get her out of it.

Pushing out a long breath, I place my hand in his. "We have a deal."

THIRTY-TWO

Haley

"Is everything okay?" I ask Beckham as I slip into the bedroom after reading to Maggie.

"Yeah. Fine." He forces a smile, but it only lasts a second before his expression falls once more.

Since he got home this afternoon, he's seemed off. Distant. I didn't bring it up during dinner, wanting to focus on spending time with Maggie before bed. But now that it's just us, I can't shake the feeling something's wrong.

While he's been a bit more reserved since I received Oliver's petition, tonight he seems even more distracted.

I don't know what to think of this version of Beckham. I don't like brooding, distant Beckham, not after being treated to fun and playful Beckham. Not to mention sexy and lascivious Beckham.

"Are you sure?" I move to my side of the bed and slide under the duvet.

Normally, the second I'm in bed, he practically attacks me, unable to keep his hands off me.

Today, he barely even looks at me.

"You can talk to me. I *am* your wife, after all." I waggle my brows, hoping to cut through the uneasy tension.

He turns his conflicted gaze to me and swallows hard, his Adam's apple bobbing up and down.

When I see his morose expression, I cup his cheek, inching toward him. "You're not still blaming yourself for all of this, are you? I told you. It's not your fault. It has nothing to do with you."

He briefly squeezes his eyes shut, as if my words physically wound him. Then he blows out a long sigh and wraps me in his embrace. "It's just some stress at work." He kisses the top of my head. "Nothing for you to worry about."

I run my fingers along his chest, tracing the pattern of the phoenix's wings spreading across his skin. Regardless of his assurances, I can't help but think he's not being honest with me.

"Are you sure that's all it is?

He touches a finger to my chin, forcing my eyes to his. "I'm sure."

"Well then…" I climb on top of him and straddle

his waist. I pull my hair free from its tie, allowing it to fall down my shoulders in waves. "You know what they say is a great way to relieve stress, don't you?"

"What's that?" He grips my thighs as I grind against him, his erection springing to life.

I reach for the bottom of my tank top and yank it off in one swift motion. When his pupils flame as his eyes focus on my breasts, relief washes over me.

"Sex, Beckham." I lower my mouth toward his. "I hear sex is a great stress reliever."

His fingers tangle in my hair, gripping it possessively as he holds me in place, keeping my lips just out of reach. Hesitation flickers in his eyes, and I almost expect for him to turn me down. A first since we started sleeping together.

Then he flips me onto my back, moving his hands to cup my face. I brace for him to slam his lips against mine like he usually does.

But that's not what happens.

Instead, his motions are slow and measured as he covers my mouth. There's no rush. No desperate need to consume every inch of me. Instead, he takes his time, his tongue sensually caressing mine as his hands explore my body.

A part of me feels somewhat relieved when he finally brings our kiss to an end, not liking the emotions he's able to bring out of me.

But when he returns to me after ridding himself of

his shorts and kisses me even more sensually, it only makes it worse.

"So beautiful," he murmurs, circling my nipple with his tongue as he slides his hand up my leg and slips a finger into my panties.

When he rubs my clit, I'm powerless to resist, a slave to his touch. His kiss. His everything.

"I need you," I beg, arching into him.

"And I need you, Haley." He hooks his fingers into the waistband of my panties.

I lift my hips, and he slides the material down my legs, tossing them to the side before returning to me, his mouth so close, yet still too far away.

"Need you so damn much."

He presses his lips back against mine, kissing me like I'm oxygen and he's been struggling to breathe for too long. One thing is certain. This isn't just a kiss. It's a dangerous combination of hunger and longing that could ruin a person.

That could ruin *me*.

But I don't have a chance to protest before he lines himself up at my entrance and eases inside with agonizing slowness.

There are no harsh drives. No wanton grunts. No carnal declarations of how good I take his cock.

Instead, the room is distressingly silent as our bodies fuse together in madness and ecstasy.

"Please, Beckham," I beg, overcome with emotion.

"Faster." I wrap my legs around his waist, attempting to encourage him to increase his rhythm.

"No, Haley. Like this." He sensually circles his hips, his motions slower than they were minutes ago. But they're even more fulfilling.

Even more dangerous.

"Let me have you like this," he rasps as he buries his head in the crook of my neck. "Let me *love* you like this."

"Beckham," I whimper.

I don't have it in me to remind him this is supposed to be just sex. It would never just be sex between us. Our connection has always been too intense. Too palpable.

Too explosive.

Instead, as I surrender to him, I have no choice but to face the awful truth that I broke the one rule I swore I wouldn't.

I've fallen in love with my husband.

THIRTY-THREE

Beckham

The stairs creak under my feet as I drag myself up to the second floor of the tasting room building, my stomach heavy with what I'm about to do.

A few months ago, I wouldn't have given up the opportunity to buy the vineyard for anything. Hell, I got married just to do it. Now, I'm ready to walk away just to keep Haley and Maggie from ever having to deal with her ex. If I don't do this, I'll never be able to live with myself. Even if it means losing Haley.

And this is the part I struggle with.

It's not losing the vineyard that makes me feel like my heart's been ripped from my chest.

It's that Haley will no longer have a reason to be married to me once I do this.

Like I told Jude, it's for the best. I've already done enough damage. The sooner we end this farce of a marriage, the better.

At least for her and Maggie.

Approaching the door to Grady's office, I draw in a deep breath and peek my head inside. "You got a minute?"

He snaps his head up from the paperwork covering the surface. "Beckham." He waves me in. "What brings you to the big house? I suppose you should get used to it, considering you'll be running the show in a couple of months."

"That's actually what I'd like to talk to you about."

He eyes me suspiciously, then gestures to the chair across from his desk. "What's on your mind, son?"

I sit, rubbing my hands along my jeans. "You know I love you like I do my own father. If it weren't for you, I don't know where I'd be today."

"You'd be right here, Beckham. You're a good man. Always have been."

A pang of guilt shoots through me. His words make me feel even worse about all the lies I've told him over the past few months, especially considering everything he did for me after I got out of prison.

And how did I repay him? By lying to him just so he'd sell me the vineyard.

"I'm not a good person, Grady."

"No one's perfect. You can't keep beating yourself

up over things you did as a teenager. That stuff doesn't define who you are now. And the man you are now—"

"I lied to you," I interject before he can bestow any more praise I don't deserve on me. "My marriage to Haley isn't real. It's a sham. After you told me you didn't want to sell to me because you were worried I'd miss out on having a family, I made a deal with her."

It's silent for several protracted moments. It's probably only a matter of seconds, but with my confession lingering heavy in the air, it feels like an eternity.

"I see." He relaxes into his chair and stares out the window at the acres of vines, the California sun shining brightly on them.

I study his face, searching for any hint of how he might be reacting to the truth. But his expression is as impassive as ever.

"Do you think you're telling me anything I don't already know?" he says when he finally looks my way.

I blink repeatedly. "You knew?"

He chuckles lightly. "I've known since the beginning. When you told me you were getting married, I had a feeling it was because of the condition I placed on you."

"Why didn't you say anything?"

"I was curious to see how it would play out. And maybe the romantic in me hoped it would not only help you realize there are more important things than work, but would also bring the two of you back together. From where I'm sitting, it worked. I haven't seen you this happy in years. Hell, I don't think I've ever seen you take time off from work."

"Most employers would hate that," I remark.

"Not me. Not when it means you've finally found something to live for other than work."

"It doesn't matter, Grady. It still wasn't real. At least not for her."

He narrows his gaze on me. "Are you sure about that? I've seen the way she looks at you. Seen—"

"*It's. Not. Real,*" I bark, my voice thundering against the walls.

I've never raised my voice to him before. Not like this. I just can't stomach sitting here and listening to him go on about how Haley looks at me or how happy I've been these past few months without it feeling like there's a vice squeezing my heart.

"I'm sorry. I just…" I blow out a long breath and lift my eyes back to his. "I still lied to you. You don't deserve that, especially after everything you've done for me. Which is why I've decided to rescind my offer to buy the vineyard."

He straightens, concern creasing his brow. "Didn't you hear me? I've known the truth all along. I'm just as guilty of lying as you think you are. Hell, I essentially forced you to get married."

I shake my head. "No, Grady. You didn't. You were just looking out for me. Like you have all my life. Now it's my turn to repay the favor. I overheard what Benson and Associates offered you for this land. It's more than double what I can afford. You've sacrificed enough for me over the years. You should sell to them. Have the retirement you deserve and not have to worry about money. You won't have that if you sell to me."

"I don't care about the money." He waves me off. "I've saved enough over the years to be able to enjoy my retirement, so—"

"Regardless, I'll still be rescinding my offer. I'm sorry for the inconvenience."

I start to stand, but before I can, Grady asks, "What's going on, Beckham? Why are you really doing this?"

"I thought I wanted to run my own vineyard, but I've realized I'm not cut out for it." I gesture to the paperwork piled high on his desk. "I'd miss making wine too much."

"That's the beauty of being the owner. You get to make the rules. The only reason I stopped being as involved in the process is because you're better at it than I ever was. You don't want to deal with the paperwork? You can hire someone to do it for you."

"I'm just not ready for the added stress. I've already spoken with my lawyer, and according to the terms of my offer, I'll lose my down payment."

"I'm not keeping your money, Beckham."

"My lawyer will have the paperwork to you in the next day or two. I just wanted to tell you now. That way you can reach out to Benson and reopen negotiations."

He furrows his brow, his analytical stare studying me

intently. "Why do you seem so adamant about me selling to Benson?"

"I did some research. They've bought other vineyards and turned them into one-stop vacation destinations for wine-enthusiasts. It would be a win, not just for us, but all the other small vineyards in the area."

He exhales, shaking his head. Then he slowly lifts his gaze back to mine. "Are you sure this is what you really want? Think about everything you're giving up."

I swallow hard. He has no idea how much I'm giving up. Then again, he just might.

Still, I have to do this. For Haley. And Maggie.

"This is what I really want."

THIRTY-FOUR

Haley

My eyes glide over the words on the page, each one blending into the next. It doesn't matter how many times I've read them, they still don't sink in. I keep waiting to wake up, to learn I've been dreaming and that's the only reason Oliver would do this.

But I'm not dreaming. This is real.

Oliver has withdrawn his petition for custody modification.

I have no idea what could have prompted him to change his mind. According to my lawyer, he made it sound like Oliver wasn't willing to negotiate on the matter. Why would he change his mind and withdraw his petition altogether?

My lawyer reminded me this doesn't mean he won't file again at a later date. The only guaranteed way to prevent him from doing that would be if he were to voluntarily terminate his parental rights. Most courts in the state are only likely to grant that in the case of extreme abuse or if a stepparent were seeking to adopt and the biological parent had never been a part of the child's life.

I'd be lying if I said I didn't briefly consider this route with Beckham. Then I remembered our marriage isn't real.

In the beginning, it wasn't even a chore to remember that. But over the past several weeks, everything about it has felt real. From waking up in his arms. To dropping off Maggie at preschool together. To him coming home for lunch just so we could have sex without worrying about Maggie hearing us. To him sinking into me before I fall asleep in his embrace.

After Oliver abandoned me, I swore I'd never let anyone else in again. Would always guard my heart with everything I had.

That was before Beckham weaseled his way back in.

If he ever left.

I doubt he had.

"What's that?"

At the sound of Beckham's voice, I whirl around to see him standing at the edge of the kitchen.

Normally, he rushes toward me and sweeps me into

his arms, unable to wait another second to feel my lips on his.

Then again, he hasn't been doing that this week.

I keep telling myself it doesn't matter. Like he mentioned when I asked him about it, he's under some stress at work. I don't know a lot about making wine, but it sounds like each month has its own challenges.

Still, I sense something else is bothering him.

"Mark Sellers called me earlier and asked me to come see him."

"Oh, yeah?" Beckham moves toward the refrigerator and grabs a bottle of water, cracking it open and taking a long sip. "Is everything okay?" He shifts his eyes toward me but doesn't look directly at me.

"Better than okay, actually. Oliver withdrew his petition for custody. He's even paying my attorney's fees."

"That's great, Haley." He approaches and wraps me in his somewhat lackluster embrace. "I'm happy for you."

I draw in a breath, savoring in the feel of his warmth. But something still seems off. His voice is calm, as if I just told him I scored a great deal at the grocery store. Not that my daughter's sperm donor is no longer attempting to rip my life to shreds.

"After we pick Maggie up from preschool, we should go to the Wicked Hop and celebrate. Even if she has no idea what we're celebrating."

His expression falls as he drops his hold on me, averting his gaze. "Actually, I can't make it."

"Oh. Okay. Maybe some other time." I smile, but can't shake the unsettled feeling in my gut. "I should head out and get her," I tell him, even though I don't have to leave for another hour. "I need to run a few errands. Should I expect you for dinner?"

He pinches his lips together, conflicted.

It's a simple question. One I've asked countless times.

But today, it feels like I'm asking him to decide between two impossible choices.

"Haley," he sighs, running a hand over his face. When he finally manages to return his gaze to mine, my heart squeezes at what I see within.

"What's going on, Beckham?" I ask nervously, although I'm not sure I want to know the answer. "And don't tell me it's because of stress at work."

He pinches his eyes shut before dragging them up to meet mine. "Grady will no longer be selling the vineyard to me."

My heart drops to the pit of my stomach, all the oxygen whooshing out of me. This doesn't make sense. A few weeks ago, we were celebrating that Grady agreed to sell to Beckham. And now he's changed his mind? I can only think of one reason for his sudden about face.

"Did he find out—"

Beckham holds up a hand, cutting me off. "It doesn't matter why. All that does is he'll no longer be selling to me."

I blink, my limbs heavy, my stomach turning sour.

"Where… Where does this leave us?" I ask timidly, my voice barely above a whisper.

"With no sale, there's no reason to stay married." His tone is neutral, but his eyes betray a hint of sadness over the prospect.

"Won't Grady get suspicious if we split up now? You wanted to stay married for six months after the sale went through so he didn't know it wasn't real. The same could be said for now," I argue, grasping onto any shred of hope that might give me a little more time with him.

I thought we had another year. Now I'm just supposed to be okay with walking away and pretending the past few months never happened?

"He already knows, Haley."

"Knows what?"

"He know it's not real."

"Is that… Is that why he won't sell? Because I…" I trail off, attempting to get my thoughts in order.

"Because what?"

I meet his eyes, debating my next course of action. I can just let it go. I *should* let it go.

A few weeks ago, we agreed we'd take it one day at a time. That we wouldn't make any grand plans for a future. I didn't think we *could* have a future, not with all the baggage we still carried.

But if this is potentially our last day together — hell, our last minute — I need to put it all out there, let the chips fall where they may.

"It's real for me, Beckham," I admit.

"Haley…"

"Maybe it wasn't in the beginning," I continue, ignoring the warning in his tone. "But right now, it's real." I move closer and bring my hand up to his face, cupping his cheek. "And I know it is for you, too."

He closes his eyes as he leans into my touch. But his moment of tranquility is fleeting, quickly morphing into painful realization. He jerks away from me as if the feel of my skin is a searing brand on his flesh.

"We agreed this would eventually come to an end," he declares.

"We also agreed to take things one day at a time. And I don't want this to end. Not anymore. I don't want to walk away just because things have changed. We've amended our agreement before. Let's do it again."

"I…" He pinches the bridge of his nose. "I can't, Haley."

"Why? Tell me why," I demand, tears threatening to spill over. "Tell me why you're pushing me away. Why you pushed me away all those years ago."

He levels me with a piercing stare filled with self-loathing. "We both know you're better off without me."

I open my mouth to argue, but he cuts me off.

"I'm the reason you could have lost custody of Maggie. Just like I'm the reason you almost died four-teen years ago. The reason you never got to go to college. The reason you lost out on so much, Haley. I've already caused enough damage. Already ruined your life."

My throat tightens at the guilt I see weighing him down. "You didn't ruin my life, Beckham. If anything, you *gave* me life. If I never fell off that deck, I probably would have kept doing whatever my parents told me to. Has my life always been easy? Not even close. But I wouldn't trade the past several years for anything."

I reach for him again, but he steps back.

"I love you, Beckham," I whisper desperately.

He shakes his head, his expression twisted with pain and regret. "No, Haley. You don't."

"You don't get to tell me how I feel. I've had enough of that to last one lifetime, thanks to my parents. You may not like it. May not think you deserve to be loved because of this blame you keep placing on your shoulders. But you do, Beckham. You deserve so much more than you give yourself credit for. If you would just finally forgive yourself."

He stares at me for what feels like an eternity, my confession hanging heavy between us. He parts his lips, and hope builds inside me for a brief second. Then he catches a glimpse of the scar running down the length of my thigh and his expression tightens once more.

"The state requires a married couple to be physically separated for six months before granting a divorce," he says after a beat, his voice even. Empty. Cold. "You'll be able to stay here until the end of October. I stopped taking bookings at my townhouse so I'll just stay there for now."

He turns and heads out of the house, acting as if I hadn't just poured out my heart to him. It's not until I hear the click of the door closing that I snap out of my stupor and go after him.

"So that's it?" I call out just as he's about to climb into his truck, my voice echoing against the peaceful serenity surrounding us, birds chirping and tree frogs croaking. "You're really okay pretending you feel nothing for me? With this ending?"

He pauses and curses under his breath, but eventually faces me. "How could this end when we never even began?"

"Bullshit, Beckham. Bull. Shit. You love me. I know you do."

His jaw ticks, but he remains silent as his stare bores into me.

"You can't even deny it. Can you? If you really feel nothing, tell me you don't love me. Say it and we can go back to barely acknowledging each other. But I need you to look me in the eyes and tell me you feel absolutely nothing for me. Can you do that?"

His chest heaving, he eats up the distance between us and digs his fingers into my hair. I wince at the pressure but still hold his gaze steady as his eyes skate over my face. I can physically feel his indecision, his brain at war with his heart. Or perhaps his past at war with his present.

When he leans toward me, his mouth a whisper from mine, I hitch a breath, anticipation filling me.

"I. Feel. *Nothing*."

His angry response shatters what little hope I somehow managed to hold on to.

Then he releases me and storms back to his truck, the tires kicking up dust as he makes his escape.

THIRTY-FIVE

Beckham

"Let me see if I have this straight," Jude says from across a table in the corner of the brewery.

I've been sitting here for the past twenty minutes telling him all about Oliver's surprise visit, as well as his proposition.

How I didn't think twice about accepting and rescinding my offer to buy Vivanza.

How I told Haley we'd no longer have to be married.

Then how she told me those three little words that were like a dagger to my heart.

They still are.

I wasn't sure how she'd take the news. I figured she might be somewhat upset.

I never could have anticipated she'd tell me she loved me.

And how did I respond?

I pretended those three words didn't shatter my entire world.

But what was I supposed to do? Say them back?

She deserves better.

"You give up the vineyard, the place that's been your life for the past decade, just so Haley doesn't have to deal with that asshole. Then when she tells you she loves you, you blow her off?"

"What did you expect me to do?" I shoot back, taking a sip of my pale ale. It tastes bitter, and not because I'm too much of a wine snob to enjoy a cold beer once in a while.

I have a feeling even the most highly praised wine will also taste bitter right now.

Everything will.

"Here's a novel thought."

He relaxes into the booth, scanning the bustling brewery to make sure everything's under control. It doesn't escape my notice that his eyes settle on Abbey, his new runaway bride bartender, a bit longer than necessary. But I don't have time to call him out on it before he continues his relentless badgering.

"You could have told her how you feel about her. You can't even sit there and tell me you don't feel the same way. That it didn't kill you to walk away from her."

"She's better off without me," I snip out, bringing my beer to my lips and hoping he takes the hint I'm in no mood to talk about this.

Then again, if I really didn't want to talk about it, I wouldn't have come here. But where else could I go?

I couldn't stay at the house, not with Haley and Maggie there.

Haley's probably getting her ready for bed. Was tonight a bath night? I think it might have been. If that's the case, Maggie probably has her bucket of bath toys next to the tub as she concocts extravagant stories in her head with her wild imagination. Then she'll beg Haley to read four books instead of her normal three because she's been extra good and deserves an extra book. At first, Haley will refuse, but eventually she'll compromise by saying if she's still awake by the time she finishes the third book, she'll read her one more.

If I were there, that's around the time I'd peek my head in and see Maggie fast asleep against Haley as they relax in the chaise lounge. Haley would attempt to pick her up, but I'd intervene.

Even when it wasn't my night to read, I still liked carrying her over to her bed and putting her in it, brushing a kiss to her innocent face as she slept.

I'll never get to do that again.

I remind myself it's for the better.

Just like I have since I walked away from Haley today.

And pushed her out of my life all those years ago.

"Are you still stuck on that?" Jude retorts, yanking me out of my thoughts.

"What? She is. She always has been."

"Why do you think that?"

"Because it's true," I bark out, my voice carrying over the rock music playing through the sound system.

A few patrons look our way and I temper my anger.

"Because it's true," I repeat, this time softer. "In case you've forgotten, it's my fault she almost died right before she left for college. She was stuck in a hospital for weeks because of me. Then had to have a live-in nurse teach her how to fucking walk again. Do you have any idea how much it kills me every time I've made love to her, only to see that damn scar running from her hip to her knee? All. Because. Of me. I couldn't control my anger. And she paid the price. She would have paid the price again if I didn't withdraw my offer. This time, it wasn't just Haley's life I fucked up. I could have fucked up Maggie's life, too. This asshole may have withdrawn his petition today, but he can try again later. I'd rather not be the cause of it again."

"Don't you think you've punished yourself enough? Haley loves you, Beck. That proves she doesn't care about any of this shit."

"She's better off without me," I reiterate. "Her *daughter* is better off without me."

"Did she tell you that?"

"It doesn't matter," I answer evasively, not wanting to share exactly what Haley did say. That I didn't ruin her life. That instead, I *saved* her life. "It's done. It's over. We can both move on and pretend this never happened."

He studies me for several long moments with his penetrating gaze. As if the longer he glowers at me, the sooner I'll crack and finally admit the truth.

"So you're really okay with this?" he asks finally.

"With what?"

"With watching Haley date another guy. Fall in love. Start a family with him, all the while wondering what would have happened if you hadn't been such a goddamn pussy?"

"I'm not a pussy," I argue, rubbing the ache in my chest at the thought.

"Oh, no?"

"Like I told you…this is for the best." I'm not sure if I'm saying this for him or me. A part of me keeps hoping the more times I say it, the more I'll actually believe it.

Because right now, I don't know what to think.

All I *do* know is I'll never be able to live with myself if anything happened to Haley or Maggie because of me.

"You know what? Fuck it." Jude jumps to his feet and leans toward me, his eyes on fire.

Unlike me, my brother doesn't get worked up easily. Not unless it's something or someone he cares about.

"If you want to convince yourself and everyone else you don't love her because you're too much of a coward to admit your true feelings, then fine. Go ahead. But I'm not going to tell you that you did the right thing. Or say I agree with it. As far as I'm concerned, this is a giant fucking mistake. And if you don't see that…" He shakes his head. "Then maybe you don't deserve her." He holds my gaze for a beat, then retreats, leaving me alone once more.

"I've never deserved her," I mutter to myself.

THIRTY-SIX

Haley

"Eat up, sweetie," I tell Maggie with a saccharine smile. "We need to leave in ten minutes."

"Okay, Mama," she replies, but her voice lacks any enthusiasm.

It's her first morning waking up without Beckham around.

Or Monte.

When she questioned me about it, I didn't know what to say. Didn't know if I could get the words out without breaking down. Instead, I did what I swore I never would.

I lied to her.

Told her he's at work.

He probably is.

But that isn't why he's not here.

He's gone because we're not together anymore.

If we ever were.

Just as I throw the mixing bowl into the sink and soak it in some water, there's a knock on the door.

A glimmer of hope builds inside me that it's Beckham. Would he knock, though? After yesterday, he might.

But when I check the peephole, my expression falls.

"Grady, hey," I greet, opening the door. "Beckham's not here."

"I know. He was in his lab before the sun rose this morning."

"Then why—"

"I was hoping I could talk to you for a moment. I won't be long."

"Of course." I grit a smile, feeling equal parts guilty and angry.

Guilty about lying to him.

Angry that he's now refusing to sell the vineyard to Beckham because of it. I didn't take Grady for the type of person who'd hold something like this against him.

Maybe I was wrong.

"Come on in." I step back, allowing him to enter, the unsteady rhythm of his cane echoing as he walks.

"Hiya, Mr. Grady," Maggie says when he enters the kitchen.

"Hey, cutie. Did your mom make you pancakes?"

"She did." Her brow furrows. "Can you give Beck

tomorrow morning off from work so he can be home for breakfast? I don't like it when he's not here when I wake up in the morning."

It takes everything I have to blink back the tears that are about to break free, especially when I see the look of sympathy on Grady's face.

"I'll see what I can do," he says sweetly.

"Thanks."

"Maggie, why don't you run upstairs and get dressed for school while I talk to Mr. Grady?"

"Okay, Mama." She slides off the barstool and runs up the stairs.

Once I hear her door close, I turn to Grady. "It was my idea," I tell him without giving him a chance to say anything.

"What are you talking about?"

"The fake marriage. If you want to take it out on anyone, take it out on me. Not Beckham. This vineyard is his life. It's why he went so far as to get married. I know you care about him and don't want him to miss out on anything, but please reconsider, Grady. This vineyard has always been the one good thing in his life. Don't take it away."

He gives me a quizzical look, tilting his head slightly as he leans on his cane. "What makes you think I would?"

His response catches me off guard. "He came home yesterday for lunch and told me you would no longer be selling to him."

Grady chuckles, shaking his head ruefully. "I always said that boy would make a good lawyer," he remarks with a hint of fondness. "He has a knack for phrasing things a certain way so it's not a complete lie, but not exactly the truth, either."

I furrow my brow in confusion. "What do you mean?"

"The reason I'm no longer selling to him is because he rescinded his offer."

"He…did?" I blink repeatedly. "Why would he do that?"

A million different scenarios run through my brain, but all I can hear are the words he couldn't say last night. Was he really so desperate to get rid of me, he retracted his offer in order to do so?

"I was wondering the same thing. All afternoon, I kept replaying our conversation over in my mind. Do you know what stood out?"

"What's that?" I ask shakily.

"He kept insisting I sell to a development firm by the name of Benson and Associates."

I dart my eyes toward his, inhaling a sharp breath.

"I gather it rings a bell."

"Yeah. It…uh——"

"Maggie's birth father is a junior partner there," he says in a low voice. "Isn't that right?"

"Yes."

"The same birth father who recently filed a petition for custody."

I don't even bother asking how he knows. "Yes."

"And the same birth father who, the same day as Beckham rescinded his offer to buy my vineyard, withdrew his petition for custody."

My heart squeezes, and it feels like the ground is about to give out from under me. "What are you saying?" I ask, resting my hand on the island to steady myself.

"I'm saying it's curious. We both know Beckham wouldn't give up this vineyard unless he had a damn good reason. And it's certainly not because he lied to me, or whatever he believes. Hell, the reason I put the condition on the sale is because Estelle and I were hoping to play matchmaker."

"What a minute. Grandma Estelle was behind this, too?" My eyes widen, although I shouldn't be surprised.

For a woman who never married herself, she does like to play matchmaker quite a bit. She certainly played a hand in getting Parker and Callum together.

"We knew if Beckham would ask anyone to marry him, even for a short period of time, it would probably be you. He's always had a soft spot for you, Haley. I think he always will."

"I'm not so sure about that," I scoff.

"Don't count him out yet. Beckham can be…stubborn."

I cross my arms in front of my chest. "Don't I know it."

"I think he's holding onto his guilt about what

happened to you because without it, he'll have to face the truth."

"What's that?"

Grady gives me a knowing look. "I think we both know. And I think he's just too scared to face that right now. Just be patient with him. Forgiveness is a process."

"I've already forgiven him."

"I'm not talking about you. I'm talking about him finally forgiving himself." He gives my bicep a reassuring squeeze. "I'll see myself out."

I watch as he retreats, replaying the entire conversation in my mind. I still can't believe Beckham would give up the vineyard just so I wouldn't have to endure a custody battle.

The weight of his sacrifice hits me like a ton of bricks, a knot forming in my throat. If I'd known, I never would have allowed him to do that. I would have fought Oliver. I was *ready* to fight him. Was ready to prove to the world that, just because someone made a mistake in their past, it doesn't define who they are.

My past mistakes don't define me.

And Beckham's past mistakes don't define him.

Except he seems to be clinging onto those past mistakes as a reason for everything.

Or maybe an excuse.

"Was Mr. Grady talking about Beck?"

I whirl around, finding Maggie lingering at the top of the staircase. Her bottom lip trembles and tears glisten in her big gray eyes.

I want to lie to her. Assure her everything's okay.

But as much as I wish I could protect her from all the pain and hurt in the world, it's not possible.

No one has that kind of power.

"Yes."

"Is that why he's not here?" she squeaks out. "Because he's scared?"

My heart aches at the sadness in her voice. "Yes, baby. He's scared. But it'll be okay. Remember what I always say? You and me against the world."

She gives me a lackluster nod.

"Now come on. Let's get to school."

"Okay, Mama." She shuffles down the stairs, and I help her put her socks and shoes on before leaving the house.

As I buckle her into her car seat, something that was usually Beckham's job, she suggests, "Maybe he needs a stuffy."

"A…stuffy?

"He doesn't have any stuffed animals. When I'm scared, my stuffies make me feel better, especially Fred. Maybe a stuffy will make him feel better, too."

I press a soft kiss to her forehead. "Maybe so."

THIRTY-SEVEN

Beckham

"Beckham Lawrence. Been a while since I've seen you in here," an older man says as I approach the counter of the hardware store.

Now that I've temporarily moved back into my old townhouse, I have time to make some of the repairs I've been putting off. Like fixing the loose faucet in the kitchen and replacing the doorknob leading out to the back porch. I've also been giving the place a fresh coat of paint to get it ready for whatever's next.

Right now, I'm not sure what that is.

When word spread about Grady's retirement, I started receiving quite a few offers from vineyards up and down the west coast. Initially, I ignored them, hoping I'd be the one to buy the vineyard. Now that I won't be, I've been reaching out to some of them to see what they have to say.

I hate the idea of leaving Sycamore Falls, but the more time I spend here, the more I realize it's probably the best thing for me.

And Haley.

"I've been busy," I tell Mitch Howard, who's owned the local hardware store here for as long as I can remember.

"Married life can do that." He winks. "How's Haley?"

I do my best to hide the sadness washing over me at the mere mention of her name.

This is why I need to get out of this place. Go somewhere bigger. Where no one knows who I am and my history. Have the fresh start I've needed for years. Where my mistakes can no longer haunt me.

"She's busy, too," I reply as I insert my card into the reader on the counter. I don't know what else to say. I haven't seen Haley in over a week now. Anytime I've needed to grab something from the house, I made sure to sneak in when I knew she wouldn't be around.

Jude's right. I am a fucking coward.

I spent a year in prison surrounded by men who committed far worse crimes than me. Yet I'm more petrified of a petite redhead and her daughter than I ever was of any of those men.

"Just be sure you make time for each other," Mitch advises. "Work will always be there. Time… Well, that you can't get back."

I take the bag he hands me. I know more than most how fleeting time is.

"Thanks, Mr. Howard."

"Sure thing, Beckham."

I turn and head out of the hardware store, the downtown area busy with a mixture of locals and tourists soaking up yet another beautiful spring day. The sky is a brilliant shade of blue, dotted with a few fluffy white clouds.

It's the kind of day I would have taken Maggie to get ice cream after picking her up from preschool. The thought brings a sharp pang to my chest.

Even though she's not mine, I loved our afternoons together while Haley made a cake delivery. Loved spoiling her with ice cream. Loved watching her play. Loved hearing her giggles fill my otherwise empty world.

"Maggie, watch where you're going, sweetie."

At the sound of the familiar voice, I'm ripped out of my memories. I suck in a deep breath when I see Haley and Maggie come out of the ice cream store, Maggie's sweet face already covered in chocolate.

The instant the little girl sees me, her eyes light up. "Beck!"

Not even caring that she's holding an oversized ice

cream cone, she rushes toward me. Instinct takes over, and I crouch down to her level, deftly grabbing the ice cream from her hands before wrapping my arms around her. I close my eyes, basking in her unwavering affection.

"I've missed you," she says softly against my t-shirt.

I don't even care that it's probably stained with chocolate.

"I've missed you, too." I brush a kiss to her head.

"Then why don't you come home?"

I pull back and meet her gaze, unsure of what to say.

"Sweetie, we've talked about this." Haley touches a hand to Maggie's shoulder, and I drop my hold on her, pulling myself to my full height. "Beck and me, we're not together anymore."

She's not telling her anything new. But hearing it out loud still stings.

"I found a new place to live, so we'll be out of your house by the end of the month," Haley states, her expression even and devoid of emotion. "Figured it would help with the physical separation requirement."

I hand Maggie her ice cream, then step toward Haley. "You don't have to rush anything."

"I'd rather not stay there." Her voice rises in pitch, and she glances at the sky, unshed tears glistening in her eyes.

It would be so easy to beg her to stay. Tell her I was

an idiot. That it killed me to push her away. That I did it for her own good.

But I don't.

Because like Jude said… I'm a fucking coward.

"Understood. I'll let you get on with your day."

I continue down the sidewalk, each step I take away from Haley and Maggie requiring immense effort. Like some force is trying to keep me here. With them.

"Beck! Wait!"

When I hear Maggie call out to me, I stop and face her, watching as she trades her ice cream for her favorite stuffed animal, an elephant named Fred.

"What is it, pipsqueak?"

"Mommy said you're scared, and that's why you're not living with us right now."

"She did, did she?" I steal a glance at Haley before refocusing my attention on Maggie, her gray eyes filled with sadness and innocence.

"Do you know what helps me when I'm scared?"

"What's that?" I manage to say through the lump in my throat.

"Fred." She looks down at the weathered stuffed animal, its color faded and trunk wrapped in bandages from when Maggie played doctor and he was one of her unfortunate patients. Then she extends him toward me. "I want you to have him. Not for keeps, but for borrows."

"I don't want to take your stuffy."

"Can you at least try, Beck?" Her expression falls as she looks at her feet. "I don't like hearing Mommy cry."

I dart my eyes toward Haley again, a single tear sliding down her cheek.

"Please?" Maggie begs.

Pushing out a long sigh, I take Fred from her. "Okay. I'll try."

THIRTY-EIGHT

Haley

The scent of dust and cardboard surrounds me as I continue to pack up my belongings at Beckham's house. When I moved out of my last apartment, I was diligent about keeping everything organized.

Not this time. Now, I want to get out of here as quickly as I can. Especially this bedroom. I haven't even been able to sleep in the bed since Beckham left, resorting to my old ways of sleeping on the couch at night.

"You don't think he'll change his mind?" Parker asks as I use my shoulder to prop my phone up to my ear so I can use both hands to pack.

"My daughter gave the man her favorite stuffy, for

crying out loud," I reply. "If that doesn't thaw his cold, uncaring heart, I doubt anything will."

"I know, but…" she trails off with a heavy sigh. "I really thought this was the second chance you both deserved."

"It wasn't a second chance, Parker. It was a carefully orchestrated manipulation by Grady and Grandma Estelle that backfired spectacularly. I should have known it would never work. Beckham proved he doesn't care about me years ago. This farce of a marriage was the reminder I needed."

"Can you really say that, though? He gave up the vineyard for you. That's got to count for something. That's got to *mean* something."

"Apparently not."

Although, I still struggle to make sense of it all. If he doesn't care about me, if he doesn't *love* me, why would he sacrifice the one thing he's always loved for me? But I can't cling onto whatever glimmer of hope this one act has left me with, not when the rest of his actions prove otherwise.

"This just doesn't feel right, Haley."

"I can't put my life on hold for someone who will always keep me just out of reach." I take a long swallow of wine, then continue throwing my belongings into a box. "I'm just pissed it just took me this long to finally realize it."

"Haley, I'm—"

"It's okay," I interrupt before she can say she's sorry. I'm not sure I can handle hearing it right now.

"How about this? I'll bring over some liquor from the bar here at the inn and we can get sloppy-ass drunk."

I laugh slightly, and it feels good. It's probably the first time I've laughed since Beckham left.

"As much as I'd love to, I've learned the hard way that hangovers and kids don't mix well. I'm in the middle of packing anyway."

"Need any help?"

"I'm okay. Plus, isn't Callum there for the weekend?"

"He is."

"Then why are you talking to me? You should be spending time with your man before he has to head back out again."

"He can deal. If you need me, I'm there. You know that."

I push out a tired sigh. "And I love you for it. But really. I'm fine. Promise."

"Okay," she concedes reluctantly. "But if you change your mind or want to go toilet paper Beckham's yard, I'm your girl."

"I know you are. Love you."

"Love you, too."

I end the call, then set my cell on the dresser. After another large gulp of wine, I grab a new box and head into the giant walk-in closet. Beckham's clothes still hang on his side, although I've noticed more and more of his things disappear over the past few days.

I have to push down the lump building in my throat when my eyes fall on the suit he wore on our wedding day. A bittersweet ache fills me as I remember how incredible he looked in it. And the way he admired me as he called me his wife for the first time before kissing me…

I shake off the memories. Remind myself it wasn't real.

At least not for him.

Setting the box on the floor, I stalk toward the shelves at the far end of the closet. I start pulling down box after box of shoes, packing them as quickly as possible so I can get out of this room. Out of this space that holds so many memories, despite the short amount of time I've lived here.

But as I reach for a box toward the back, it slips from my grasp, heavy enough to catch me off guard. When it spills open onto the floor, I see why it was so weighty. Instead of shoes, it's filled with hundreds of envelopes, the papers yellowed with age, some frayed at the edges.

My pulse increases as I gather them up, seeing Beckham's name, address, and inmate number written in my flowing girlish handwriting.

Lowering myself to the floor, I open one of the

already-torn envelopes and pull out a letter on delicate stationary. As I unfold it and begin to read, tears prick at the corners of my eyes.

Dear Beckham,

I've been out of the hospital for a month now. And you've been away for a month. I still can't bring myself to say where you are. In my mind, you left for college like you planned and are having the time of your life. You're going to parties and learning that signing up for a math class at 8 AM probably wasn't the smartest idea. And you tell everyone about your girl off at a different college. How you can't wait until the long weekend next month so you can go see her.

It's a bit of a pipe dream, isn't it? But it's what I tell myself to get through the day. Maybe I'm in denial. Maybe I should just face reality, but I hate what happened.

Hate what you're going through.

Hate that it's my fault.

I don't blame you for not replying. If I were in your shoes, I probably wouldn't want a reminder of my biggest mistake. But writing you these letters has been the one good thing in my life. It's helped me cope with, well...everything.

I don't care if you never write me back. I'm going to keep writing to you.

I just wish you'd write back.

Wish you'd forgive me.

Wish you'd forgive yourself.

Yours,

Haley

I run my fingers over the faded paper, the words I once wrote to Beckham causing a myriad of emotions to stir within me. They're words I didn't think he read. Not only did he read them, he saved them. Even all these years later.

"You sprayed the paper with your perfume."

I jump to my feet at the unexpected voice, sucking in a sharp breath when I see him standing in the doorway of the closet, clutching Fred in his hands.

"I didn't even care that some of the guys teased me about it. Your letters were the only thing that kept me going," he admits, his voice filled with raw emotion. "I looked forward to them every damn day, Haley. Read them over and over again until I fell asleep with them under my pillow, pretending I was falling asleep with you."

I wipe away the tears moistening my cheeks. "Why

didn't you write back? Why did you refuse to see me whenever I tried to visit?" I suck in a quivering breath. "Why did you ignore me when I showed up the day you were released?"

He pulls his lips into a tight line as he briefly looks to the ceiling. It doesn't escape my notice that he squeezes Fred even tighter. Just like Maggie does whenever she's scared.

"I couldn't, Haley," he says, his voice barely above a whisper. "I wanted to. I just…" He steps toward me. "You had a bright future ahead of you. I was a convicted felon. I didn't want to bring you down. I figured if I didn't write you back, if I refused to see you, if I made you think I didn't care about you, you'd forget about me and have the life you deserved. I didn't want to ruin your life more than I already had."

"I told you. You didn't ruin my life, Beckham. You *gave* me life."

"Maybe. But at the time…" He shakes his head, agony and regret covering the lines of his face. "When I saw your lifeless body on the pavement…"

He steals a glance at my leg. My once-prominent scar has faded, but it's still there. It will always be there. A reminder of everything we've been through.

"Even before that night, your dad wanted me to stay away from you because he thought I was bad news. That I'd ruin your life. And in that moment, I realized he was right."

"It wasn't your fault."

"It was, Haley. You didn't fall off that deck by accident. I was so angry, I couldn't think or see straight, and you paid the price. So I made a promise to myself I'd do whatever was necessary never to ruin your life again." He clutches Fred tighter still. "And now… I'm fucking petrified I'll keep ruining your life. That I'll ruin Maggie's life. It's what I do. What I've always done. I have a criminal record. No one should want to be with me. No one should love me. I don't deserve it. Don't deserve you. And I certainly don't deserve Maggie." He draws in a deep breath as he looks at Fred.

"But as I was sitting in my ridiculously quiet townhouse with the walls distressingly vacant of Maggie's art, I realized something. Or maybe Fred helped me realize something."

"What's that?" I ask somewhat timidly.

He focuses his gaze on me. "Maggie was willing to risk being scared for me."

A tear slides down my cheek, my heart expanding at how amazing my little girl is.

"Maybe it's time for me to risk being scared for her. And you. Please tell me it's not too late for us, Haley." He hesitates, swallowing hard. Then he chokes out, "I love you."

"What did you say?" I ask.

He takes a deep breath before closing the gap between us and placing a warm hand against my cheek.

"I love you, Haley. And I hope you still love me. Hope I haven't completely fucked this up. I was just…

scared. Still am. I'm scared of hurting you. Scared of hurting Maggie. Scared of not being enough for either of you. Scared you'll wake up one day and realize what a colossal fuck up I am. But I'd rather be fucking petrified with you than live another day without you."

Neither one of us says anything for several long moments as his confession rings out around us.

Then a slow smile curves across my lips as I drape an arm over his shoulder. "Now that wasn't so hard, was it?"

His muscles relax as he inches closer. "Loving you is probably the easiest thing I've ever done. You make it easy."

"Better be careful, or I might just find you tolerable again."

A low chuckle rumbles from his chest as his mouth hovers over mine. "We wouldn't want that now, would we?"

"Certainly not," I reply breathlessly, anticipation coiling through my veins.

"Should I say something to make you find me insufferable again?"

"Definitely."

"Okay." Licking his lips, he places a hand on my hip and guides me backwards out of the closet. "I hate how much life you've brought to this house in the past few months. Hate coming home to the sound of you and Maggie singing and playing."

He nuzzles my neck, his teeth lightly biting my skin.

"I hate having to share our time with you," I pant. "You're a horrible addition to our little family."

"I also hate the fact that my former bachelor pad is now covered with amateur drawings."

"It must really be inhibiting your ability to get laid," I retort as he peppers kisses along the column of my neck.

"You have no idea. It's been absolute torture."

He pulls back as my legs hit the side of the bed. The playfulness in his expression mere moments ago is gone. Instead, there's a look of peace and serenity.

"Do you know what I hate the most, though?"

"What's that?" I ask shakily.

"I hate how much I love you. How much I want to stop taking it one day at a time and go all in on you." He cups my cheeks. "On *us*."

I swallow hard, the intensity in his stare unraveling me.

"So what's the verdict?" he asks softly. "Do you find me intolerable again?"

I hoist myself onto my toes and skim my lips against his. "Incredibly so."

"Good," he whispers before pressing his mouth firmly against mine.

I melt into him, all the tension that's plagued me since he left evaporating as I surrender to him. To us. To this love. And as he swipes his tongue against mine, I feel him surrender to it, too.

Even better, I feel him do the one thing I didn't think he ever would.

I feel him forgive himself.

No more guilt. No more regret. No more blame. Instead, we allow ourselves to be the perfectly imperfect couple we've always been.

Who needs perfect when we have something real?

THIRTY-NINE

Beckham

The sound of wrapping paper being ripped and excited squeals surrounds me, creating a symphony of holiday cheer. I relax into the plush cushions of the couch in the living room, a contented smile crawling on my face as I take in the scene in front of me.

The twinkling lights of the Christmas tree in the corner cast a warm glow over the room, illuminating the handmade ornaments adorned with photos of Maggie. It's a lot more personal than any tree I've put up in the past.

But everything's different now with Haley and Maggie in my life, and I couldn't be happier.

I love waking up with Haley in my arms. I love

driving Maggie to school in the morning and listening to her chatter about the latest kindergarten gossip. I love coming home after a long day of work to my two best girls.

But most of all, I love walking through the vineyard with my family by my side, especially now that I'm the owner.

Despite rescinding my offer to buy Vivanza, Grady ended up pulling one over on everyone when he gave me the vineyard instead. I tried to refuse, but he wouldn't hear it. Said I deserved it.

I still question whether it's true, but I'm trying to be better about not punishing myself for things I did in the past. Trying to forgive myself.

"Do you think we may have gone a little over-board?" Haley asks under her breath as she surveys the pile of presents surrounding Maggie.

"No such thing." I kiss the top of her head. "She deserves it. If it weren't for her, I'd probably still have my head shoved up my ass."

She laughs as she snuggles in closer, her red and green checkered pajama bottoms matching mine.

Last year, if you told me I'd be wearing matching pajamas with my wife as her daughter opened presents in front of our Christmas tree, I would have laughed. Hell, most years, I spent Christmas morning in the fields or experimenting in my lab.

Not this year.

"It's a good thing I have her then," Haley remarks.

"*We* have her," I correct, tilting her chin.

"We have her." She repeats as my lips touch hers.

"Ugh. Crush business? Again?" Maggie exclaims with a slight lisp due to a missing tooth.

Haley and I laugh, but don't stop kissing. I went years keeping my true feelings for her locked up and punishing myself for my past mistakes. Never again.

"Stop complaining, pipsqueak."

"Whatever," Maggie says, returning her attention to another one of her new toys.

I narrow my gaze at Haley. "Did she just *whatever* me?"

"Wait until she's a teenager. It'll be even worse."

I run a hand over my face. "I'm not sure I'll survive her as a teenager. And dating? I may end up back in prison."

"You'll be fine. You're a good dad." She gives me an encouraging smile. "Speaking of which…" She nods toward Maggie. "Now might be a good time."

I draw in a deep breath as a bout of nerves overtakes me. I wasn't even this nervous when I drove over to Haley's to ask her to be my fake wife. Because I knew it wasn't real. What I'm about to ask Maggie *is* real. And it has lifelong consequences. It absolutely terrifies me, but like I promised Haley when she agreed to give me another chance, I'm not going to walk away from things that scare me. Not anymore.

"Hey, Maggie?"

She looks up. "Yes, Beck?"

"Can you come here? I think I found one more present for you."

Her eyes light up at the mention of another present and she jumps to her feet, running toward me. I reach behind the lamp on the side table and grab the small wrapped box, handing it to her.

My heart thunders in my chest as I watch her sit on the floor and open it. Sensing my anxiety, Haley grabs my hand and squeezes.

"It's jewelry!" Maggie exclaims as she lifts the lid off the white box. "I love jewelry. I love being fancy, you know."

"I know you do."

As if I need another reminder of just how fancy Maggie likes to be. Her closet is filled with princess dresses, and I've been forced to attend my fair share of tea parties and makeovers. I've stopped even noticing when I go to work with my nails painted different colors. It's all part of having a little girl in my life.

"Do you know what that says?" I gesture to the letters on the friendship bracelet.

"Those are our names."

"That's right. And do you know what the charm says? The one in the middle?"

She returns her attention to it, but shakes her head. "Not all the words."

"That's okay. Want me to read it to you?" I ask, struggling to keep the emotion out of my voice.

With a nod, she stands and crawls onto my lap, handing me the bracelet.

"It says, 'It is not flesh and blood but the heart that makes us father and daughter'."

I glance from Maggie to Haley, a few tears escaping her eyes.

"Does this mean you're my daddy now?" Maggie asks, her brow wrinkled in confusion.

I situate her so she's facing me. "I want to be, Maggie. But only if it's what you want."

"So you *want* to be my daddy?"

"More than anything."

She stares at me for several moments with those wide, innocent eyes of hers. Then she wraps her tiny arms around me and squeezes. "I want that, too."

I hug her tighter, inhaling the familiar smell of her shampoo. "I love you, Maggie."

"I love you, too, Beck— I mean, Daddy."

"You can still call me Beck if you want."

"I've never had anyone I could call Daddy before, so I want to call you Daddy."

"Good." I hug her against me once more, my heart so full I fear it'll burst.

I wasn't sure if this would ever be a possibility, not with Oliver in the picture. To my surprise, he didn't put up much of a fight when I essentially demanded he terminate his parental rights so I could adopt Maggie. Then again, he's dealing with enough as it is with his wife divorcing him and his boss firing him once he learned what he did in order to convince Grady to sell to his firm.

He said he believed in karma. I'm glad it finally caught up with him.

"That just leaves one more thing," I say as Maggie crawls off me and slides her bracelet onto her wrist. I reach into the pocket of my pajama pants and retrieve a tiny black box, facing Haley.

"What's that?" She eyes the box with suspicion.

"A ring." I flip open the box to reveal a sparkling round cut diamond.

She gasps, her eyes widening. Then a smirk curves on her lips.

"In case you've forgotten, we're already married, Beck." She holds up her hand to show me the simple wedding band still adorning her finger.

Since we were already married, we didn't think it made sense to go through with the divorce. Not to mention, we would have a hard time proving physical separation, considering we've been living together ever since I finally stopped being a fucking coward, as my brother put it.

"I want a do-over. Want to give you the wedding of your dreams. Want you to go dress shopping with all your friends as you gush about how excited you are. Want to watch you walk down the aisle and think what a lucky guy I am." I blow out a nervous laugh. "I thought that last time, but still. I never want you to doubt how much I love you. How real my feelings for you are. How goddamn happy I am with you. You're the best thing that's ever happened to me, Haley. So what do you say? Will you marry me again, but for real this time?"

Several seconds pass as she looks from me to the ring and back again. I shouldn't be anxious. After all, she's already my wife. But a part of me will always think I don't deserve her.

Finally, she cups my cheek. "It's always been real for me." Her soft lips press against mine in a tender kiss. "But I'm more than happy to marry you again." She moves her mouth to my cheek. "And again." She kisses my other cheek. "And again." She returns her lips to mine.

I slide the ring onto her finger and deepen the kiss, Maggie's snickers the perfect background noise to this moment.

"Don't look, Monte," she says in a loud whisper. "They're doing crush business again."

I briefly pull away, glancing toward my little girl. "Get used to it, kid."

Then I kiss my wife again.

Wondering about the runaway bride Jude hired? Find out in Resisting my Roommate! Just type the link into your web browser or scan the code with your mobile phone.

Falling for the runaway bride is the last thing I need right now. And I definitely shouldn't offer her a job and a place to live. But somehow, that's precisely what I do.

https://getbook.at/RoommateTL

Want one last taste of Beckham and Haley? Then sign up for my mailing list to get a bonus chapter.

https://geni.us/Frenemy-Bonus

Thank you so much for taking the time to read this book. If you enjoyed it, please let your friends know by leaving a review so more people can fall in love with Beckham and Haley.

RESISTING *my* ROOMMATE

Falling for the runaway bride is the last thing I need right now. And I definitely shouldn't offer her a job and a place to live. But somehow, that's precisely what I do.

Once upon a time, I thought I had it all figured out. Until my life as I knew it turned on its head.

Now I stick to what I know — running my bar, brewing my own beer, and keeping my heart firmly off the menu.

Then Abbey Rhodes walks into my bar, still wearing her wedding dress, looking like she just escaped a rom-com gone wrong. She's fierce, funny, and her heart's as bruised as mine. The smart thing would be to send her on her way and avoid the trouble she brings.

As it turns out, I'm not as smart as I thought.

Which is why I find myself not only offering her a job, but also my spare bedroom.

The last thing either of us needs is another complication. But there's something about Abbey that makes me wonder if there might be more to life than playing it safe.

Do I keep my heart locked up tight, or can I take a chance on a runaway bride who might just make me believe in love again?

ACKNOWLEDGMENTS

Thank you so much for reading *Married to the Frenemy*. I hope you enjoyed reading Beckham and Haley's story as much as I enjoyed writing it.

While I'm typically known for my more suspenseful stories that I write under my T.K. Leigh pen name, it's refreshing to take a break from all the murder and write something a little lighter but that still packs an emotional punch.

I hope I hit the mark for you with this one.

Before I reach the last page, I just wanted to send a quick thank you to all the people who've helped with this book.

First of all, a big thank you to my little family — Stan and Harper Leigh. Especially Harper Leigh.

If you're wondering where little Maggie got most of her quirky phrases from, it's my kiddo. She calls heaven "haven", refers to cemeteries as "the stones", and whenever she sees kissing on TV, she instantly covers her eyes and says "ewe crush business."

So thank you to my precocious little girl for always filling my life with laughter as well as plenty of material for my books.

To my wonderful PA, Melissa Crump — thanks for all your help as I switch gears from one genre to the next from month to month.

To my fantastic beta readers — Melissa, Stacy, and Vicky — thanks for always reading for me and offering feedback. I don't know what I'd do without you amazing ladies.

To my admin team — Melissa and Vicky. Thanks for keeping my reader group and page running.

To my review team — Thank you for always not only reading my books but also taking the time to write reviews, regardless of whether something dark and suspenseful or light and heartfelt.

To my reader group — Thanks for being my superfans and giving me a place to go when I need a break from writing.

And last but not least, a big thank you to **YOU**!

Thank you so much for picking up this book and taking a chance on it. Whether you've been a longtime T.K. Leigh reader or are just finding me now in this new genre, I'm so happy you took the time to read my words.

Can't wait to share even more stories with you very soon.

Love & Peace,
~ Tracy

ABOUT *the* AUTHOR

Tracy Leigh is the spicy small town alter ego of USA Today Bestselling author T.K. Leigh. She lives outside of Raleigh with her husband, daughter, special needs rescue dog, and three cats.

When she's not penning her next small town romance filled with heat and heart, she can be found reading, spending time with her family, or planning her next escape to Hawaii.

facebook.com/tracyleighbooks

instagram.com/tkleigh

tiktok.com/@tracyleighauthor

bookbub.com/authors/t-k-leigh

pinterest.com/tkleighauthor